Under the Mango Tree

Short stories from Goa

Published in December 2018 by

Goa 1556

Goa,1556, Sonarbhat, Saligão 403511 Goa, India. http://goa1556.goa-india.org,
goa1556@gmail.com +91-832-2409490
with

FUNDAÇÃO
ORIENTE

Fundação Oriente Delegation in India
175, Filipe Neri Road, Fontainhas – Panjim
Goa 403001 India foriente@dataone.in +91 832 2230728
and

Golden Heart Emporium

The Margao (Rua Abade Faria) bookshop with a difference

Cover design and all illustrations by Bina Nayak http://www.binanayak.com
Editing: Anjali Dar SenGupta
Printed and bound in India by Brilliant Printers Pvt. Ltd, Bengaluru - 562 123
http://www.brilliantprinters.com
Typeset using LyX, http://www.lyx.org in Utopia (Fourier) 9.8/13
Cover photo courtesy pxhere.com. First edition 1000 copies.
Typeset with LyX, http://www.lyx.org. Text: Bitstream Charter, 9.7/13.2
ISBN 978-81-938140-1-7

See Goa,1556's catalogue at: http://goa1556.in

The shade of the mango tree beckons, tantalisingly...

Come, tarry a while in the cool shadows

Contents

Introduction

Savia Viegas

THE Fundação Oriente Short Story Competition began as a maiden initiative in 2012. It has now entrenched itself, creating a niche in the quilted patchwork of Goa's literary endeavours. It is here in Goa that some of the established writers come to be inspired and fledgling aspirants follow the scent of that trail. It is here that writers' groups abound and writing is everywhere. This literary initiative now, in its fourth edition, garners some of these energies to map the pulse of the short story in the Goan imagination. There is something endearing about the practice that encourages writing and literary completion in four languages, and encourages access to these works by simultaneously publishing them in translation. The mood for the competition is created by a Fiction Writing and Publishing Workshop which is popular and well-attended.

The short story has gone through a process of evolution and is today a genre that bears a relationship to the world of fiction the way watercolour does to painting. It has had its masters in Anton Chekov, Guy de Maupassant, O Henry and Eudora Welty, to name but a very few. The Indian subcontinent has also produced master storytellers like Munshi Premchand, Saadat Hasan Manto, R.K. Narayan, Mulk Raj Anand, Ismat Chugtai, Mahasweta Devi and Sarat Chandra Chattopadhyay whose works are known for their Indian imagination. Closer home in Goa writers like Francisco Luís Gomes, Adeodato Barretto and Paulino Dias are known for their contribution to Indo-Portuguese literature.

In this edition of the Short Story Competition, there were 79 entries in English, Konkani, Marathi and Portuguese languages. It was time for us in the jury to think technique, societal idiom, nuance of language, development of character, sense of mystery and manners.

The jury comprised Xavier Cota, Jessica Faleiro, Oscar de Noronha, Prakash Parienkar and me. Xavier Cota is a former banker and now translator from Konkani to English. Jessica Faleiro is a fiction writer and author of *Afterlife: Ghost Stories from Goa* and the recently-released *The Delicate Balance of Little Lives*. Oscar de Noronha is Professor of English and heads the English Literature department in the Government College of Arts and Commerce, Pernem. He translates from Portuguese to English. Prakash Parienkar is Professor of Konkani Language in the Goa University and is proficient in Marathi, Konkani and English. He writes fiction and scripts plays.

The largest number of entries were in English (59), followed by 11 in Konkani, four in Marathi and two in Portuguese. In the stories we received and read, we evidenced a significant shift in the themes from issues of land ownership and caste complexities in earlier years to issues of everyday life. Clearly, this swing also marked a move from looking inward and focusing outward but vitally, a vein of *Goanity* throbbed through all these stories – shocking, entertaining and seducing. Some stories had vignettes of intimate observations on Goa's complex yet unique past, narrated in strong, authentic voices.

Finally, after weeks of deliberation, long phone conversations, and on the basis of combined scores, the jury unanimously decided to award the Alban Couto first prize to the Marathi short story 'Kahat Kabira' ('Says Kabira') by Vithal L. Gawas. The lucidly-narrated story is set in a nondescript border town that could be any one of those dotting Goa's hinterland, home to mixed populations of Hindus and Muslims. The narrative looks at how perfectly amicable relations between the two communities, where cultural values of one enrich the lives of the other, get communalised and vitiated. So much so that finally the Muslim protagonist is driven away from something he loves doing best – participating in community *bhajans*.

The Semana da Cultura Indo-Portuguesa second prize was

bagged by the English story 'Murder?' by Rajyashree Dutt. This racy, tightly-edited and humour-laced murder story, with several twists, delved around the capabilities of portly Inspector Kunkolienkar to solve the mystery of a dead body lying spreadeagled in a bedroom. A motley village crowd watches his every move as he ambles about gathering clues. The author deftly handled action by showing a rich minutiae of detail-accumulating. It offered some striking cameos of local landscape which is the life-blood of good fiction.

The Fundação Oriente third prize was awarded to the English story 'Dhirio' by Mayabhushan Nagvenkar. The powerful local tradition where bull meets bull in an impromptu fight arena, crowds gather and place huge bets is a popular sport across Goa. However, the ensuing events do not augur well for Rocky and his master Caitu, the protagonist in the story. The loss of a bullfight, entrapment in debt, disillusionment of Caitu's family and the veterinarian's reluctance to treat the injured bull, all lead to a redeeming finale. This poignant story had a distinctive sense of local life.

The Special Jury Prize went to the Konkani story 'Pavlli' ('The Dripping Stream') by young writer Sushmita Dessai. In this special jury prize winner, the central character Reshma reminisces about her college years and friendship with Vidya, the stormy petrel who had been lucky in her choices and her loves.

One of the concerns of the jury was that most entries were by mature writers and there was a paucity of strong, young voices telling their stories. This was in contrast to the jury's expectations and hope that younger and newer writers should participate in telling stories of their generation and strengthen the writing culture of Goa. It is imperative that the young voices be encouraged either by creating niche awards or by encouraging writing programmes that perform the dual task of mentoring and motivation. Moreover, Fundação Oriente could organise a short story conference which will add value to its present activities.

Many of the entries that did not get selected in the shortlist for the book compilation began remarkably well but lost their sense of gravity and meandered, unable to retain the unity and coherence of the story. Some entries fell short because not enough time and adequate efforts were put into technique. Reworking the stories is as equally important as the act of putting down a story. It is here that the act of crafting takes precedence. Issues of language, local idiom and characterisation can be played around with and honed to give a story its final dressing, the two qualities that make fiction – a sense of manners and a sense of mystery.

The jury members saw the immense potential that this programme has to grow further. The creative writing workshop which sets the tone for the competition occurs in mid-year and draws participation from across the state. I had conducted the first workshop in 2011 and was pleasantly amazed by the kind of enthusiasm that it generated. Subsequent workshops were conducted by Victor Rangel-Ribeiro and Isabel de Santa-Rita Vaz. This year, we had four writers conducting the Fiction Writing and Publishing Workshop: Alexandre Moniz Barbosa, Sheela Jaywant, Manohar Shetty and Frederick Noronha.

A corpus of twenty-five stories was selected to become part of the fourth edition of the publication entitled *Under the Mango Tree*. The earlier editions were titled *Shell Windows* (2012), *Coconut Fronds* (2014) and *Monsoon Winds* (2016), respectively. This is the fourth volume of short stories – a dedicated effort by Fundação Oriente to extensively mine and encourage the short story.

The arduous task of translation of Konkani short stories was enthusiastically performed by Xavier Cota. The Portuguese story was translated by Oscar de Noronha and the Marathi translations into English were done by Damodar K.K. Ghanekar.

I congratulate Fundação Oriente, its former Delegate Eduardo Kol de Carvalho and current delegate Maria Inês Figueira, for starting and continuing this wonderful initiative. Yvonne Rebello of Fundação Oriente works tirelessly behind the scenes to provide logistical support to the competition.

Savia Viegas
Chairperson of the Jury
Fundação Oriente Short Story Competition, 2017

Validated by the Bell

Suvarna Bandekar

J UST as she was about to doze off in the bus, Sumi heard some loud altercation going on.

"What's the problem with you, old lady?"

"What's my problem? Be careful what you say! Don't think I will tolerate such nonsense from you!"

"What's going on here? Why are you both shouting?"

"Look, conductor, this drunkard who has entered the bus, is 'high' – see how he's swaying! And he's slyly touching that school-girl's back. I just caught him in the act. These guys should be punished."

"You there, what's wrong with you? Can't you stand up properly?"

"Can't you see how crowded the bus is – there's no place to stand, and the vehicle is moving fast too."

"Don't talk too much. Look, over there, on the back seat there is a police officer. I'll hand you over to her immediately!"

When the conductor mentioned 'Police Officer', the girl sitting next to her gently prodded Sumi with her elbow. Sumi had to get up. She thought, 'Damn this conductor,' and began to make her way forward. Hearing what the woman had to say, she delivered a stern warning to the drunkard. The problem was solved there and then. Whilst getting down, she heard a couple of words, "*Rau re*, wait, my stop has come."

"When the board clearly states 'Standing 11 allowed', you keep filling the bus! This is what you get." Saying this, Sumati alighted from the bus.

"Madam, the only solution for this is to ring their *ghant* hard!" said the old woman who had started it all, as she got down behind her.

"Wait a minute. Did you just say *ghant?* The way you said it seems to remind me of someone. Is your name Rekha *maushi?*"

"Yes, but how do you know my name, madam?"

"Oh god! Is it really you? I'm meeting you after so long. Aunty, I am Sumi," said Sumati, hugging Rekha *maushi.*

"Sumi, who?" Aunty had still not recognised her.

"Aunty, I'm talking of twenty years ago. But I have not forgotten you. *Maushi,* I am the Sumi who used to play and roam with Minu."

"Oh, it's Sumi! Now I remember. You were around ten years old then, weren't you? And now you're a policewoman. How's that you're here? I haven't seen you around before?" Rekha *maushi* exclaimed.

"Yes, aunty. I've just been transferred here this month. Tell me, how are you?"

"I'm okay, just getting through my days. But Sumi, I'm surprised how you recognised me. How could you possibly remember me?"

"Aunty, there's only one person who pronounces bell as *ghant* in that peculiar way, so when you said *ghant* I immediately recognised you!"

"So, it was actually the bell that made us meet!" remarked *maushi* with a laugh.

"That's true! Aunty, come, let's go to the police station. We can sit in my cabin and talk. The station is just a five-minute walk."

"No, my dear. Not now. I'll come some other time to talk. Otherwise, when you have the time, you come over. Walk from the station and when you get down, the first blue house with the *balcão* is mine. You can drop in any time," said *maushi,* giving Sumi directions.

"Okay, aunty. We'll talk again later," said Sumi as *maushi* walked away. But Sumi remained there.

"Good morning, madam. You've come by bus today?" said D'Souza, saluting her.

"Yes, D'Souza. The jeep wasn't ready this morning, so I sent Sabnis to the garage. But it was a good thing that I came by bus. I

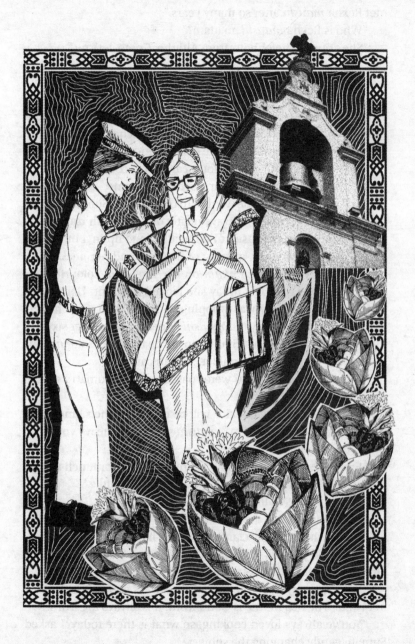

met Rekha *maushi* after so many years."

"Who is Rekha *maushi*, madam?"

"She's our old neighbour from Altinho. Come, let's go."

"A-u-n-t-y," Sumi called out as she entered the gate of Rekha *maushi's* house, and looked in through the kitchen window.

She was standing alone in the kitchen and was startled.

"Yes? Oh, it's you, Sumi. You scared me completely. Come, please come in and sit. I'm happy that you came," said *maushi*, opening the back door. She went in to bring water. Sumati remembered the *maushi* of old. Always neatly dressed, with ornaments on her hands. Her hair used to be neatly done up in a bun, with a plait of *mogra* flowers, a string of beads round her neck and a rupee-sized bright red *kumkum* on her forehead, colourful sari and living quite well. But today she looked different. Her vitality was not there and she was stooping. Her forehead was creased. She must be around fifty but *maushi* appeared to be over sixty.

"Keep coming like this, Sumi. You are dear to me," said *maushi*, putting her hand on her shoulder. Sumati came out.

"*Maushi*, looks like you were roasting *polle*," Sumati's glance went to the fireplace.

"Yes, my dear. Now the kids will be crying for their lunch. I've made *polle* because of them," *maushi* said with a heavy voice.

"Whose children?"

"From the neighbourhood. I've invited them for lunch today," said *maushi*, turning over the flatbread on the griddle.

"Maushi, you still like to cook and serve?"

Ding, ding, dong... the noon bells were ringing at the church.

"That is the truth," exclaimed *maushi* happily.

"Aunty, do you still believe that? That when the bells ring, they affirm the truth?" asked Sumati in surprise.

"You know my dear, the bells have always shown me the way in my life. The bell for me is God's word. It is always the truth."

"You've always loved cooking, so what is there today?" asked Sumati, gently changing the subject.

"Nothing much. What is that bag in your hand?" *maushi* asked, hiding the note of sadness in her voice.

"Oh god! Just see, I've forgotten. Take this, *maushi*. Today is the full moon of the banyan tree. I've brought you a small *vainn*." Sumi offered the bag to *maushi*. At that moment, *maushi* turned around and, holding on to a pole for support, she stood up. "Sumi please take that gift and give it to the crows and from today don't come here again."

Maushi's words jolted Sumi's heart.

When she got up and went towards *maushi*, she saw that she was crying and asked, "What happened, *maushi*? Why are you crying?"

"Nothing Sumi. You can go. And please do come again."

Sumati went towards the door on leaden feet. "But go straight and give the *vainn* to the crows," *maushi* said without looking back.

Sumati entered her cabin quickly and, pacing up and down, asked D'Souza to bring her a Pepsi. Taking the bottle, she came inside. "D'Souza, I am upset today. Once upon a time that Rekha *maushi* was so good. It was she who taught me about *vainn*, the gift to be given on the full moon of the banyan tree. She taught us that the gift was for the intention of the well-being of the husband. And today she is telling me to take that gift and give it to the crows!" said Sumati pacing up and down.

"Who is this Rekha *maushi* and what has happened to her?" D'Souza asked.

"It's a story of more than twenty years ago. She was our neighbour in Altinho. We were not immediate neighbours. At that time Altinho was just hills. Unlike today, there weren't many houses or any buildings then. The houses were of mud and the floors were plastered with cow dung. There were very few things. Even our houses were scattered. Rekha *maushi's* daughter Minu and I were in the same class. We were close friends, and used to go to each other's houses quite often. Rekha *maushi* used to give us a lot of things to eat and tell us many stories... she was very religious. She used to pray and sing hymns praising god. She had a lot of taboos – there was no bathing at nights, nails were not to be cut after sundown. You weren't supposed to leave the house at night on Wednesdays and Sundays. She used to tell us a lot of these dos and don'ts... and what was really special was her adherence to the church bells. She used to pronounce bell in a peculiarly stressful way as *ghant*."

"Did she go to church despite being a Hindu, madam?" D'Souza interrupted her.

"I don't know that, but when the bells of Mary Immaculate Church tolled, she would stop whatever she was doing, join her hands and pray to god. And she would pray at least once if not at all the three bells – morning, afternoon and dusk. And the funny thing was that when the bells rang as she was speaking, she would say, 'That is the truth'!

"Once I had asked her, 'Why do you do this?' At that time, she had explained, 'God is one. We tend to forget Him. The bell reminds us of Him and shows us the way.' She would say this quite often – that the bell reminded her of god. She did everything well. But to my mind, one thing that wasn't good, was that she was too outspoken. I have heard her arguing roughly with Minu's *baba*.

"*Baba*, meaning Minu's father, too was a hot-tempered man, angry-looking in appearance. He was lean. But he loved his daughter Minu a lot. He was a man of few words. I don't remember him much, but I still remember all the things that *maushi* taught me. You know that on the day of *Voda Punov* – the banyan tree full moon – *maushi* would get up at 3:30 in the morning to make the preparations. First, she would draw water from the well and fill the cauldron. She would stoke the cauldron firewood with a pipe to bring the flame to life. By the time the bath water was ready, she would tuck in her sari at the waist and plaster the whole floor with cow-dung. She would use the *tulsi* and hibiscus flowers to make a pretty *rangoli* design at the front door. After doing all the work, she would have a bath, dress up, plait her hair and begin the *puja* with everyone. She would hum songs of praise. The preparations for the *puja* – meaning rolling the wicks for the oil lamps, preparing the flowers – these were the things she taught us. Rolling banyan leaves into cones and filling them up with the batter for sweets. Whilst teaching this, she would tell us tales from religious mythology. Then we would offer these cones in a *puja* before god. After that, we would apply turmeric to these cones and put these *vainn* in a tray. Then Minu and I would have to take these gifts and distribute them to the neighbours.

"One *Voda Punov* day, I was confined to the house with fever. I could not go to *maushi's* house. I could not even get up. Minu came to our place with the *vainn*.

"But after that day, I never saw Minu or *maushi*. Their relative Mandar too was not be seen. At the time, I had only understood that they had left the house and gone away.

"The other day when I met *maushi*, it was after a gap of many, many years. I really felt very good to meet her. But I just could not understand why she behaved this way today? I grew very pensive about it."

It was a couple of days after that banyan tree full moon day episode. Sumi didn't have the courage to go to *maushi's* house. But even as she was pondering over the next case with closed eyes, she couldn't help thinking of *maushi*. No matter how much she tried, she couldn't solve the riddle. 'If I keep thinking this way, I won't be able to finish my work,' she thought, mumbling to herself. Then she stood up in her cabin when she saw *maushi* pushing open the door and entering.

"Hello *maushi*, you have come here to see me? Come, come in, I hope everything is all right."

"Yes Sumi, everything is okay. How are you? Lots of work?"

"I'm fine, *maushi*. The usual work. Come, sit down," Sumi said, pulling up a chair for her.

"What will you have, *maushi*... tea, coffee or something cold? I'll order a cold drink. You must have come through the hot sun, right?"

"What sun, it's barely 10:30 in the morning! And I've just had my breakfast before coming."

"So, where are you going?" Sumi asked, sitting down in her chair.

"I've come just to see you. To ask your forgiveness. That day you came to our house for the first time and I asked you to leave. Till today I've never sent away anyone who comes to our house around lunchtime, without having a meal. But I sent you back. I've not been at peace for the last two days. That is why I have made some nice *polle-bhaji* and brought it for you. Forget the anger you had for me, Sumi," said *maushi*, taking out the cloth-wrapped tiffin and keeping it on the table.

"*Maushi*, what is this? I don't have any anger against you. But I have an unanswered question. What did I say that caused tears to fill your eyes?"

"No, my dear. You didn't say anything wrong. It is all in my destiny. Today, I want to place before you the burden I've been carrying for the last twenty years. Please try to understand me, Sumi," *maushi* said in a low voice.

"*Maushi*, you can talk freely. I'll see that nobody disturbs us," said Sumi, giving some orders over the phone.

"Sumi... it happened twenty years ago on the day of the banyan tree full moon – the blackest day of my life. On that one day, my life turned to mud... my Minu... my darling Minu left me..." As *maushi* spoke, Sumati rolled back the twenty years.

It was the day of the banyan tree full moon. *Maushi* had begun her work from the morning. From her work, *maushi* had called out to Minu, "Minu, dear, it's almost 12. Go to Sumi's house and give her this *vainn* gift. She's not well it seems. That's why she probably can't get out of the house."

"I'm going. I too want to show her my new *ghagra* blouse and *odhni*," Minu had said as she got up. As she left with the *vainn*, 'ding, ding dong' the church bells rang. "Minu, wait a while. One does not get out of the house at 12 o'clock," *maushi* said, but Minu had already left.

Maushi said a prayer and resumed her work after a while.

Minu's *dada* returned home. So did Mandar. Uttering 'suk suk', he began to dance and play around by himself.

"Mandar my boy, after Minu *tai* returns, we can all sit down for lunch. Till then, have this apple," *maushi* said to him soothingly.

"Get up you! Go and see where Minu *tai* is and bring her back. Go!" *Dada* said somewhat sternly.

"What is this, *dada*? He's only five years old. Where will he go to search for her? He won't know. He may go into the forest and get lost."

"He certainly knows how to guzzle down food. Nothing will happen to him," said *dada*, taking him by the hand and leading him out. After about ten minutes, *dada* returned alone. "You have come back alone? What's happened to Minu? And where is Mandar?"

"He went with Caetan to look for Minu," said *dada* averting her gaze, and he began to sweep.

"*Dada*, it's not right to sweep after 12 o'clock. That Mandar also just went out."

"Let him go. It's a good thing he's gone. He eats up everything greedily – it's as if we are in the rare thirteenth month," said Dada crossly.

"Why do you say this about him? What has he done to you?"

"What more can I say? He's some stranger's child. He's come to our house and eats away my food. Am I supposed to keep quiet?"

"How can you say stranger? He's my cousin's son. Both his parents died in the epidemic. This poor fellow is the only one who survived. Because he didn't have anybody, he's at our place. The neighbours brought and kept him here. Whatever it may be, he's now a part of our family and my son," she added.

Dada was spoiling for a fight.

"But I don't accept that. The only person I love is my god-given Minu – there's no one else. I don't even feel like calling out the name of that urchin. Every time I see him, he keeps bumping into me. Have I to struggle and earn money only to push it down his throat? Why should I? I wonder why he too did not die with his parents?"

"Oh my god! When you say such obnoxious things, why aren't you struck dumb? It's not good to talk like this."

"God? I just don't want to see him! My head whirls. I told you so many times that we should take him and keep him at your brother's house, but you...."

"Enough of that. You keep raking it up again and again. You will not get a different answer from me. It's a month since he was left with us, but you haven't shown even the slightest kindness to the poor boy. In the first place, he's lost both his parents, but your heart will not soften." Maushi too had raised her voice.

"I hope he does not come back, the problem will be solved once and for all," *dada* said in anger and went inside. In a short while, he had a bath and came out in his *lungi*.

"Why did you have to have a bath in the afternoon?"

"I hope to get some peace away from that devil."

Just hearing this, a shriek escaped from *maushi*. They used to have these family fights often. Since she didn't want to escalate the fight, she did not respond.

As there was no news of Minu and Mandar for more than forty-five minutes, *maushi* was worried. Suddenly, Mandar ran in crying. "Minu *tai*, fox; Minu *tai*, fox" were the only words he uttered. Hearing this, *maushi* had only one thought, 'How did Minu land in the forest?' *Dada* picked up a heavy stick from the corner, tucked his *lungi* at the waist and went out mouthing profanities. Taking the hand of *maushi's* who was calling upon god for help, Mandar began to run with her. Other people too came with sticks and spikes and went towards the woods.

At the foot of a hill, there was a big drop. Minu's *odhni* was caught in the thorny shrubs on the side. *Maushi's* heart skipped a beat. Everyone knew that if Minu had fallen from here, it would be very difficult to survive. Ahead, *dada* also squatted on his knees.

Without warning, *dada* landed a resounding slap across Mandar's face. Mandar was frightened. He went crying and stuck to *maushi*.

"Why are you beating him? How is it his fault?" she shouted angrily.

"It is his fault. All this happened because of him. He must have brought Minu here. He must be a demon with reverse feet. First he swallowed his parents, and now he must have jumped on Minu's life. He switched fates with her. I won't let him be!" Saying this, *dada* grabbed Mandar's hand and tried to drag him.

"What rage has possessed you? In your anger, you're talking nonsense. Instead of venting your anger on him, first go and find Minu. She'll be around here somewhere," *maushi* said, freeing Mandar from *dada's* hand.

Mandar began to cry, "*Kaki*, it wasn't me. Uncle said... I had taken Minu *tai* to the forest... but the foxes came after me... Minu *tai* came to save me... but I could not do anything..." Sobbing, he clung tight to *maushi*.

"Hush, baby hush, don't cry like this. Minu *tai* will be alright. Everyone has gone to search for her. Don't cry. You're a smart boy, aren't you? Smart boys don't cry." *Maushi* was wondering whom to look after. On the one hand, she was worried about Minu and on the other here was Mandar's face looking beseechingly at her.

Everyone went to look for Minu in the forest. But *maushi's* feet would not move. She caught Mandar's fingers and squatted down by the side of a tree. Some of the neighbours were consoling *maushi* and heading back home. By the time it was dark, the howling of the foxes began and Mandar was hungry from noon. She decided that she should go back at least because of him. *Maushi* got up. The first thing she thought of was, 'Minu, is this our last meeting?' At that moment, the evening Angelus bell tolled in the church. *Maushi* got the message. A stream of tears began to flow from her eyes. She sat on the ground for a long time, patting Mandar and sobbing copiously.

Afterwards, she steeled herself, wiped her tears and went back home.

Late that night, *dada* returned home with his head drooping. Seeing *maushi* in the house, he said, "Caetan and others have gone ahead. They'll find Minu by morning." When she saw *dada*, she lost her mental control. "You say Minu will return? There is no more Minu. We'll never see her anymore. And for this you are responsible. Because of you, my Minu has died. I had told you not to sweep. The children had just gone out. You sent poor Mandar outside. You got what you wanted? You managed to bring death into the house. Death came to my Minu. I don't want to see your face. You killed my Minu," she said, beginning to sob. Hearing her words, *dada* slumped down by the door.

In the morning at dawn, someone woke *maushi*. It was Caetan who was running, and saying "Look at *dada*, look at *dada*!" He caught her hand and dragged *maushi*. Pulling her, he took her to the place where Minu's *odhni* was caught in the branches. *Dada's* body was swinging by the halter round his neck. *Maushi* fell unconscious.

"But, *maushi*, why did *dada* take his own life?" Sumi asked, after hearing the whole story.

"Sumi, *dada* loved Minu very dearly. We lost our first son to polio. At that time *dada* was very sad. Our situation too was very bad, but just as the temple priest had predicted, after Minu was born, *dada* got a job as a peon and good times came for our family. From then on, *dada* began to love Minu a lot. People thought that *dada* had committed suicide because of Minu. But you want to know the truth? He was cut up with my words and went off. That is why, every year, on *Voda Punov* day, I send food in memory of Minu to children and the *vainn* to crows in the hope that my sins will be forgiven."

"But *maushi*, I have some doubts. You may think that it is your fault, but I am speaking from the objective viewpoint of the police."

"Go on."

"Look *maushi*, Mandar was always scared of *dada*. *Dada* used to treat him badly. On that day, *dada* sent him to search for Minu and he lied to you that Mandar had gone with Caetan. According to what Mandar related, *dada* had sent him into the jungle with the intention of him either falling into the hands of the foxes or falling down the ravine. Otherwise, tell me, why did *dada* sweep the floor? Why did he bathe himself after Mandar's departure? And why did he slap Mandar across the cheeks, saying that he HAD switched fates with Minu. In my opinion, *dada* had made preparations for Mandar's death, but it rebounded ON HIM and his beloved Minu died. And in his remorse, *dada* took his own life."

Ding, ding dong! The noon bells rang out in the church.

"It is indeed the truth," *maushi* said as usual and quickly bit her tongue. Sumi too kept her words in her mouth.

Maushi turned pensive and did not speak for a couple of minutes. Then, picking up her bag, she left the police station.

Once again the bells had endorsed the truth.

Glossary

Ghant: Bell

Maushi: Aunt, also a term used to respectfully address an elderly woman

Balcão: Balcony

Mogra: Jasmine

Kumkum: Mark applied to the forehead by a Hindu woman (earlier by a married woman, who had to stop using it after widowhood, but now used by unmarried, married and widowed women)

Polle: In Goa, leavened bread prepared from wheat flour and bran

Vainn: Gift of fruits and sweets distributed to married women in the neighbourhood on the day of the full moon of the banyan tree (in July–August) for the well-being of husbands

Tulsi: Holy Basil

Puja: Prayers

Rangoli: Art form (originating in the Indian subcontinent) of patterns created on the floors of living rooms or courtyards using rice or flour mixed with colour or even with flower petals. Besides decoration, it is considered auspicious and a necessary preliminary in any Hindu religious ritual

Bhaji: Vegetables

Ghagra: Ankle-length loose skirt pleated at the waist, worn with a blouse (*choli*) by girls and women

Odhni: Thin shawl worn by South Asian women around the neck

Lungi: Loose ankle-length garment worn around the waist, mostly by men

Tai: Elder sister
Baba, dada: Father
Kaki: Paternal uncle's wife

Originally written in Konkani as 'Gantthen Sot Kelem'.
Translated by Xavier Cota.

The Migrant

Maria do Céu Barreto

VINOD just couldn't sleep. He tossed and turned in his bed and lay on his back again, unable to doze off. He thought it better to keep his eyes open and treasure in his heart the little room he shared with his brothers, all of them younger than him. Through the gaps, the faint light of dawn was already visible inside the hut. He knew it was time to be on his feet, yet he kept lazing in his straw bed for a few minutes, thinking about his impending adventure.

What would Goa, where he was going to hunt for a job, be like? He was told by his country-cousins there that the land was bathed by the sea and its blue waters mirrored the clouds. There were long, seemingly endless, beaches of white sand. He rejoiced at the thought that it must be a very beautiful location indeed. He had seen the sea in the movies; now he would get to soak in its waters.

But then, he wasn't going to Goa for its beauty. A job, however modest, is what he was looking for. He was gutsy and painstaking; work never intimidated him. Even as a little boy he had helped out in the fields. His father had tried to make sure his children would have a decent future; he had taken a bank loan and spent it all on those fields. But alas, the soil had been ungrateful; the gods did not help, despite the family *pujas* every morning. The hot sun had burnt up all the plantations that he had seen grow. The rain gods had abandoned them. Only wealthy farmers had managed to live through the drought: they had the money for irrigation and to buy electric pumps to draw groundwater. Debts were mounting with every passing month, and one day when he came home, he found his father's body hanging from the ceiling. Unable to pay off the loan, he had committed suicide, like many other peasants in despair.

Vinod rose from his straw bed resolutely. He sat in the doorway to take in the morning air. He looked around. It was all arid. There was no other way out; he had to set off, to help his mother support the little ones, who were still asleep. The school was two kilometres away and they walked to and fro every day. Poor little chaps! Mother tried to persuade him to stay on. She needed him; it would be hard to bear it all alone. He put across his point of view in the best way he could, asking her to pray to the gods as she always did, without ceasing. And then, no more hesitation; his fate was sealed. But today he had still to fetch water from the well – his last chance to help out. With the little liquid left over from the previous days, he had a wash and, as usual, went to the bushes to answer Nature's call. Toilets were a rare sight in the rural set up. All governments had promised to build lavatories; those were only election campaign promises, forgotten as soon as the aspirants rose to power.

It was still very early in the morning, yet he wasn't among the first ones to turn up at the well. There was already a queue for men and another for women. The menfolk usually drew the water and the women headed home with those pots held on their heads. Vinod was glad to see this line-up of women draped in multihued saris; they talked, giggled and looked askance at the boys. Lakshmi was there too. She had captured his heart and, by the looks she gave, his passion for her seemed to be reciprocated. How good it would feel to be back from Goa with money and to marry her! He had heard of many such success stories. He too would do well; he sensed success from deep within his soul.

Back from the well, he saw his mother preparing breakfast at the firewood stove. She handed him a plate of *rotis* and *bhaji*. He ate every bit, for he couldn't say when his next meal would be. By now his siblings had woken up and were gearing up for school. Vinod thought of taking the eldest one with him to Goa one day, and then maybe the whole family! At construction sites there was always employment for everyone.

The train was due to leave at noon, and it would be two hours before he got to the station. He thought it better to start out before he had a change of mind. He had written to some of his village friends in Goa but hadn't heard from them. He hoped at least one of them would pick him up from the station; it would be a relief if they got him accommodation, even if only for a week. His mother handed him whatever she had saved up for emergencies – a thousand rupees, quite a fortune, he thought. He tucked it away, picked up his suitcase, and humbly kissing his mother's feet bid her farewell.

"God be with you, my son," said his mother, embracing him. "Krishna will protect you."

He couldn't pluck up his courage to hug his siblings, who had started to cry. He patted them on the head and left for the station. He turned round before the last bend of the road: his mother and brothers were there waving at him. He paused for a moment and waved back. He was all alone now.

Vinod heard the whistle in the distance. The train had arrived, a little late as usual. The passengers stood where they thought their wagons would stop and were ready to pick up their suitcases. Travelling as he did, third class, Vinod had no reserved seat. He had to be in readiness, too, as it would now turn quite messy with people jostling for the best of places. As soon as the train halted, he picked his suitcase and dashed off to grab a good seat, and grab one he did. He placed his luggage on the rack and stretched his legs. He was very tired. Lack of sleep, anxiety, tension... Now he was sure to drift off. A few minutes after the train was in motion and had gathered speed, Vinod leaned on the headrest and shut his eyes.

He could not say how long it had been – maybe all night and a good part of the day – but when he woke up he found the landscape had changed. He tried to strike up a conversation with his fellow passengers.

"Have we reached?" he asked a young man who was going to Goa, or so he thought.

"Not yet. It's still a little too early. We will get there by evening," said the young man.

He wished to ask him a few more questions about Goa but noticed that he had dozed off. With a few more hours to go, he thought of walking up and down the corridor but feared for his seat. Patience! He would have to remain seated there throughout. He noticed some passengers preparing to eat their home-packed breakfast and, famished as he was, avoided looking at the food-stuff. Just then, a co-passenger invited him to share his breakfast, an offer he gladly accepted.

What a long journey it was! He closed his eyes again, knowing well he would not get even a wink of sleep amid the bustle of hawk-ers. The train had halted at a station and the peddlers were crying their wares – food, fruits, artefacts and other items. They did ev-erything to draw the attention of the passengers and win them over. Vinod smiled. He hoped to have Lakshmi by his side on his next trip. A slim and pretty girl she was, whose long hair, charcoal-black eyes and tanned skin made his heart stop. He had not bid her goodbye, for in the village boys seldom talked to girls without their parents' permission. And badly off as he was, they would ig-nore him. But everything would change when he returned with his pockets stuffed with cash. Where would he celebrate his mar-riage? Back at his native place for sure, in keeping with tradition. All expenses would be borne by the bride's parents. He would not ask for a dowry; he knew that her parents did not have the means and he had no intention to get them into debt, like many families did... But would she wait for him until he came back?

Vinod fell asleep, lulled by these thoughts and unmindful of the noise. On waking up, all he saw was lush green countryside and water, water, water everywhere. There were lakes and rivers, and as the train carried on, he saw waterfalls too. He had never encountered anything like this before; he was sure it was Goa. Half an hour later he felt the train grind to a halt. The whistle blew; they were at Vasco da Gama, the port city of Goa.

A motley crowd welcomed their friends and relatives. Vinod felt his ears numbed by the numerous languages he heard: it was a real Babel. He even heard some words in his language! Was it his friends? He saw none; it was hard to locate people amidst the chatter. He let the other passengers exit first; he was not in a hurry. Then, all of a sudden, someone called out his name.

"Here, here we are!" Turning around he spotted Rama and Vishnu, his childhood friends. A strange joy seized his heart: he was no longer alone. They hugged him; they were thirsting for news from their land, family, friends, but Vinod, not in the mood for all that, promised to field questions a little later. He noticed that they looked very different, well dressed and cheerful as they were. Obviously, life had not treated them badly. He was happy for them.

"You're staying with us tonight! Mother is waiting for you. Let's see, if you like, you can even stay longer, until you get a job," said Rama.

Vinod was thrilled. He did not know what to say.

"How are we going? Shall we take a rickshaw?" he asked.

"No, no, we'll take our motorbikes." Vinod was amazed. Their bikes? How did they manage to buy bikes? Questions and questions that would have to wait for answers...

On arriving at Rama's house, Vinod found the pleasant aroma of food engaging his senses. It was a small house compared with the others around there, but it had electricity, piped water and even a gas stove – luxuries for people from poor, parched areas.

"Miss our land and our friends so much!" Rama exclaimed at the post-dinner chat. "No doubt it's great out here, you know! Communities live in peace; no one interferes with you. Yet, it's not the same as your own land. It's a different culture; language and food are so different. To fit in, we've had to learn the local language, so much so that many of us speak better than the locals do!"

"And do the locals treat you well?" inquired Vinod.

"Well, they bear with us. They feel we are robbing them of their jobs and that in future they'll be outnumbered by the migrant population. Maybe they will; I don't know. However, they shouldn't forget that we've helped them develop this state. We do all the hard work, so I think we're a part of this land, although they don't think so. They are proud of their half-Western culture and dub us *ghantis* and shower insults, which we pay no heed to... To make sure we do well, we must avoid squabbles."

"And why can't they get those jobs?" Vinod retorted.

"They can, except that they don't want to work hard; they try to find jobs that won't have them dirty their hands. The educated lot opt for the civil services or private company jobs. They think this fetches them better security and better respect. And those who don't get such jobs or aren't happy with what they have, simply migrate. I know families and families that have migrated."

"Where do they go?"

"Don't ask! Maybe Dubai, England, Canada... I think there are Goans scattered around the world."

"Are they happy?"

"Hard to say... They earn better and enjoy a better quality of life... And who knows, maybe they even suffer humiliations like we do and are treated as second-class citizens."

"And they sure miss their land," observed Vinod.

"Of course, they do. They celebrate their respective village religious festivals, cook typical Goan dishes and even have exclusive Goan associations, where they meet regularly. You see, no one can forget their own little land."

"So they are like us!" exclaimed Vinod.

"Yes; only that we are migrants and they are emigrants."

Vinod was very tired and, by now, dying to go to bed, but the conversation was so interesting that he decided to linger.

"I don't understand how you guys have all these things at home, and bikes too."

"That wasn't easy. We had to work hard. Of course, we have to also be in the politicians' good books. At election time they grant whatever we ask for, in exchange for votes. The larger the family, the greater the bargaining power. For instance, you are alone and won't get much, but if you tag your family along, you'll get much more."

"And how did you secure this place?"

"That wasn't difficult. In fact, one has only to build a hut in some vacant space, live there and in time government legalises everything."

"Incredible!" said Vinod. "I think coming here was the right thing to do. I'll bring my family here as soon as I can."

Just then they overheard some commotion outside. "What's that?" said Vinod. "Who's fighting?"

"Not to worry! That's Vishnu; he drinks every night and creates a racket in the neighbourhood. He spends all his earnings on drink. He has three children, and, to support the family, his poor wife works at several households. This is a real hazard in Goa. Alcohol and drugs are easily available. There's a bar every few hundred metres. That's a great temptation. Make sure you don't fall into this trap, for then it's tough to get out of it. We've come here to make money and have to focus on that."

"Rama, thanks for the warmth and advice... I won't do any such thing. I've suffered enough back home; I've seen misfortunes caused by the lack of money. The first thing I'll do now is look for a job."

"I'll help you if you like. I know the builder of the nearby constructions. If I recommend your name, he'll find you a job."

"Yes, please do."

Vinod thanked him once more and went off to bed. The morrow would be another day. So far so good! The future was in God's hands. He smiled and fell asleep with these thoughts. Was he dreaming of Lakshmi?

Glossary

Roti: An Indian unleavened flatbread made from wholewheat flour and water that is combined into a dough. It is rolled out and cooked on a griddle over a flame

Bhaji: A vegetable preparation

Puja: Prayers

Ghantis: lit. From across the ghats. *coll.* Outsider. A derogatory term directed at people, especially non-Goans, who come to Goa, whether they are from across the ghats or not

Originally written in Portuguese as 'O Migrante'.
Translated by Óscar de Noronha.

Margie Pereira Learns How to Swim

Francesca Cotta

MARGIE Pereira had arrived at that point in her life where it had started to sink in that she, much like the faces she'd invariably recognise in the obituary section of *The Navhind Times*, was going to someday die. She realised she'd better start enjoying the little pleasures in life that she had long ago forgotten to appreciate when she took up the full time job of being a good wife and mother to two girls. It was just one of those things that happened, unbeknownst to everybody including herself. The little pleasures, for as long as she could remember, were only reserved for the young, perhaps also for men and maybe for some distinguished old ladies from rich families.

She decided that she would start by learning how to swim. The fear of water bodies, be it the Mandovi river or the sea at Miramar beach, had been instilled in her in the 'sixties – when she was just a little girl – by her overprotective mother. She would regale Margie and her older brother and sister with horror stories of picnics at the beach gone awry when the tide changed, or of toddlers who waded in too deep when their parents happened to be distracted for a moment. Margie didn't really know where she got these tales from. Some of them were not even reported in the newspapers, but she never doubted their veracity, as a result of which she grew up frightened of even entering a swimming pool, when those became commonplace in Goa.

In her adult life, the most she would do was sit at the edge of the baby pool during annual family getaways or São João celebrations, sipping gingerly on a gimlet and making small talk with a septuagenarian or octogenarian relative also wetting their feet for a bit, while often glancing fretfully at the bigger pool to check that her children hadn't sunk to the bottom of the deep end. Occasionally, she would call out anxious instructions: "Don't go to the deep end without a float!" or "No doing underwater races, it's too scary!" or "Please stick to the wall if you're swimming alone", and her daughters would flash a big grin and a thumbs up in her direction and promptly ignore her commands. They'd dart in and out of the water with their cousins like a shoal of minnows, the parts of their limbs that poked out of the surface every now and then gleaming wetly in the sunlight.

This swimming pool phobia was such a defining characteristic of Margie that when she marched up to where her sixteen-year-old youngest daughter Giselle was sitting slumped breadthwise across an armchair, legs dangling languidly while she tap-tap-tapped on her phone, and announced that she would like to learn to swim, the girl barely looked up from her screen.

"You're scared of entering a pool, mama," Giselle stated matter-of-factly, in a voice filled with tremendous patience, as if she were explaining a basic algebraic premise to a toddler for the first time.

"Correct. I'm bloody scared to do the silliest of things and I'm tired of it! That's why I want to learn!"

She said this with enough vigour to cause Giselle to look up from her phone and cock an eyebrow at her in surprise.

"Okay," she said slowly, "if you want to learn so badly, why don't you ask papa to teach you? He goes swimming almost every day, no?"

"I don't want papa to teach me..." Margie could just imagine how he would infantilise and patronise her while giving instructions and, while not intending to be mean, still hurt her feelings by not taking her wish to learn all too seriously. No, her husband was not suited for this task.

As her mother let her sentence trail off, smiling at her meaningfully, Giselle caught her drift and groaned theatrically. "You've got to be kidding me! You want ME to teach you? I barely have the time these days!"

"Oh come on, Gigi, you can spare an hour thrice a week for your ma. You can even pick which days of the week we go."

Giselle started to grumble, but Margie cut her off, saying, "It wasn't as easy for me to learn when I was a girl as it was for you, you know – what with the sea or some almost-opaque river being the only feasible options, and my paranoid mother, and girls not particularly being encouraged to do sports and all!"

"My fault or what, that things were hard for you back then?" her daughter shot back, on the defensive, but Margie could tell from experience that she was beginning to soften her stance on the matter.

"Oh, don't be a hypocrite! What's the point in sharing those feminist poetry videos on Facebook like you do all the time if you can't even be thoughtful towards your own mother?" she faked a wounded expression, raising her voice histrionically. She knew this would seal the deal as far as convincing her daughter was concerned.

"Alright, alright," Giselle muttered guiltily, "no need to get personal now, I'll do it. I'll teach you how to swim. But I really am busy these days so I don't know how we'll mana...."

"Busy doing what? Only messaging this fellow all the time, no? Your boyfriend, Sameer. What's it you call him? *Samster.*" Margie pronounced the nickname with an Americanised accent and chuckled.

"Mama, don't start now, ah..." the younger Pereira said warningly.

"Sorry, baby. Just joking," she said, and kissed the top of her daughter's head.

"Everyone's staring at me!" Margie gulped, gaping at the Marriott swimming pool. It was a balmy Monday evening, and the pool was half-filled with people of all ages, regulars from the way they seemed to instinctively know how to navigate their way past each other with few collisions. She tightened the towel round her hips, suddenly conscious of the cellulite above her knees and the stray strands of hair growing on her shins. She felt stupid standing there with her grey-streaked shoulder-length hair tucked into a lavender-coloured swim cap. That morning, she'd carefully laid out her favourite swimsuit, a sensible and stylish navy blue thick-strapped halter-neck one-piece with a white band across the waist. It was a gift from her sister in Braga, who insisted on sending her the latest 'hip' swimwear every two years regardless of the fact that Margie didn't swim. "Since you're seen OUTSIDE the pool in your swimwear rather than INSIDE it, it is even more imperative that you wear something nice when you go on holiday since everyone can see you!" her sister stated matter-of-factly when Margie once objected to having a plethora of swimsuits she could hardly put to good use.

Now, noting that the only people being taught how to swim were toddlers, she felt embarrassed. What had she been thinking! Surely, they were doing a much better job of learning to swim than she would, she thought, morosely.

Picking up on her mother's trepidation, Giselle nudged her gently and said, "C'mon, mama, the water looks nice and warm. Let's get in quick!"

The pressure she was feeling on seeing so many people in the pool helped Margie momentarily forget about her fear of water and she began her descent down the steel ladder. The second she was up to her chest, however, she lost her nerve. Her old paralysing phobia seeped in, and she started to wail, "I CAN'T DO THIS! GET ME OUT OF HERE!"

Giselle kept her hand firmly grasped in her mother's and refused to budge, saying, "I'm right here, don't worry."

After the shock from the coldness of the water and the novelty of standing upright in a pool for the first time ever wore off, Margie started to appreciate sensations she was experiencing: the cool of the water enveloping her body, the sea breeze from Miramar beach right across, the sudden lightness of movement. Amazingly, rather than her body becoming an anchor, dropping to the bottom of the pool, she felt lithe and supple as a dancer, and took a few steps forward joyfully.

For the next few days, Giselle and Margie merely practiced walking the length of the pool. They would do this for a whole hour, taking breaks only to relax on the shallower side at the lip of the infinity pool overlooking the beach and taking in the sights and sounds of scores of people walking the length of the shore; children yelling, groups of young men calling out to each other as they passed a ball between them, idle chatter and laughter from miscellaneous groups frequenting the beach.

By the end of the third week, Margie was able to float, paddle in the water with her head submerged for a few seconds at a time, and kick her legs for a short while. Sometimes, and much to her husband's amusement, tucked up in bed at night, she would practice kicking her legs a little under the blanket with her knees straight like Giselle had taught her. When a while later she learnt how to come up for breath *while* moving through the water, he commemorated the day by gifting her with a pool membership in Marriott's and a pair of goggles that matched the colour of her swim cap.

But the most glorious achievement for Margie was learning to float on her back. She discovered a whole new world there, just her and the cerulean blue sky and the pillowy clouds, and the ripples of water carrying her along. Over there, she could truly abandon all cares – be it paranoia about her slowly ageing body, or fretting about a quarrel she'd had with her brother the week before or pending domestic duties. Floating on her back, she was not Margie. She was a lotus on a pond, or a beautiful Broadway dancer in her own private pool somewhere where the real estate was ridiculously expensive, or best of all, nobody at all.

Margie's first display of her new skill to her social circle was at a weekend getaway two months later, with three of her closest friends whom she'd known since her time in college. They were staying at a resort in Agonda, to bring in their friend Jacinta's sixtieth birthday. The revelation was such a surprise to her friends that Jacinta laughingly accused her of stealing her birthday thunder. When they popped a bottle of champagne at 12, they toasted both to the birthday girl's good health and to Margie's "sexy bum-shake when she does the doggie paddle" as Tania, the more rambunctious of the four, declared, grinning from ear to ear. Margie went pink in the face and thwacked her on the head with the room service menu card, but didn't look altogether displeased.

These days, Margie can be seen floating as naturally as a dry leaf on water in the Marriott swimming pool. She is finally putting her swimsuit collection to good use. She no longer needs Giselle's help to navigate the sparkling blue depths of the swimming pool. She is sometimes accompanied by her husband, and on days that she is not, she is perfectly content with the company of six-year-old Rehan, a regular at the pool who comes every day with his mother. She is not yet brave enough to venture into the sea, but she knows now that crossing that hurdle is always a possibility if she really wanted to. She is considering learning to drive – a skill she briefly took up years ago and soon abandoned out of wariness of the busy inroads around Panjim, and the fact that no one seemed to mind whether she was able to drive or not.

However, on second thoughts, she'd rather not. "Driving is that *one* activity in the family in which other people invest more time and energy than I do," she recently announced to a friend, "and I'm more than content to keep it that way!"

The Dripping Stream

Sushmita Dessai

FOR the last few years, the rains had begun to bug Reshma. She had never felt troubled by the rains as long as her mother was alive. But two monsoons had gone by since her mother had passed away. Now she just could not tolerate the rains. Why did the rain irritate her? Why should she tolerate it?

She casually clicked on *shaadi.com*, the online matchmaking site. Her uploaded photo stared back at her. 'I should have touched-up the picture before uploading it. At least one person would have called back. But till now...' But if the photo were touched up, would Reshma have changed? But again, if a nice photo is put up and someone gets attracted to it, how long would such an attraction last? Such contradictory thoughts crowded into Reshma's head. And then she got engrossed looking at the photos on Facebook. It was past 7 in the evening. Outside, the steady drip-drip of the rain continued. But inside, there was a fire raging. Some photos were adding fuel to the fire, while others were rubbing salt into the wound...

Reshma kept fiddling with the laptop. She didn't have to worry about cooking tonight. After returning from college, Reshma had finished her cooking by 4 in the evening. Even otherwise, how much does one need to cook for a single person? Nevertheless, after her mother had passed away, Reshma used to cook and eat regularly. Her mother used to always say, "No matter how educated a woman is or how much she earns, her work always ends in the kitchen and the bedroom." She'd earned success in her work in the kitchen. But the other room... that was still vacant. Her blood would begin to boil... And then it would cool down. Though she was in her thirty-seventh year, nothing was cooking as it should have.

Vidya Naik... yes indeed it was Vidya! Looking at the photo on Facebook, the volcano which had been dormant for long now, had started boiling and threatened to spill out of Reshma. But she didn't stop looking at the photo. The next photo showed Vidya with both her children. The elder boy was holding her tight from behind. And Vidya's younger daughter was playing at her feet. Vidya's husband had taken this selfie. He was trying to get himself into the frame. Vidya! What flirty escapades she'd had... and now... the symbol of chaste womanhood! Reshma couldn't help but remember the question. Reshma removed the laptop from her folded legs and stretched herself on the bed. Once again her glance went back to Vidya's family photo. Like a flashback in films, Reshma's memories rolled back and stopped around more than twenty-two years or so back.

Vidya and Reshma had become friends from the first day of college. The first few days went by as they felt like lost kids trying to get their moorings. Both came from similar backgrounds. They had both lost their fathers. They both depended on their fathers' family pensions and both the mothers leaned on their sons to propel the vehicles of their lives forward. Vidya had an elder brother who was not much educated. He was working in some small job. This alleviated Vidya's mother's burden a little. Reshma's father did not have much savings, but he had ensured that after his death his wife and daughter would not be left to fend for themselves. Besides, Reshma's mother used to sew people's clothes. They didn't exhibit their poverty and managed to pull on and present a respectable front... in any case, whoever says that they have enough?

The first month of getting to know one other was over. Now they could see each other in their true colours. Their friendship grew strong. But the fact was that, till today, Reshma was not that close to Vidya because, deep inside, she was envious of Vidya. Reshma had occupied herself with studies while Vidya was busy with other distractions.

In the third month of college, Vidya got very friendly with Vishal from the third year. One day, whilst going home from college, Vidya confided in her, "Reshu... I like Vishal!"

"What?" Reshma expressed surprise.

"Why are you looking as if you've just seen a ghost?"

Reshma did not respond to the question. 'Perhaps they were together. But then, if not now, when should they get attracted to boys – in old age? But again, this is the time for studies, not for making love...' Perhaps this was the way Reshma was thinking.

That night, Reshma hardly studied. 'Vidya and I are studying together. We go to the canteen together. We sit together in class. Often, Vidya comes to our place to study... Despite this, I wonder why Vidya behaved in this way? And how's that she did not tell me earlier...'

Vishal was a heartthrob... like a hero from the Hindi movies. Ninety percent of the girls in college were longing to have him as their boyfriend. As if this slip of a girl would get him?! When this thought came to her, she turned over and her eyes opened in the night. 'I wonder if Vidya has kept it away from me till the affair has gone well ahead.' It was difficult to get sleep now, but she was convinced that Vidya had quietly carried on without giving her the slightest hint about it and taken a huge leap.

Next day, whilst going to college, Reshma decided to keep a track on Vidya's behaviour. Vidya was sitting in the canteen. She'd worn a pink *churidar*. The *churidar* had a thin matching *odhni*. Reshma felt that her neckline was quite daringly low. The thin *odhni* was barely covering Vidya's blossoming bosom. Perhaps if it were brought to her notice, she might have hidden her youthful splendour! But again, it made no difference to Vidya. Admiring glances from boys would put her on a high.

'This is it! This was what I haven't seen till today.' Reshma had got the answer to one of last night's questions. Seeing Reshma, Vidya's excitement had reached sky high. She'd come running, hugged Reshma and given her a kiss. This was a side that astonished Reshma. She didn't know what had happened but she displayed enthusiasm. Vidya put a paper into Reshma's hand and whispered into her ears, "Vishal gave it. Read and return it to me." The reason for Vidya's excitement was now clear. The paper she'd put into her hands was a love letter from Vishal!

The laptop beeped an alert, raising Reshma's hopes... From flashback she came back to the present. She got up from the bed and began to grope for the charger. She didn't take long to find the charger in her college bag. But along with the charger, a paper fell out. Reshma picked up the paper, connected the charger to the laptop and began to read the paper. Since the students' exam was approaching, the principal had instructed all the lecturers to set the question papers and submit them to the examination committee. When she read the order, Reshma was irritated. She drew the books which were lying around close to her and started typing on the keyboard slowly. Outside, the continuous dripping of the rain; inside, barring the clicking keyboard, everything else was peaceful.

In the morning, when Reshma woke up, the laptop was still on. All the papers were typed. Outside too, the rain had taken a break. Reshma yawned and stretched herself as she got up and went and stood before the mirror. She could not look for long at the face of the nearly forty-year-old in the mirror. Her body had become flabby. Reshma did not feel like going out. Around eight years ago, the children around had begun to call her aunty, which irritated her. Her mother would gesture to her that they were just kids. Reshma felt that she'd rather be addressed as a sister. 'How are you, Reshma *didi*?' would be nice. She was greatly troubled by people calling her 'aunty', but was it their fault? *Bai, didi, tai, mauxi,* aunty – she knew that these nicknames are bestowed by society based on a person's looks and shape!

She finished all the morning chores and hurried out of the house. She found it difficult to wake up early. She usually had her morning tea in the college canteen or at a restaurant. Today also, despite waking early, she went to college without having her tea. College would begin at 9:30, and it was only 8 now. What did a single person need? The college campus was quite empty. There weren't any cars in the parking lot. In fact, there was one car belonging to the canteen operator. At least I'll be able to get a tea, she thought, as she locked her car and headed straight to the canteen. To get to the canteen, there was a straight passage, and then some steps. After climbing those, on one side was the library and behind that was the front door of the canteen. After climbing the staircase, Reshma's glance fell on a couple. They were having a good time. Both were college students. They were sucking on each other's youthful lips and the boy's hand was round her neck and inside the top...! Reshma saw the picture for a moment. The girl came back to reality and they became conscious that Reshma madam had seen their indiscretion with her own eyes. Both of them sprang apart. Reshma gave them a disgusted look and walked towards the canteen.

'What appalling behaviour from these youngsters! Do they come to college for this business?' The *canteenwala* brought tea and some *bhajjias* and kept them before Reshma. 'I didn't say anything to them!' The thought came to Reshma, of course... and the very next moment, 'How lucky that girl is,' she thought. 'I wonder what sort of magic those fingers work on that girl's youthful womanhood?'

Immediately, the morning scene played out before her eyes... her ears sizzled and her body heated up. Engrossed in her thoughts, she looked towards the sky and closed her eyes... The girl's closed eyes, the whole picture... 'And just then, I had reached there...' Reshma was annoyed with herself. Had I not reached there...? What would have happened? *Shi-shi*... these thoughts are unbecoming of a lecturer. She finished her *bhajjias* and began to walk towards the staff-room. Her eyes were seeking out the couple from the morning episode... What was their fault? Why did I look at them with anger? Such thoughts started drumming at her heart. But she couldn't get an answer to any of them.

Once she was in class, Reshma would forget everything. Me and my existence... it's my life... the fire burning at night... that scene this morning... everything. And then, the students and even

Reshma herself got an opportunity to see and experience historic intellectuals. The bell signalled the end of the lecture – and with it began the picture of a lost soul come back to life.

Reshma exerted herself a lot for two lectures and then she felt exhausted. She did not have any close friends in the college. Everybody else's life was blooming. Some would come flaunting their baby bumps. Others would be glowing after frolicking with their husbands the whole night... some would announce that their marriages had been arranged. Some would get proposals. But none of these things had happened to Reshma. She was still hoping that these things would happen to her, but she thought, 'If these things are to happen in my life, there should be a miracle.' With this realisation, she kept away from others and became a loner. Reshma walked towards the canteen. She went to an empty table and sat on a chair. She looked around and her disapproving glance fell on the couple of the morning. The couple got up and, walking past Reshma, went out. 'Why did I behave this way?' Reshma's conscience began to trouble her.

It was 3 in the afternoon by the time she reached home. She cooked and had her lunch and it was past four. And her hard time began to trouble Reshma again. Closing her eyes, Reshma lay down on her bed... Vidya... yes, Vidya came back in flashback.

Reshma had reached home with Vishal's love letter given to her by Vidya. Closing the door, she'd opened the letter.... her heart began to race... her body began to heat up for no reason... The letter was written by Vishal to Vidya, but the one who was excited was Reshma! By that night, Reshma had read and re-read the letter several times. Each time, she was aroused. Her heart was thudding. 'Why Vidya, why?' was the question Reshma kept asking herself. After that, all the love letters that Vidya received were safeguarded by Reshma. Reshma used to read those letters again and again. Now, Reshma and Vidya had an added member to their pair... Vishal!

"Shall we go to the movies today?" Vishal asked.

"What?" Reshma asked in surprise.

Vidya was just behind them. Seeing Reshma's confusion, both of them burst out laughing.

Vishal and Vidya would remain glued to each other. He used to put his arms around Vidya's shoulders. Vidya would cling to him. When they felt no one was looking, they would kiss each other and burst out laughing. They never felt that Reshma was intruding. 'When I am so close, they do this... god knows what they do behind my back!' Even at the thought of it, Reshma's body would heat up. And with all this, Reshma went with Vidya and Vishal to the movies.

There was some Hindi movie playing at the theatre. Vishal sat in one place, Vidya next to him in the middle. The seats in that row were vacant.

"Not many people today... otherwise, the place is packed," Vidya remarked. 'Today, meaning... they've been going without me knowing?' Reshma was shocked... so this thing has been going on for quite some time!'

The morning show was only for college students bunking lectures. They were crowded into the corners. The movie began. Around ten minutes later, Reshma's glance went towards Vidya... and Reshma's body was aroused much more than it had ever been. Reshma feasted her eyes on the unfolding drama. Besides Reshma nobody else seemed interested in the movie. Reshma's heart beat increased. She said softly to herself, 'Don't look to the side,' but in a few minutes, her glance went that way again... Vidya's cleavage which used to be otherwise covered by the *odhni* was now exposed and Reshma could see it... and Vishal's lips were feasting on it... Reshma kept looking without stopping...

Reshma was now thoroughly aroused and her heart was thumping. After all these years too, the memory used to burn her. After a year, Vishal's place was taken by Ajay. Suraj and Vidya had spent a night together at Reshma's house and now who is this guy...! Had

Vidya erred? Or had Reshma erred? Reshma got up from the bed...
She went straight to the bathroom.

There was no one in the house. Nobody. Yet she closed the
bathroom door. She latched it. She removed her clothes one by
one. Looking at the mirror, she closed her eyes. She could see the
body that nobody wanted in the mirror. Her heart was still thumping. Cold water sprayed from the shower. The first stream of water came over her nose, over her lips, through the valley of her
breasts, seeking a way to her navel. It filled her belly button and
continued on its way down. Another stream joined it coursing its
way from her eyes. This stream calmed her down. And the streams
kept coursing for quite some time.

Glossary

Churidar: Tightly fitting trousers worn in the Indian subcontinent
by women with a *kameez* (tunic) and by men with a *kurta*
Odhni: Thin shawl worn by South Asian women around the shoul-
ders
Didi: Sister
Bai: coll. Used here to refer to a woman
Tai: elder sister
Mauxi: Aunt
Canteenwala: Canteen operator
Bhajjias: (singular. *Bhajjia*) A savoury fried snack
Pao: In Goa, leavened bread prepared from wheat flour and bran
Shi-shi: Sound of disapproval

Originally written in Konkani as 'Pavlli'.
Translated by Xavier Cota.

This story won the Special Jury Prize at the Fundação Oriente
Short Story Competition, 2017.

Kashmir to Goa – A Love Story

Sunil Kumar Damodaran

THE explosion could be heard miles away from the site of the blast, shattering the window panes of the neighbouring houses, and debris was spread over vehicles and homes as far as a block away.

A tramp who was rummaging through the dustbin across the road was lucky; the blast toppled a dustbin, spilling the trash on the road. He fell on top of it, dazed but unhurt.

The coffee shop was in the bye-lanes of Fontainhas, an old Latin quarter in Panaji.

Sophia was sitting with her aunt, having coffee. Salim entered the shop along with three sombre looking foreigners and occupied the table on the other side of the aisle.

Their eyes met and though it was a fleeting glance, it was evident that something magical clicked. The chemistry was so instant and undeniable. Every time she stole a glance at him, she found him looking her way, trying to do the same.

Finally she smiled at him. Though caught by surprise, he recovered in time and smiled back. Soon their bill arrived and her aunt moved towards the cash counter, with her in tow. She had one last look behind while exiting the shop and found him smiling and waving *bye-bye*.

It was only when Sophia wanted to make a call home at around 10 o'clock in the night that she realised that her mobile was not in her handbag. She had forgotten to pick her mobile up when she placed it on the restaurant table, before leaving the shop. It was too late to go back to the restaurant as shops in that area closed by 8 o'clock at night.

After fretting for some time over the loss of her mobile, she decided to track her phone by making a call from her aunt's mobile.

Salim's heart skipped a beat when the mobile phone he had taken from the owner of the coffee shop began to ring next to his bedside. He had intended to hand it over to the girl personally, in case she came back to the shop to collect it. He had waited patiently for about three hours outside the shop, till it closed at around 8 o'clock at night.

He picked the phone and the found the name 'Ana Aunty' flashing on her mobile. He accepted the call and waited.

"Hello," Sophia managed to whisper.

Silence.

"Hello, who is this? That's my mobile you have got. Please hand it over back to me, please, I beg you," she said fumbling for words.

He took a deep breath and asked, "Coffee shop?"

"You?" she asked.

"Yes, you left the phone on the table and the waiter handed it over to the owner sitting on the cash counter."

"And...?" prompted Sophia.

"I asked the owner to hand it over to me."

"And he gave it to you!"

"No, initially he refused, saying that he will give it only to the owner."

"Ummm, then?"

"I told him that we are related. He then handed it over to me immediately."

"What relation?" she asked curiously.

"I told him that you're my fiancée and I will be going to your place soon."

"How dare you," she said, a huge smile stretched across her face.

"I am sorry, I don't know what I was thinking. This is the first time I have done something like this. Tell me your address and I will personally deliver it to you at your residence."

"Oh no, Please don't take that trouble."

"Can you come to the coffee shop tomorrow?" Salim asked. "I will hand it over to you."

Silence.

"Are you there?" he asked.

Silence again.

"Okay, I will leave it at the coffee shop tomorrow and you can collect it whenever you want," he said.

"Noooo!" she said, before he could disconnect. "I will meet you at the shop, but I won't sit with you there, I will leave immediately," she added.

She was beginning to enjoy the conversation and did not want to stop.

"Hold on," she said, and went slowly to the next room where her aunt slept. She found her fast asleep. She tiptoed back to her room.

"Should I call you later from my phone?" he asked.

"No, continue," she said, "there are no charges for calls made between these two numbers even if we talk the whole night."

"So you want to talk to me the whole night?" he asked laughing.

"No, that's not what I meant," she said, blushing.

"Tell me about yourself," he said.

"You first," she replied.

Salim then narrated the sequence of events that had landed him here in Panaji, Goa, a distance of more than two thousand kilometres from his village near Kargil, in the state of Kashmir, which was close to the Pakistan border.

A few weeks back Abdul Hamid had come to his house accompanied by three people. Abdul was well known in the locality; till recently he had been an instructor at the local *madrassa*. However, he had not been seen in the valley for the past few months and there was talk that he had joined some outfit that were helping Muslims in distress in other parts of the world.

After exchanging greetings, Abdul introduced the men to Salim's father. The tallest of them, with his mop of red hair, closely trimmed moustache and long beard, Abusaid Ali, was from Chechnya. The short stout man, who too sported a beard like Abusaid, was Makhdoom from Saudi Arabia. The third person, who looked like an ex-army person with his crew-cut hair and thick moustache and had the big hulk of a Pathan, was simply introduced as Major.

Abdul then informed his father that these men had come to the valley to recruit young men and take them to Saudi Arabia for carrying out the work of God. He said that as Salim was a very disciplined and religious student of the *madrassa*, he had recommended his name. Abdul also told his father that he was fortunate that God chose his son for more important tasks in life.

His father had protested and said that Salim was the eldest among his five children and the sole breadwinner of the family. If Salim left them his other children would starve, as he himself could not do any work after he had lost his foot in a landmine explosion.

Hearing this, Makhdoom started laughing and said that he need not worry as Salim would be paid more than five times what he earned here, besides reimbursement of other family expenses like the school fees for his younger brothers and medical expenses for the entire family.

The family was paid an advance of fifty thousand rupees and Salim was told to be ready to travel within a week. He landed in Goa a few days back along with Abusaid, Makhdoom and Major, and was put up in a two-storey bungalow situated on the banks of the scenic river Mandovi in Panaji. He was told to occupy the bedroom on the ground floor. The other men occupied the bedrooms on the floor above, as and when they were in town.

"So what's your work here?" Sophia asked.

"Nothing much," he said. "I was told by the people who have recruited me that they intend to set up a tourist venture here in Goa and that I am supposed to familiarise myself with various places of tourist interest in Goa, especially the ones visited by foreign tourists."

"That's all?" she asked

"No, besides that I also have to carry out a survey of all the vital defence installations in and around Goa and get familiarised with the surrounding areas. I was told that I will be given necessary instruction and guidance by them from time to time."

"Wow," she said. "But I don't see any connection with God and your task at hand."

"So don't I, but I was told by my employers that it will become clear later on."

"Oh! Divine suspense!" she said.

"Well, I have said enough, now it's your turn."

Sophia told him that she was from Canacona, a town in south Goa, and was pursing her Management degree from the Goa University. She was staying with her aunt, a spinster and a retired headmistress of a local school. She had one more year to go and after completion of the course she would go back to her native place.

They spoke for a very long time that night, about their childhood, hopes and dreams, likes and dislikes and many other things.

More than six months had passed since they first met. Salim had recently informed Sophia that his employers were likely to depute him for some training out of the state for a few months. By now both of them were madly in love and could not bear the thought of not seeing each other even for a day.

They both loved to meet at the ruins of an old fort built by the Portuguese colonists in the sixteenth century and watch the sunset from the ramparts of the fort. The area around the fort was overgrown with vegetation and the locals from nearby places stayed far from it as there were tales about the place being haunted. Salim and Sophia had the whole place all to themselves. The only other regular visitor there was a tramp from the town. He had made the old fort his home. He, however, was in his own world and always walking around with a set of earphones plugged into his ears, mumbling to himself all the time.

They usually met after 5 o'clock in the evening. However, on that day, it was well past 6 and Salim had not turned up. His phone was switched off. She waited till sundown at their meeting place, constantly checking her phone to see if he had sent her a message.

Little did she know that it would be a long time before she met Salim again.

Salim checked the message he received from Abusaid, on his phone, again. "Pack your bags and be ready to leave within an hour," it said.

He had tried calling Sophia, but found her phone engaged. He was about to send her a message when a car pulled into the driveway and Major stepped out from the driver's seat. He said that there was a change of plan and they had to leave immediately.

Salim placed his bag in the boot of the car and sat in the front seat. Abusaid and Makhdoom occupied the back seats.

"You will no longer require that," Major said, pointing to the mobile in Salim's hand as he entered the car. "Give it to Abusaid."

Abusaid held out his hand and said, "Don't worry, you'll get it when we come back."

The drive and the subsequent hopping flights lasted for twenty hours. The next day, another journey of eight hours, through the desert in an old open jeep. The last stretch of the journey was long and tiring. They walked for six consecutive nights crossing mountains and plains, resting during the days, before reaching a camp situated in a valley. They were in the no man's land between the borders of Afghanistan and Pakistan.

Rabbani was the commander of the north-western frontier training camp, under the direct supervision of Mullah Najib Rehman, the Supreme Commander of the outfit.

For the next six months Salim lived in the camp. A typical day began with morning prayers, followed by a sermon on the significance of *jihad*. Physical drills and operational training took place during the day. Instructors were typically veteran jihadists. Recruits were given lessons on how to handle small arms, sniper rifles and machine guns as well as rocket-propelled grenades, explosives training. They were instructed about making and planting bombs.

Evenings were for indoctrination. To dispel any doubts about the cause of *jihad*, recruits were shown hours upon hours of video depicting Indian and Western atrocities and of troops raping women and girls – a fate which their trainers said awaited their own female relatives if they did not carry out operations against their enemies.

Some students found to be eager learners and who could be easily motivated and radicalised were selected for further training and grooming as suicide bombers. Suicide bombings were depicted as glorious martyrdom operations, with rewards promised in the afterlife. On the final day, the Supreme Commander gave blessings before the suicide bombers took their vows.

Salim was one of them.

The Supreme Commander was listening intently to the information Rabbani had to give him, lines of fury marked his face. The surgical strike by the Indian Army had wiped out three of their camps. Twenty-three highly trained disciples and two area commanders had perished in the onslaught.

"It's time to send Salim to Goa," he said. "We have to get our revenge."

Salim had managed to mislead his handlers so far without raising any doubts. He was one of their most eager students and a very fast learner too. He excelled in almost all the training given to him.

In the meantime, Sophia was contacted by the Indian Intelligence Bureau (IB). An official informed her that the three men associated with Salim had been on the radar of the IB for a long time and it was suspected that their company was a front of a terrorist organisation waging war against India. He told her that the tramp who stayed in the ruins of the fort was their agent and kept tabs on all of them. He also said that Salim's life was in danger and she could help save him if she cooperated with the authorities.

The night they reached Goa, Salim managed to slip out and contact Sophia from a local payphone booth nearby. He had a lot of explaining to do regarding his sudden disappearance and absence for the last six months. They spoke for a very long time.

Salim narrated his ordeal to her and the intentions of his handlers. Sophia then informed Salim about the IB contacting her. She said that she could help him escape from the clutches of his recruiters with the help of the IB. She told him that for the moment he should do as directed by his handlers, so as to not raise any suspicions.

The D-day for Salim came much earlier than expected.

The ex-Chief Minister of Goa, now elevated as the Central Defence Minister, was to commission a naval aircraft carrier built by Goa Shipyard at its works in Vasco da Gama, and dedicate it to the nation. The function would be attended by top Union Ministers, Members of Parliament and Ministers of State. The heads of all the three wings of the armed forces would also be present.

The terrorist organisation wanted to strike on the day of the inauguration so as to have maximum casualties and wipe out many top politicians of India. On the fixed day, Abusaid dropped Salim to Vasco da Gama, near the shipyard, and left the place. His suicide vest was rigged to his body in such a way that it would explode if anybody tried to detach it from his body.

The function which was open for the general public was to begin in five hours' time. After waiting for some time and confirming that Abusaid had left the place, Salim waved down a taxi and asked the driver to take him back to Panaji.

According to the plans he had made with Sophia, she was to collect his car from his residence and meet him near the Campal football stadium. He had placed the keys of the car in the glove compartment of the vehicle the previous night.

Salim reached at the designated place in time. However, there was no sign of Sophia. After waiting for some time Salim decided to go and check if Sophia had managed to collect the car from his residence. He told the taxi driver to drop him a few blocks away from the house. He then cautiously walked towards the bungalow. From far he was able to see that his car was still in the garage. Major's car was parked next to it. The front door of the house was open.

He cautiously approached the house and found no one around. He next checked his room and found it empty. Hearing loud noises from the floor above, he slowly climbed the staircase and cautiously opened the door to the Major's bedroom.

Lying on the floor covered in blood, head to toe, was his love, Sophia. She was stark naked. Blood-stained broken bottles, knives, rods and her clothes were strewn across the room, mute testimony to the torture she had undergone.

Major came out from the attached bathroom in the room, zipping up his pants. "Get up you bitch," he said, and landed a kick to her midriff.

Sophia grimaced in pain and made an effort to get up. It was then that she saw Salim at the door. He ran towards her and lifted her.

She held on to him and barely managed to whisper, "I did not tell them anything." And then she closed her eyes and went limp.

Abusaid and Makhdoom were trying to pull her away from him.

Salim held her in a tight embrace, looked around the room, his eyes vacant, and pressed the button on his suicide vest.

The tramp scrambled to his feet and started searching frantically in the rubbish strewn on the road. He found his wireless set under a pile of dirt. He wiped it clean, adjusted the channel and spoke into it, "Threat neutralised, but lost the pigeons."

The Chief of the Intelligence Bureau camping in the control office of Goa Shipyard heaved a sigh and gave the all clear signal to his officers assembled in the room to go ahead with the inaugural ceremony as planned.

Murder?

Rajyashree Dutt

I NSPECTOR Kunkolienkar hitched up his pants and sucked his teeth. It was not a pretty sight. The body lay spread-eagled like a rag doll in the doorway between the tiny hall of the old house and what appeared to be a bedroom. Bare-chested. Deep blue shorts with white palm trees. He could not see the face. It was obscured by a curtain – large purple flowers sailing against a blue sky.

A thin young woman in a red dress scrunched her hanky to her nose and moaned. She sat in the stiff white plastic chair next to the TV, rocking back and forth. Eyes unseeing.

A man in a dirty vest paced up and down, hugging himself. The stubble on his face and the deeply furrowed brow pointed to a very disturbed mind.

Several pairs of eyes followed him. The many family members who lived in the village had crowded into the room and stood around the walls, craning their necks to catch every movement, every word spoken. Those who were not in the inner circle had to be content with standing in the overgrown garden and peering in through the bars of the windows. And the passersby stopped when they saw the crowd and lined the narrow road, concaving their bottoms to let the occasional vehicle go past – a car, the *poder* balancing a large basket of the warm and fragrant *poi* on his cycle, or the *nusteykar* on his scooter with the not-so-fragrant catch of the day in a bright yellow plastic box.

"What happened?"

"Don't know."

"I think it is a murder."

"Murder! Who got murdered?"

"Some man."

"Who?"

"Don't know."

Inspector Kunkolienkar walked up to the body. The crowd surged forward.

"Back, back, everybody back, otherwise I will clear the room," he roared.

The crowd retreated. Outside the windows they were standing on upturned flowerpots, stones, anything they could find, trying to get a clear view of what was happening inside. Then someone slipped off a stone and landed on someone else's foot. A yowl, followed by curses, apologies, more abuses.

"Quiet," yelled Inspector Kunkolienkar.

"Ssshhh... shhh... shhh..."

To view the face of the 'victim' Inspector Kunkolienkar had to first lift the curtain in the doorway and tuck it into the carved wooden pelmet above the door. This was not easy given that the body occupied most of the space in the doorway, leaving him not much room for manoeuvre. Inspector Kunkolienkar was a portly man. He inched his way up to the left of the body and lifted his right leg over to straddle it. His tight trousers strained at the seams and the bulging belly rippled against the buttons on his uniform. A few titters broke out.

"Silence," yelled Inspector Kunkolienkar as he teetered for a moment before landing on firm ground. With his baton he lifted the curtain. And he managed to place it over the pelmet.

A frisson of excitement passed through the crowd as they finally saw the face. Surging and jumping each one confirmed for themselves that there did not seem to be any marks of injury on the beautiful visage, serene in death. "But," they whispered, "the neck is at a peculiar angle, no?"

Sweating with the effort, Inspector Kunkolienkar bent forward to examine the face and the curtain slid off in slow motion and fell on his head.

This time there were spontaneous giggles. Inspector Kunkolienkar's backside quivered with indignation, but he kept quiet. Once again he lifted the curtain with the baton and tried to loop it

over the pelmet. And again it came swooshing down.

"*Arre baba*, use your hands," came some useful advice.

"This is a crime scene," thundered Inspector Kunkolienkar. "You cannot do things like that with a crime scene."

He looked around and discovered a thin wire strung from wall to wall. If he could reach it, he could perhaps hitch the curtain over it. But he was stuck in this somewhat compromising position with no idea how to go forward. One of the spectators had had enough. He marched up to the door, lifted up the curtain with his hands, and before Inspector Kunkolienkar could finish the third, "*Oi, oi, oi...*," had slung the curtain over the wire and out of the way.

With his legs splayed at an impossible angle, Inspector Kunkolienkar waddled up, over and beyond the body. The audience lapped up the show, stifling their laughter, nudging each other and rolling their eyes.

Now he was in the bedroom which was obviously where the crime had been committed. The rumpled bed sheet halfway off the bed. One pillow on the floor. The other still where it had been slept on.

Inspector Kunkolienkar was in his element. He drew himself up to his full five feet, tucked his baton under his left armpit, pulled out his mobile phone and began taking photographs. A small room dominated by a carved old four-poster bed. A table along the wall with delicate legs peeping out from under a plastic table cloth. On it the detritus of everyday life – yesterday's copy of *The Navhind Times*; a steel glass half full of water; a bottle of medicine, rich ruby red liquid behind the label; a strip of tablets from which a couple had been torn out, leaving a supplicatory aluminium finger pointing to the sky; a small orange face towel, neatly folded; a bunch of keys. Inspector Kunkolienkar's eyes and clicking mobile phone swept over the table and moved on. They came to rest on the cupboard built into the wall. One of the lightly carved wooden doors was open, revealing neat rows of clothes – his and hers. And a small, bilious green steel cupboard, with an old fly-blown photograph of a couple on their wedding day on top, snuggled into a corner. A gloomy room with light filtering in through the tiny spaces between the roof tiles and a single arched window. Beyond the window the pink and white hibiscus bloomed. A profusion of ferns fought for footholds on the craggy surface of the damp red laterite wall.

There was no access to this room except through the door in which the body lay. Inspector Kunkolienkar switched off his phone and walked around the bed to the other side. The *janta* in the hall craned their necks to see what he was up to, but did not dare walk up to the doorway. Suddenly, there was a yapping and a snarling as a little white dog emerged from under the bed and flung itself at Inspector Kunkolienkar's foot. Luckily for him his thick boots protected his feet, but as he leapt into the sky with a loud "*Aiyaaa*" he could not do much to protect his already crumbling image as a modern-day Sherlock Holmes. Having fulfilled its mission in life, the tiny ball of fur disappeared under the bed and Inspector Kunkolienkar, wiping his brow with a dirty brown handkerchief, beat a hasty retreat towards the door.

He was now face-to-face with the body. He took several pictures of it from various angles. Then he put away his phone and pulled out a little blue notebook and plastic ballpoint pen from his breast pocket.

"Does anyone know this person?" he asked loudly.

The woman in the red dress started wailing. The man in the dirty vest became more agitated.

Inspector Kunkolienkar peered out from the bedroom. From his position he could not see the woman who obviously knew something. And the man kept appearing and disappearing as he walked like a caged animal across the floor.

Inspector Kunkolienkar needed to go back into the hall. With his back pressed against the door jamb he tried to sidle past the body. But he could not see beyond his belly. So he finally had to lean forward, and shuffle along like a penguin nursing an egg. Inside the room they suppressed their laughter. But through the windows came the sound of whispering and chuckling and the unmistakable click of phone cameras.

Finally his rotund body surged through. Planting his feet firmly on the ground, his back to the body, Inspector Kunkolienkar looked around, lifted up his notebook with a flourish and stood poised for action, pen hovering in the air.

"Who is this man?" he asked, pointing vaguely in the direction of the floor.

Inspector Kunkolienkar looked around at the gathered folk with an enquiring look. Some shrugged, some averted their eyes.

The woman in red muttered something very softly.

"What?" barked Inspector Kunkolienkar, looking fiercely at her, "Please speak loudly. I cannot hear you."

"Joe," she whispered as she buried her face in her hanky.

"Joe... Joe what?" he asked.

"Joe Rozario," she said, barely audible.

"And who is he?"

The woman resumed her sobbing.

"He's... he's my friend," said shabby vest.

Inspector Kunkolienkar spun around. "And you are...?"

"Agnel... Agnel Gomes," said the surly one.

"Mr Agnel Gomes," barked Inspector Kunkolienkar, beginning to feel he had things under control, "who are you?"

"This is my house," said Agnel, looking around the room for corroboration. Several heads nodded in confirmation.

"Aha!" exclaimed Inspector Kunkolienkar as if he had unravelled the whole mystery, when in fact he was even more at sea. "This is your house... good... good... so who is that lady there?" he asked pointing to the woman in red.

"That is my wife..."

"Ahhaaa!" said Inspector Kunkolienkar, almost shaking with excitement.

He glowered at the man and his wife. Then he looked at the body. He remembered his notebook and scribbled a few things in it. The audience approved. Now he was looking more professional.

Inspector Kunkolienkar looked up from his notebook and fixed the woman with a baleful stare. He pursed his lips and scowled. "So Mrs... err... Mrs..."

"Mercy," said Agnel.

"What?" asked Inspector Kunkolienkar.

"Mercy. My wife's name is Mercy," said Agnel.

"Oh, I see. I see," said Inspector Kunkolienkar, but in fact he saw nothing.

This was taking too long. Some of the people standing around on the road in the hot morning sun decided they would leave and perhaps catch up with the story in the evening.

A young boy, nose stuck to the windowsill, called out, "Police uncle, what happened to that dead man?"

"Hmm..." said Inspector Kunkolienkar, turning around to look at the body, "... neck is broken. I think someone has broken his neck."

An immediate buzz arose within and outside the room.

"Broken neck."

"How?"

"No idea."

"What is the policeman thinking?"

"Am I god? How will I know what he is thinking?"

"I don't think he is thinking at all."

Which wasn't true. Inspector Kunkolienkar was thinking very hard. Crumpled bed sheet trailing on the floor... signs of a struggle? Yes, yes, definitely a struggle. He turned around and peered back into the bedroom. Well, maybe not a struggle. Maybe someone jumped out of the bed in a hurry. That was why the sheet was half on and half off. But who? The dead man? The woman? The husband? Inspector Kunkolienkar chewed the back of his pen. Two men and one woman. Love triangle. That's it. Of course. Open and shut case.

With renewed confidence he looked at Agnel. "Who found this body?" he asked.

Agnel and Mercy exchanged a quick glance. Inspector Kunkolienkar was scowling at his notebook and missed it, but the sharp young lad at the back of the room caught it.

"Well? I asked who found this body?" snapped Inspector Kunkolienkar.

"We both found it," said Agnel.

Mercy opened her mouth as if to say something but shut it immediately, looking away from the policeman as she did so.

"When did you find it?"

"This morning."

"I see. Hmmm... So tell me what happened this morning."

"Well, I was sleeping and..."

"And your wife?" glowered Inspector Kunkolienkar at the poor wife, who was knotting her handkerchief and twisting it round her fingers.

"I... I..."

"My wife was also asleep in the bed next to me," said Agnel quickly. Too quickly.

"No, I wasn't," came the strangled response from Mercy.

"Shut up, woman," muttered Agnel, but it was too late.

Inspector Kunkolienkar smelt a large rat.

"Quiet," he barked at Agnel, "let her speak."

Angling her body away from the wrath of her husband, Mercy babbled. There was a hush in the room as people edged forward to listen to her.

"I was away. I was visiting my mother in Vasco. I was supposed to come back next week but my sister in Bangalore fell ill so Mother had to go to her. I decided to come home. I could not inform Agnel. His phone was switched off."

"Switched off? Why?" scowled Inspector Kunkolienkar.

"Maybe it was not switched off. That is what it said. But you know the signal here is very poor. You cannot connect," explained Mercy.

"Okay, I see. Carry on. Then what happened?"

"I came home on the early morning bus and the pilot dropped me home."

"What time was that?"

"I think it was 7 o'clock."

"Yes, yes, 7:15," said a voice. Inspector Kunkolienkar peered over the heads of the rapt audience and saw a man leaping up and down in the garden. "Yes, sir. I am Tony. The pilot. I brought this *bai* from the bus stop this morning," said the man, basking in his moment of fame.

"Hmm," said Inspector Kunkolienkar, "come inside, Mr Tony."

There was much scuffling and shifting as the witness made his way inside.

"Okay, madam, continue," said Inspector Kunkolienkar, turning back to the distraught wife.

"I came into the house. The bedroom door was shut. Snowy was inside."

"Snowy? What is snowy?" asked Inspector Kunkolienkar.

"My dog."

"Oh... Okay. Carry on."

"Snowy... my dog... he heard me and started barking. Then everything happened very quickly... ," she sobbed.

"What? What happened?"

"I was trying to open the door. But it jerked opened from inside. That... that man came running out..."

"That man," said Inspector Kunkolienkar, quickly referring to his trusty notebook, "you are talking about Mr Joe?"

"Yes, yes, Joe."

"Okay, carry on."

Agnel shuffled up to the door between the hall and the bedroom like a broken man. He leaned his back against the wall and slowly lowered himself to the floor. He sat there very still. His face in his hands.

"I was trying to go in. Snowy was trying to run out to greet me. The man... Joe... he tripped over the dog and fell. I heard a loud noise. Like a crack. I think he hit his head on the door. And he fell down."

"He fell here?" asked Inspector Kunkolienkar indicating the body. Mercy nodded soundlessly, the tears streaming down her cheeks.

Inspector Kunkolienkar turned to Agnel, "And where were you?"

"In bed," hissed Mercy, spinning around, eyes blazing with hate, "he was still in bed..."

Inspector Kunkolienkar frowned. Something did not add up. If this was a love triangle and the dead man was the third person... how come... how come...

"How is that possible?" he sneered. "This man... Joe... how was he inside the bedroom if your husband was still in the bed? Why was he inside if you were outside?"

Mercy's face contorted with rage. "What do you think? You can't see, or what? Do I have to explain everything to you?"

Inspector Kunkolienkar stared at her. His eyes opened wide. His gaze shifted slowly to the body and then he looked at Agnel. And as the penny dropped he pursed his lips and gently shook his head.

Glossary

Poder: Baker
Nusteykar: Fish vendor
Arre baba: An exclamation indicating irritation
Janta: coll. The general public. Used here to refer to the crowd of onlookers
Bai: coll. Used here to refer to a woman

This story won the second prize (the Indo-Portuguese Friendship Society Prize) at the Fundação Oriente Short Story Competition, 2017.

Says Kabira

Vithal L. Gawas

"COME on, get up now, the sun has come up, and you are still sleeping like a child. Does this behove a man like you?" He woke up as he heard his wife's voice. Now there was no escape. He knew by experience that his wife would nitpick if he did not rise. He sat on the bed, eyes tingling. Sleep was overpowering him. This situation would continue till the month of Shravan was over. Once Shravan begins, this village is overwhelmed by an auspicious environment. Religious activities get a boost. Somewhere there is a Satyanarayan *puja*; at another's place there is some religious activity... And then the *bhajan* at night is sure to follow. *Bhajans* in the village would not take place without his participation. The same thing happened last night. There was a *bhajan* at the residence of the Shanbhags on the occasion of a *puja*. The *bhajans* ended late, at 1 am in the night. It was 2 am by the time he ate, went home and slept. Hence, his sleep was incomplete.

He rose, kept the bedding at the usual place, finished his ablutions and came into the kitchen.

His wife had kept breakfast ready. After breakfast he went and sat in the balcony. The notes of last night's *bhajan* were still resounding in his ears. The *bhajan* had kept people engrossed. He had sung beyond his comfort level. Listeners were seen swinging their heads to his singing. When the *bhajan* ended people had been taken to a heavenly level. Everyone praised him. They were appreciating the way he had come down slowly after raising the highest pitch.

Today is Monday, the day of *bhajan* at the Mahadev temple. He would never go elsewhere when there was a *bhajan* at the Mahadev temple, even if anyone urged him. People would throng to the temple on the first Monday of Shravan. Connoisseurs from all the wards would be present. 'I must sing the newest *abhang* in the *bhajan* tonight, one which people have never heard. Listeners must swing,' he had decided. He began to sing within himself by holding the rhythm in both hands. He practised thus for a very long while...

"Day in and day out just sit there clapping hands and do '*aa aa*'," his wife said in rage.

"What happened?" he suddenly became conscious.

"You did not go to *namaz* this morning?"

"Did not feel like rising due to the sleeplessness of last night."

"That is routine for you."

"Okay. I shall go this evening."

"What about shopping?"

"Today is Monday. We don't eat fish."

"We don't eat only fish. A lot of things are needed in the house."

"Okay then, I will go." So saying he got up, put on his *salwaar-kameez* and slippers and, taking the bag from his wife, descended the steps of the balcony.

While he was so descending, the wife began to tell him names of items one by one... He said "yes, yes" to all of them and went away.

He walked towards the market. While walking he was humming the new *abhang* to be sung later that night.

There was a lot of crowd at the market. Everyone was in a hurry to finish with their shopping. He bought the things his wife had told him to bring. He stood there for a while, recalling if he had not forgotten anything. 'Every time l tend to forget something and get a scolding from my wife.' He thought he had time and, as usual, went and stood outside Ibrahim's beef shop.

He suddenly heard loud slogans. He looked in the direction of the sound. Around fifteen-twenty people were shouting slogans from a truck. They stopped a truck. When the curtain at the back of the truck was withdrawn, they saw that there were five or six cows inside. Two people climbed in and released the cows. At that the cows jumped out to freedom and ran away. Those people then

began to hit the persons on the truck and its driver. The helpless persons were shouting for help, which was not forthcoming. After a while, they left them there and came towards the beef shops. They began to stone the shops. They brought out persons from the shops and began to thrash them. They told them to stop selling beef from the very next day.

He was watching everything from Ibrahim's corner beef shop. Suddenly a stone went whizzing past his ear. He saw the crowd coming towards Ibrahim's shop and he began to run home. He ran non-stop but looked back again and again. He was wary of someone chasing him. Finally he reached home panting. His body was shivering. He felt tired.

"Bibijaan," he called out to his wife.

"What happened?" She came out running.

"Give me some water first," he said, handing the bag to her.

"What happened? You look frightened." She handed him a glass of water.

He finished the water in one gulp.

"What happened?" she asked again.

"Nothing."

"Tell me what happened."

"I told you, no? Nothing."

"If you do not want to tell, don't tell." She went in angrily.

"I am hungry. Serve me if food is ready."

"Okay, okay," she said as she went in.

He sat on the bench in the balcony. His breathing became normal. For some time he just sat there.

"Food is ready," his wife called out.

He got up, went in and sat in front of the plate.

"You also sit with me."

"You eat first, I shall eat later."

Before, they used to eat from the same plate. But nowadays she had given up sitting together. When asked, she used to say, "Have those days of love remained now?"

He began to eat. She sat watching him.

"There was a fight in the market," he said after a while.

"Fight...?" she asked eagerly.

"Yes, those people had come."

"Who are they?"

"Those *gorakshawallahs.*"

"What did they do?"

"They hit those transporting cows and selling beef... They have warned them to keep the beef shops closed from tomorrow."

"What is the world coming to! Oh, Allah!"

He finished eating, washed his hands and wiped them on a towel.

He spread out the bedding and lay down. It was usual for him to take a nap after lunch. Normally he would fall asleep soon but today's events began to haunt him. He kept tossing and turning, but could not sleep.

Nowadays it had become routine. Small fights had begun to erupt. At times, due to Pakistan's win in cricket someone would burst crackers and fights would erupt, or because of the killing of Indian soldiers by Pakistan or by terrorists in Kashmir. Or due to some small incidents in a foreign country. There were oral encounters over killing of cows and eating beef. The Muslim habitation was away from the centre of the village. A few years ago there were only fifteen or twenty Muslim houses. Tiny ones. With tiled roofs. There was a dilapidated masjid without paint. Nobody was aware of when and who had built it. Young, active persons used to be busy with their jobs all day. Only the old used to do the *namaz.* Most of the people were poor. People used to do menial jobs. Someone sold bangles or another had a bicycle repair shop; someone else sold beef. All the butchers in the market were Muslims. Even in poverty, the people were happy. There was no bitterness among religions. Muslims used to participate in the Diwali and Chaturthi celebrations. Sweets would be sent to their homes, and Hindus would partake in *sheer korma.* Any childless Hindu woman would make a vow for a child at the dargah where the three roads met. The dargah was famous in the surrounding villages as one which fulfilled vows. The dargah's name would also be mentioned by Hindus seeking a boon. But the situation had begun to change over the last few years. Some years ago the vagrant son of Mohiddin, Rafiq, had gone to Dubai. When he returned to the village he was a changed man. Well-built and handsome with fine clothes. Each finger had a gold ring and there was a shining chain around his neck. After that, young people began to go to the Gulf. Now there is at least one boy from every household in the Gulf. Due to abundant salaries, the village has transformed. The mud houses with tiled roofs are being demolished. Their place has been taken by colourful cement concrete houses. Young people have built a shining new masjid in place of the old one. Muslims in all their finery have begun to say *namaz* there. With money, thoughts have also transformed. They think they are different. In that, some people from outside the state have begun to incite them to violence.

His house was still unchanged. His wife becomes angry on seeing the shining new houses of others. "If I had a son he would also have gone to the Gulf. He would have built a bungalow. I would have shown off in shining new clothes. 'You have only done *aa aa* all your life. The hundred or two hundred rupees you get from it does not feed us. Our luck is bad', the wife keeps on prattling." He does not know how to quieten her. He keeps silent.

When he woke up, the sun had set. He had kept tossing and turning but he did not know when sleep overtook him. He went in and splashed water on his eyes. Then he came out and sat in the balcony.

After a while his wife brought him tea.

"The cry for prayer was long over. You have still not gone for *namaz*." She handed him the glass of tea.

He kept mum.

"Nowadays you avoid going to *namaz*.'

"Who said so? Yesterday evening I was there."

"Yesterday evening? A true Muslim has to pray six times a day."

"The Muslims are otiose. They don't have work to do. Just go on praying throughout the day," he said angrily.

"This is it."

"Shut up. Don't teach me."

"You behave thus and...?"

"Don't speak. I know what you'll say."

"You won't listen to me. It's only my misfortune," so saying she went in stomping her feet.

He finished his tea and kept the glass aside. His head had begun to spin while recalling the afternoon's incident. He could not think of anything else. Just this morning he had rehearsed the new *abhang* to be sung at the temple. But all that had vanished after the incident. If there was a *bhajan* somewhere he would be meditating on it through the day. His fans from surrounding villages were eager to listen to a new *abhang*. He knew people would throng the temple tonight to listen to his *abhang*. He could not understand what to do. There was still an hour and a half for the *bhajan*. Thinking that he would rehearse for awhile, he got down from the bench. He sat cross-legged on the floor and began to sing the *abhang* to the beat of his hand. He raised the pitch and began to modulate his voice. He became engrossed in his singing.

He saw someone coming towards the house and came to his senses. He felt sure that the man was approaching his house. He got up with a start, came down the steps and with twinkling eyes saw Shakeel, the moulana's man.

"Who? Shakeel?"

"Yes."

"What is it?"

"You have been called."

"By whom?"

"By the moulana."

"Why?"

"Don't know."

"Proceed. I will follow."

"He has called you quickly."

"I am following you."

"Okay." So saying that fellow left.

He took his *kurta* and *pyjama* from the peg on the wall and wore them. He put on his cap and *chappals*.

"Where to?" the wife asked.

"To the masjid."

"Why?"

"The moulana has called."

"Why?"

"I don't know."

"Come back soon. The situation is not conducive."

"Okay, okay." So saying he went on his way.

'Why would the moulana call me? Yesterday evening I was the last to go to the masjid. After that, I have not stepped inside the masjid. Did he call me because of that? Or some other matter?' In fact, he had decided in the afternoon itself that he would not go for *namaz* that evening. He knew for sure that the reaction to the incident in the afternoon would come after *namaz*. Everyone would raise their pitch. They would seek revenge. "If we keep quiet, we shall get a beating," they would say. "What if our number is less? We cannot remain a frightened lot." If anybody tries to pacify them with advice of patience, they would shout him down and attack him. He had experienced all this.

He reached the masjid with these thoughts. He entered it with a slow pace. The moulana was seated in his place. Eight to ten men were beside him.

He stood before the moulana.

"Why did you not come for *namaz* this evening?" the moulana asked.

"I had a little headache," he lied.

"You are not regular nowadays," one of the fellows spoke.

He kept mum.

"Do you know that a true Muslim has to pray six times a day?" another spoke up.

He nodded his head positively.

"Then?"

"I shall come from tomorrow."

"You know about the afternoon incident?" a third one asked.

"Yes."

"If we keep quiet, we will get beaten many more times."

"We have to remain together," said another.

"I am with you," he said.

"Then why did you not come for *namaz*?"

"I told you I had a headache."

"Liar, you are with them."

"'With them' means?" he feigned ignorance.

"You sing *bhajans* with them."

"I like to sing *bhajans*."

"Singing *bhajans* is against the shariyat."

He kept silent.

"If you have to sing, sing qawali in our programmes."

"Don't go with them anymore."

He again kept silent.

"You will not go, won't you?"

"I will not," he answered in a voice that none could hear.

"Really?"

"Yes. I will not go."

"Go now. Come for *namaz* regularly from tomorrow," said the moulana.

"Okay." So saying he left.

While walking back home he could see the faces of the moulana and his colleagues. He recalled their words. The moulana asked him only the first question. His colleagues spoke the most and asked questions. 'They have incited the moulana by telling him some unpalatable things about me,' he thought. He knew that it was inevitable. These days everyone raised the same point at the time of *namaz*. They were telling him not to go to the bhajan. At times he felt he should listen to them. Be with the public. Else they would boycott him. They would not hesitate to even kill him by calling him an infidel. 'When I hear the *bhajan* tunes, I feel uneasy. The mind is restive, I cannot sit in one place. And then, unknowingly, my steps take me towards the direction of the tunes.'

From the time he was eight or ten years old, he had become passionate about *bhajans*. There were five to six young friends in the neighbourhood. They used to visit the Mahadev temple every Monday... Not for their liking of *bhajans* but for the sprouted grain, *usali*, and *puri* which was distributed after the *bhajans*. Those days were different. Poor children would not get to eat what they wanted. Hence, children would crowd the temple. He also went along. Slowly he was attracted to the tune and rhythm of the *bhajans*. He used to catch the rhythm while seated behind the main singers. He sang in the chorus. He also caught the fineness of some singers. At home, in his spare time, he hummed the *abhang* he had heard on the earlier night. His voice was sweet and everybody began to love his singing. Everybody prodded him to sing the *abhang*. He also sang without hesitation and soon became the main singer. *Bhajan* programmes mandatorily included him. He did not miss the *bhajan* at the Mahadev temple on even a single Monday. He did not take any fee for singing in the temple. But he got it when he sang at public or private functions. His mundane affairs eased with the money he received. There was no bitterness amongst various religions like today. That is why nobody had objected to his singing; none expressed resentment.

With these thoughts he reached home. His wife was on the balcony. She stood up on seeing him.

"Why had the moulana called?" Bibi asked, as he climbed the balcony.

"Let me at least come inside."

He came up and sat on the bench. He sighed deeply. He sat quietly for a while.

"Why were you called?" Bibi asked again.

"They do not want me to sing *bhajans*."

"Why?"

"They say *bhajans* are against the shariyat."

"If everybody says so, don't sing."

"You will not understand why I sing the *bhajan*."

"Why?"

"When I sing the *abhang*, I forget all my woes."

"What use is it forgetting?"

"Meaning?" he asked confused.

"Our difficulties have to be resolved. I have not told you?"

"What's that?"

"Just the other day, Rukhsana was saying the reason for our being childless is that."

"What?" he shouted.

"Yes. The *bhajan* is against the shariyat. That is why Allah does not bless us."

He kept silent.

"Then what did you tell the moulana?"

"That I will not go."

"You did well," she said and went in.

He was shocked at Bibi's words. Nobody had told him such a thing till date. This thought had not crossed his mind. Someone has planted this madness in her head. He laughed it off. It's madness that l am childless because l sing *bhajans*!

'Fools....! If God is one, isn't singing *bhajan* like paying obeisance of *namaz* to Allah? Very many Muslim saints have penned *abhangs*. They are sung with devotion in temples. I purposely sing the *abhang* like "Sheikh Mohammed Khavind, in his heart Govind." Kabir has said Ram and Rahim are one. Then why this difference?'

He came to his senses when he heard the sound of the tunes of *bhajans* and cymbals. The *bhajans* had begun in the temple. He became excited; he could not sit still. He began to pace up and down the balcony... He began to sing along to the tunes while holding the rhythm in both hands. He remained doing that for quite a while. Suddenly he stopped. He surmised that his wife was in the kitchen. He put on his slippers and set out towards the temple. He reached it quickly. He began to climb the steps.

"Stop!" he heard a voice.

When he looked up, he saw eight or ten young people at the door.

"You cannot enter," one of them said in a hoarse voice.

"Why?" he asked.

"You are a Muslim," said another.

"I always come here," he replied.

"From today, you are prohibited from entering."

"Why?"

"You kill our holy cows, eat their meat. We respect them as god. We perform her *puja*."

"I do not eat beef."

"May not be you, but your brothers..."

He looked at them flabbergasted. He did not know what to say. All my fellow singers are singing in the temple. Even after so much noise, none of them came out. Nobody stopped those youth, made them understand or took him in. He understood the reality.

He turned and sat on the platform built around the banyan tree. Tears overwhelmed him. 'From today my *bhajan* singing comes to a halt.' He cried for quite a long time. Finally he closed his eyes, caught the rhythm in his palms and began to sing along with the sound emanating from the temple.

The *abhang* that was being sung in the temple was '*Kahat Kabira suno bhai sadho, Ram Rahim ek hai dono...*'

Glossary

Puja: Prayers

Shanbhag: A surname

Bhajan: Hindu devotional song

Shravan: Fifth month in the Hindu almanac, considered holy

Abhang: Hymn

Namaz: Prayer prescribed by Islamic law

Salwaar-kameez: A long loose dress (*kameez*), and the loose pants worn under them

Gorakshawallahs: Cow protection vigilantes

Sheer korma: lit. 'Milk with dates' (in Persian). It is a vermicelli pudding made during festivals, especially on Eid

Moulana: Title given to learned Muslims, in particular graduates of religious institutions

Chappals: Slippers

Kurta-pyjama: Long loose dress (*kurta*), and the pants worn under them

Shariyat: Sharia or Islamic religious law

Qawali: A popular form of Sufi devotional music

Usali: Dish made of unground pulses
Puri: Also spelt *poori*, it is an Indian unleavened bread made with either whole-wheat flour (*atta*), coarse wheat flour (*sooji*) or, most commonly, refined wheat flour (*maida*) that is combined with water to form a dough. It is then rolled out into small circular shapes and deep fried
Kahat Kabira ... hai dono: Kabir says listen my pious brothers, Ram and Rahim are one and the same
Dargah: The tomb of a Muslim saint

Originally written in Marathi as 'Kahat Kabira'.
Translated by Damodar K.K. Ghanekar.

This story won the first prize (the Albano Couto Prize) at the Fundação Oriente Short Story Competition, 2017.

Gouthami

R ITA waited patiently while Perpetua went in to try out the
dress. They had been friends since they were in school together. Perpetua came out looking totally different – she
was no longer the hassled housewife, the mother of two – she
came out a chic young lady in the light blue suit. Her face lit up
as she looked at the mirror and then she rushed over to Rita and
kissed her on both cheeks. "Thank you, my dear. You have magic
in your fingers. I haven't had a suit that has made me feel this
good before" she said. Rita laughed and replied, "A dress can only
highlight what is already there." "Okay, now tell me how much
it costs," Perpetua said, and when Rita was about to protest, Perpetua rushed on, "You know my brother is paying for this, not me.
It is his only son's wedding and he wants me to look good." Rita
held Perpetua's hand and guided her to the trial room saying, "It
doesn't matter who is paying. I can't take money from you or your
family. Now you take that suit off so I can finish the embroidery
on the collar."

Perpetua left to get on with her day and Rita started on the
embroidery. As always, her thoughts were far away – with her
Desmond. He would have encouraged her to be a good friend
to Perpetua and help her always. Rita and Desmond had met in
school. He waited till she finished her graduation and married
her the next day. He had had great plans for this tailoring shop,
D'Costa Tailors, that had been started by his grandfather. For six
months, they dreamed through day and night about their lives.
The accident ruined their charmed lives. Desmond died on the
spot. The shock of the news expelled the foetus from Rita, too
soon. Family and friends gathered, not quite sure how Rita would
survive this double tragedy. Rita herself wondered sometimes how

she did it. But she did. After three weeks, she got up one day, got dressed and went to the tailoring shop. While opening it, she realised that she could no longer run it as a men's tailoring shop. She went across to the painter and had two words added to the board. It now read D'Costa Tailors (for women).

As she had looked around the shop, the tears had welled up. Quickly, she had taken out a dusting cloth and started to work. Within minutes, her mother and Perpetua had been there, full of concern. "Rita," said her mother, "it is not right for you to be out so soon." Perpetua had intervened quickly, "Aunty, if she doesn't see to the shop, she will lose business. And it will keep her occupied as well. I will sit with her all day and see that she does not overwork." Her mother had tried once more, "But what will people say?" Rita had just looked at her steadily, tears lurking in her eyes.

And that was how D'Costa Tailors became exclusively for women. Business was slow to start with. Rita used the time to make the space more welcoming and comfortable. She brought in some old chairs from the house and upholstered them in cheerful checks from Mapuça market. She bought an electric kettle, so there was always a cup of tea available to those who came by. She was a popular girl, always helpful and cheerful, while in school and college. Her friends now rallied around her and made sure they visited regularly. Some of them brought some work along – a dress to be altered, edges to be stitched – and slowly, she built up her clientele. Soon all the women in Kazarlem had gotten something stitched by her. Rita hired two other girls now, but they worked out of home. Her shop remained a calm oasis for any lady who wanted a bit of quiet and a cup of tea (with as much sugar as she wanted).

Perpetua visited less and less often. Her life was full. Her parents had gotten her married to a rich man who was almost twice her age. Perpetua went to her marital home with no dreams or hopes. Her husband drank a lot, taunted her about her poverty and, if she came anywhere nearby, picked up whatever he could and flung it at her. That didn't stop him though from having sex with her every chance he could. Two children had followed in quick succession. Perpetua was actually dismayed when her mother-in-law told her to get sterilised after the two children were born. At least during her pregnancy, her husband had left her alone. A gregarious girl through school, Perpetua was now subdued and sullen. She avoided meeting any of her old friends, especially Rita.

Rita finished the embroidery and as she held it up to scrutinise it for mistakes, her thoughts went to how much she owed Perpetua – if Perpetua hadn't been there, there would be no D'Costa Tailors today. She felt a pang when she realised that she had been so caught up in her own angst that she had not quite supported Perpetua through her miserable marriage.

The next day Perpetua came in to pick up her dress. She looked terrible – Rita suddenly wondered just how bad Perpetua's life was. After Perpetua had exclaimed over the delicate embroidery, Rita had insisted she stay to have a cup of tea. While Perpetua was protesting, she called the bakers down the street and asked them to send some of their chocolate cake – she knew it was Perpetua's favourite. "Please, Perpetua, it has been so long," was all she said. There was a bit of a silence to start with. But now Rita knew the art of small talk. She shared a bit of gossip another lady had told her. A hint of a smile showed up in Perpetua's face. Two days later, Perpetua dropped in saying, "I was at the market and I just needed a glass of water. It is so hot today." Rita had installed a small fridge – she pulled out cold water as well as some soft drinks, which Perpetua waved away. "No, I have only a minute. I will come another day. Keep those for me." And she was gone.

Between firm friends, it is not difficult to revive a friendship. It was a matter of days before Perpetua was dropping in all the time, "just for a minute". Inside the shop, some of her old bubbly self came back. If there were other customers, Perpetua was sober and quiet. But when they were just the two of them, they giggled like they had back in school.

Their newest entertainment was something called Facebook that had taken their world by storm. After the birth of their second son, Perpetua's husband had taken to giving her expensive gifts. The latest had been the newest model of a smart phone. Perpetua was now connected with the world through the gadget in her hand. She felt a sense of power just holding it. However, her husband's generosity did not extend to paying for the phone recharge. Perpetua used what little money she could save from household expenses for that. So there were days when all she could do was receive calls. On one of those days she had been sitting in Rita's shop and cursing her husband. Rita had taken out a fifty-rupee note and told her to quickly recharge the phone. While Perpetua was shaking her head, Rita said, "Consider it payment for all the work you do around here. Don't think I haven't noticed you dusting, cleaning up, washing the tea cups, bringing my favourite biscuits and all the other small things you do unasked. Besides, your Facebook gives me so much fun. Don't deprive me of it."

Perpetua made sure that she never asked Rita for money. She knew that money often destroyed relationships. But she never refused when Rita gave her money. She usually used it for small pleasures – recharging her phone, a new pair of dressy earrings, an ice-cream... and Rita did all her tailoring for free. So even if her face looked haggard and drawn, she was always smartly turned out.

For some days now, Rita had noticed that there was a kind of a peaceful look on Perpetua's face. Rita knew that it was best to wait till Perpetua spoke of it herself. Meanwhile she just enjoyed watching her friend look almost happy. One day, Perpetua hung around the shop the whole morning. Her husband called her several times. Sometimes she took the call and said she was just coming and at other times she simply ignored the call. Rita was puzzled at her behaviour. Finally, just as she was about to close for lunch, she understood. Perpetua needed money and didn't know how to ask for it. But how much did she need? Rita decided to be upfront about it. She took out a fifty-rupee note and gave it to Perpetua and asked, "Is this enough?" Perpetua just sat with her head bowed down. Then Rita took out a hundred-rupee note and handed it to her. Perpetua jumped up, kissed her on both cheeks and fled. Rita was left shaking her head. What a girl Perpetua was!

It was a week before Perpetua came by again. And she was clearly downcast. Seeing her, Rita gave her a hug, before returning to her two clients who were enjoying their tea that morning. Perpetua literally hung around – did some dusting, swept the already swept floor, washed the clean cups and left the used ones untouched – clearly she was waiting to talk to Rita. Did she want more money, Rita wondered, a little apprehensive.

It seemed forever before the two clients left. By then Rita was so impatient that she almost told Perpetua, "Spit it out, woman." Instead, she asked Perpetua to sit down, offered her another cup of tea and then sat quietly, sipping her own tea.

Perpetua was clearly struggling with what to say. She made some sounds, started some sentences and then gave up. Rita was a little worried by now and put her hand on Perpetua's. She was surprised to see how strongly Perpetua held it and her apprehension grew.

"I met a guy on Facebook." Perpetua said after the long silence. It was now Rita's turn to hold Perpetua's hand tight. Several thoughts were racing through her mind. I hope it is not someone else's husband. Everyone will blame me for encouraging her. I gave her the money; I told her to sin. I should have asked her before being so generous.

Perpetua was smiling and her face had softened. It took all of Rita's strength not to say anything. After what she thought was too long a pause, she shook Perpetua's hand. Perpetua looked up and saw Rita's face. And she hurried into her story. "He sent me a friend request on Facebook and I accepted. He is part of a rock band in Shillong. He and I chatted about anything and everything. I like to listen to him talk about his life. It is filled with music and love. He was in Goa last week." And again she fell silent.

Rita had read something about this musician from Shillong in the newspaper. The picture alongside showed a cute, potbellied man, with long hair and the shortest of shorts. Surely nothing could have happened with him. He was a public figure and if he had met Perpetua it would have been in the news by now. "How old is he?" asked Rita.

D'COSTA TAILORS
(For Women)

"I never asked him," replied Perpetua, "probably mid-twenties." So it wasn't the guy in the newspaper. That must be good, thought Rita. "So did you meet him?" asked Rita, unable to bear the suspense anymore. Perpetua looked up with that dreamy smile again, "Yes, we did. That is why I needed the money from you. He was in Margão for a gig. So I needed the bus fare to go there. He met me at the bus stop and took me on a bike to Colva beach. I hugged him tight all the way there. Then we sat on the beach. He put his arm around me and we held hands and watched the waves."

Rita's mind had raced ahead in panic. "Did you use any protection?" she asked. Perpetua looked at her puzzled. "No, it wasn't raining and there were enough clouds, so we didn't need sunscreen either." Then she understood what Rita was asking her. She dropped Rita's hand, cupped her face with both hands and said a soundless "O!"

"*Scheee*, it is not like that at all. All I wanted was for someone to put his arm around me and listen when I talk and to be gentle with me. That's all. Nothing else happened. I came home after that." Perpetua lost that dreamy look and was close to tears when she said, "This will last me a few months."

Rakhandar – Part 2, Survey No 25

Narayan Mahale

BUDHU came to Dhangarwado by coming down the Vagh-bil hillock and began to carefully look at the herd of goats which was grazing. But in that herd he could not see that particular he-goat, the one with a vermilion spot on his forehead, garlands of flowers around its neck and black and brown spots below its belly. He was expecting the goat to return to Dhangarwado, trailing the other goats of the herd.

This morning he had gone to Vaghbil. He made bleating sounds at the valley just like a goat but hadn't been able to find it. He was sure that the goat would not go far off, leaving his usual surroundings. Did someone steal that goat – overnight? Or did a tiger prey on it?

He was confused. He could not understand what might have happened to the goat. Where could one search for this goat? With confused eyes he once again glanced over the whole herd.

"Hello Budhu, what are you looking for? Do you want to buy a goat?"

He turned around and saw Lakho, a stick in his hand and a coarse blanket on his shoulder. His smile had spread from the tangle of his moustache to the dimples on his unshaven cheeks.

"No. I've just been roaming around." Budhu's tongue teetered. Words rolled down his tongue like loose rocks on a hill. Lakho looked at him with appreciation and said, "Don't tell me that you are also hosting a mutton party! You will pass the exam. You will be an engineer. The other day Sadlya and Dhako took a small goat from me. I'm mentioning it because I remembered!"

He sensed that Sadlya and Dhako had lied to Lakho. In fact, it was not so. There was a plan to build a grand airport in the village. Planes from all over the world would land there. Now and then, the newspapers also had reported about it. Some people also said that there would be no airport. Whichever party forms the government, the airport won't happen. There was strong opposition to the airport. But only last month there was a public hearing held by the government. Everybody spoke in favour of the airport. Sadlya spoke against it. The villages would be destroyed, fields, forests, *aforamentos*, springs, wells – all would be destroyed.

Sadlya had said while returning from the hearing, "What shall we do? The government is not telling the truth and our MLA also does not want to listen to us. Ministers are not seen here at all. Nobody wants to raise his voice against the airport."

"We will make a vow to the Protector of this area. He alone will take care of everything," Dhako had suggested. And then, as they reached the area of the Protector, Sadlya had made a vow to sacrifice a he-goat. They had collected the money to buy a goat then and there. Sadlya himself gave five hundred rupees. Dhako gave another five hundred. And others gave big and small amounts. Budhu himself had given three notes of a hundred rupees each, as his own contribution.

He thought of telling Lakho that the goat bought by Sadlya and Dhako from him the other day had been released as a sacrifice to the Protector and that he himself was present with Sadlya and Dhako at that time. There is no intention of hosting any party. Sadlya and Dhako have been telling lies to him. Budhu felt like telling the truth.

The thoughts from his mind began to tingle on his tongue. But the very next moment, he recalled what Sadlya had insisted on while releasing the goat at the area.

"Budhu *re*, you are still in the shell. You won't understand all this. We make vows to the Protector for your success in exams, so that you become an engineer, by giving a fine party of mutton to all!"

Dhako had deliberately said, "Budhu, do not speak to anybody. If we tell others, the Protector will not fulfil our vow. He will not accept the sacrifice of the goat and then the airport will be a reality!"

He recalled everything and kept his mouth shut!

The shadow of the kumyo tree fell over his head. Lakho also came under the shade. Spreading the coarse blanket down on a rock, he sat over it and began to speak again.

"Budhu, it seems you will be an engineer. What is it? What does an illiterate goat herdsman like me understand about education? I speak what they speak in the village."

Budhu felt elated.

"You study hard. Men have to study." Suddenly Lakho began to call out to the goats. About a dozen goats were going in the direction of the far-off grazing ground. Then he turned to Budhu again and said, "What will we do staying in this village now? Can we sow ragi or should we rear the goats? If we go for the second option, where is the land left?" He suddenly shouted loudly at the goats, which had gone into the thickets. Lakho began to speak with one eye on the herd. "An airport is being constructed in this place. This village will be destroyed. We will have to leave this village and go elsewhere. The government will pay us compensation but what will happen from it? What will happen to the goats? Where will we get land from?"

He also felt that Lakho's sight had centred on the plateau meant for the airport. The herd of goats disappeared behind the thickets. Lakho quickly threw the blanket over his shoulder, took his stick and went in search of his goats, shouting loudly.

Budhu felt like shouting and telling Lakho, "The airport will not be built in our village. The Protector of this area will come to our rescue and will stop the construction of the airport. So far, he has stopped all the dangers to the village at the border of the village itself. We have vowed to sacrifice a goat to him." But the words remained on his shivering lips.

'If I tell Lakho that we have vowed to sacrifice a goat to the Protector, the Protector will not accept our vow, and he won't stop the airport.'

And, as a last-ditch effort to look for the goat in the *aforamento*, Budhu came to the pathway on the hillock from Dhangar-wado and started walking towards the *aforamento*. The wind was blowing through the peaks of trees and shrubs, cashews and jackfruits. His nostrils smelt the strong odour of the uski flowers and thoughts of goat were sidelined for a moment. His mind began to run helter-skelter, just like a galloping calf when breeze enters its ears.

He had not come to the *aforamento* for the last five years or so, because of his Tenth and Twelfth standard exams as well as the entrance tests.

During the cashew season, people came to their own *aforamento* with choppers and axes to prune the trees. A part of their household expenses would be met by the cashew and mangosteen fruits and the small branches would be used as firewood. He used to roam about these trees and pathways since he was a child. He had toiled in the fields, farms and the mire. When he had reached the Tenth standard, his mother had insisted, "I shall look after the *aforamentos*, fields and farms. You concentrate on your studies."

And now he had plenty of free time, at least a fortnight, till the Twelfth standard and the GCET results were declared. There was no pressure on him now.

He stood on a large, spread out jet-black rock and took a deep breath. His chest was filled with the sharp smell of mangosteen, mangoes, jackfruits and cashew apples. His heart was filled with happiness. Fifty-sixty monkeys had totally destroyed the fruits on the black mango tree along the narrow path. The young ones of the monkeys were swinging on the mangosteen branches which were full of ripe blood red fruits. They would just bite a small piece of the fruit and throw it down. There were heaps of fruits below the black mango and mangosteen trees. Due to unseasonal rain a few days ago, old and dried blossoms had fallen down and, at some places, fresh blossoms had sprouted. The jackfruit along the pathway had fruits just above its roots. One could not count the number of jackfruits on that tree, but there must have been more than hundred and fifty. Jackfruits would ripen on the trees and fall off. Squirrels in hordes played on the branches. A special animal drew his attention. It looked just like a squirrel but bigger, iron grey in colour and with whitish stripes over it. He recognised it at once. It was a shekru. It is a rare animal but is native to this forest. He could not control his happiness at having seen it.

On the peaks of the fig trees, crows were cawing. Crows with pieces of grass were lunging towards the fig tree peaks. He sensed that they must be building their nests.

He heard the chirping of birds in the deep ravine of the uski thicket in the forest. And then he also heard a frightening hiss. A serpent had caught a bird in its mouth. He also heard the sound of dry leaves crackling. Slowly there emerged a rabbit running helter-skelter. Then a dozen young ones of a wild fowl began to run. He saw a bright yellow rat snake coming out from the thicket. It was also running away fearing for his life. He imagined that the unbearable heat and the rocky surface must not be allowing the snake to sit in one place.

At that very moment he was witness to someone enjoying its life, someone dying and someone escaping with fear.

And just then, on the long strip of the sky a darkish cloud appeared. For a few minutes, the sun and shadows played a game of hide and seek. A drizzle of rain also showed up. He heard a shrill sound emanating from the thickets. This was a peacock. It emerged and, spreading its wings, started dancing immaculately.

Something fluttered overhead. It was a big flock of birds. He saw the yellow-beaked dhanesh and kites circling slowly in the sky. There was a woodpecker making its peculiar *tuk-tuk, tuck-tuck* sound.

At the foot of the hill there is a brook which belongs to the Protector. It flows throughout the year. Its water goes through a canal into god's pond. All the coconut trees, arecanut trees and other trees as well as the vegetable crops are fed by it. One does not catch a cold if he drinks this water. Bathing in its waters frees the skin of scabies. He was also fed on this clear, clean and medicinal water from childhood.

He could see the trees in the *aforamento* and in the forest – jackfruit trees, mango trees, teakwood trees (with a girth big enough for two big men), nano, channudo and hasano trees. He had eaten 'charava' as prasad from the channudo leaves.

While watching this blossoming nature of the trees and animals from the forest, his sight fell on the village. The long tarred roads and shiny cars running over them, colourful new houses with concrete slabs were the indications that the standard of living of the people here had improved.

The government had long taken over the lands and forests in the area needed for the airport. It had deleted the names of original landowners from the Form I & XIV for whom compensation was paid. The government had included its own name in their place. People have bought these cars from the money paid as compensation. These new houses are also due to that money.

And what else could he see?

Whatever and howsoever big the opposition, the airport is here to stay!

His mind applied brakes as he remembered the airport. The black cloud of sadness slowly hovered over his mind's screen.

"What will happen to all this forest grandeur?"

"Bulldozers will flatten and destroy everything."

"The MLAs and ministers are giving assurances, 'When the airport is built, the people from the villages will get the jobs'!"

"We will also increase the rate of compensation for the land."

"Once the airport is constructed, village people will get the jobs at the airport."

Budhu thought, "Do these people have the kind of education that will qualify them for a job at the airport? Only outsiders will get the jobs. Who can stop them? Whom can you stop?"

"People here will take the money as compensation and will then finish it in a jiffy."

He recalled the public hearing. He had opposed the airport openly. His family members had ridiculed him and shouted him down.

"Why are you under tension about the airport?",

"Who will cultivate the land on the plateau?"

"Kulith, ragi, pakhad – will you cultivate them?"

"Will you rear the bulls and hold the plough?"

"Our ancestors did all that. They stayed in the village doing *hiriri papari.* Will you be able to do that now?"

"Who needs agriculture now?"

"One does not get workers to work in the fields like before."

"The government is not taking our lands for free."

"Budhu, you are good at studies. Study well. Study a lot. Become an engineer!"

"The ministers say, and the MLAs also say, that they will give you a job at the airport."

"You are an aborigine of this land!"

"The airport has taken your land."

"Sadlya, Dhako and Pavno are your colleagues. And what do they do? They hold meetings and get their photos published. It seems the whole village is opposing the airport and they believe they are village leaders!"

"They understand a lot. They have studied a lot."

"The government is building the airport, the panchayat is not building it."

"They indulge in politics."

"Budhu, you have made a fool of yourself due to their influence."

"Give up the foolish idea of not wanting an airport."

"Budhu, you are still in a shell."

He also felt that the foolish idea of opposing the airport was simmering in his head. There was confusion of thoughts and an unexpressed tension.

His mobile rang. He checked it. There were six missed calls from Sadlya, Dhako and Pavno.

"Budhu, *arey,* are you alive or did the tiger eat you up?" he heard Sadlya's irritated voice.

"Sorry, I can't hear clearly."

"Where are you?"

"In the *aforamento.*"

"Have you seen the he-goat?"

"No, I searched everywhere."

"That means the tiger cub has eaten it up. The Protector received the goat. The airport will not be built. No need for any tension now."

He heard Dhako's voice and laughter too. And then, the network snapped.

But the goat began to bleat in his head. He felt he should look for it again. 'I did not go to the Protector's area. There is no tiger cub in the forest area. Who, then, will eat the goat? What might have happened to it?'

He began to walk on the pathway leading to the area. A thought crossed his mind. He made a bleating sound near the uski thicket. He heard a bleating response. For a moment, he could not believe it. He repeated the sound. There was a repeat response. He ran in the direction of the sound, through thickets and thorns, over stones and rocks. He saw a goat. Black, with a beard – this was not the one offered to the Protector!

He came to the plateau and saw that land was being measured under police protection. The government officers had put the tape to the stones which represented the gods of the area. Officers were working in the sacred area with their leather sandals and shoes.

This is a holy area in Gaumthane. The goat herdsmen used to burn their holi in this very area. If one wishes to make a vow, one has to come to this spot. Once a year, the *Mane* of god is offered at the same spot. The spot does not distinguish between castes. The 'chapay' of the Dhangars and the religious offerings take place at this spot. Women in their menses and inebriated men do not dare come anywhere near the spot. Nobody can tell a lie here and escape the consequences. This god is one who will put his stake and build a residence – this god has inhabited the village. This god has never allowed any calamities to enter the boundary of this village.

The village has preserved the sanctity of this place for generations with faith. And what was he seeing today?

"Hey, what are you looking at?"

An officer holding the tape accosted him.

"What are you doing here?" Budhu asked in a low voice.

Another asked him, "Which village are you from?"

"From this village," Budhu said in loud voice.

"Do you not know that an airport is being built at this spot?"

"Is this land yours?" one clerk asked him looking into a file.

Budhu replied, pointing to a far-off stone fencing, "That land is mine. Mine means, my family land, my grandfather's."

"We do not want your family history."

"Who is the owner of this land? Part No 2, Survey No 25?" he asked, looking at the Form I & XIV in the file.

"The Protector," Budhu replied stressing on the words.

"Which Protector?"

"Dev – Thalkar."

"Does he have any descendants?"

Budhu was confused. Who are the 'heirs' of this spot? Whom to ask?

"*Arey*, this boy is still a child. How will he know all these details? Close the file. If anyone comes to make a claim, we shall see," another suggested.

"Budhu... Budhu...!"

He heard a call. He turned and saw Sadu with an umbrella in his hand. He was working for the Land Survey. He used to visit this place often with the officers. He held the umbrella to protect the officers from the sun. He introduced Budhu to the officer.

"Sir, this is Budhu. He belongs to this village, very good at studies. He has appeared for the Twelfth science exam."

"Very good!" the officer said with admiration.

"Sir, the Airport Authority has taken over his family's land too. That land..." Sadu pointed to the fence.

"Did he get the compensation?"

Budhu did not speak. Sadu said quickly, "Sir, the land belongs to the family. There will be a delay in the settlement."

"Okay, what have you decided about the future?" the officer asked.

"I have not decided yet." Budhu was confused.

"I suggest you go for engineering. The airport will be built in four to five years. You belong to this place. Your land has been taken over for the airport. You will get a job with the Airport Authority."

The officer's mobile rang. He began to speak. Budhu took out his mobile. Just then a police inspector accosted him. He was observing Budhu for quite some time.

"Are you taking photos? Will you give them to newspapers?"

The inspector shook the baton. Budhu was afraid of the stick.

Then he came towards Budhu and asked, "Your leader – Sadlya – where is he? And who is the other one?"

He recollected Dhako's name and said, "Their photos have been published in today's papers. It seems they are opposing the airport. Dhako, Pavno are big leaders. They did not come here today. Have you come alone?"

Fear in Budhu's heart cast its unclear shadow on his face. Even in that condition he remembered the incident during the public hearing.

The Sarpanch was giving a speech. In his speech, he justified the construction of the new airport. At that point, Sadlya tried to shut him down by creating disturbances with hoots and boos. Dhako and Pavno also tried to disturb the meeting by standing on the chairs and by making catcalls. Budhu had tried to stand up. At that time, the same inspector had hit Sadlya on the legs and had said, "If you make a noise again I shall break your back."

He had taken them out of the pavilion and instructed them, "Whatever leadership you want to display, go home and do it." And then, putting his arm around Budhu's shoulder he had said in a persuasive voice, "You are still a child. If I see you again with these fellows, mind you – I shall lock you up."

And now, the inspector put his stick to Budhu's shoulder and asked harshly, "At this age, do you want to sit in the locker? Answer me."

Budhu was sweating. Was it due to heat or fear? He did not understand.

Budhu escaped from there, far from that place. When he looked behind, he saw officers' cars and the police jeeps going back. The shadow of fear had disappeared from his face.

It was necessary to convey to Sadlya that the government has taken over the land of the Protector for the airport. He called him over the phone. Then he called Dhako, and then Pavno. But he received only one common message: that they were out of the coverage area.

The sun was now slowly leaning down below the plateau on to the hillock. The wind was also flowing with a nice, smooth speed. He realised that his mind was becoming lighter, clearer and that he was thirsty. He went along the pathway down to the spring. Looking at the roaring spring originating directly from the rock of the hillock, he felt an urge to drink water directly from the spring. He broke off a channudo leaf. He made a cone out of that leaf, stepped down closer to the spring and gulped down the water. He splashed some water on his face and sprayed his body with water. He felt his mind and body both had become fresh and tension-less. He sat, dipping his legs into the spring water, and began to inhale the clean and clear air emanating from the green trees and bushes.

He could not come to this area for a long time due to his Tenth and Twelfth standard examinations, and later because of the GCET exam.

Twilight had spread over the surroundings. He could hear the sounds of birds returning home. Crows were beginning to gather on the mango tree. Monkeys were quietly sitting there.

Suddenly he could hear the "be... be..." bleats of the goat, from the green thicket near the spring. For a moment he thought that the goat released for the Protector was working on his mind.

His nerves had now cooled down due to the spring water. He did not pay heed to the bleating. He thought it must be the same goat he had seen some time ago, the black and bearded one. He did not feel like walking to the thicket. Guppy fishes were tickling his feet which were dangling in the water.

Again he heard the bleating right next to his ears. Startled by the sound, he looked behind to see the goat. The garland around its neck had withered. And the vermilion spot on the forehead had become indistinct. And it had black and brown spots under the belly and neck.

This is the same goat which was released for the Protector.

The goat came and stuck to Budhu's shoulder. It started brushing its body against Budhu's back.

Budhu took out his mobile and took a selfie with the goat. Once, twice and then he did it many times over. He threw water over the goat. He took a selfie again while giving it a bath.

It started getting dark near the spring. Budhu climbed up the spring. He began the descent of the hillock. Half way down he could still see the goat following him.

He came running to the pathway. It was dark there. He turned around, but this time he did not see the goat. On the way down he saw the selfies he had taken through his mobile. They were charming.

And to give this happy news, he called Sadlya, then Dhako and then Pavno.

But they all seemed to be 'out of coverage area'.

Glossary

Dhangars: A shepherd community in Goa

Wado: Hamlet, section of a village

Aforamentos: Lands on lease, *comunidade* land (land belonging to a community)

Re, arey: a call; *lit.* Hey you

Kumyo: A tree found in the forest

Ragi: Finger millet

Uski: A wild bush

Koite: A chopper; sickle-like chopping tools (singular: *koita* or *koito*)

Shekru: A Malabar giant squirrel, also known as the Indian Giant Squirrel

Dhanesh: A hornbill

Prasad: lit. A gracious gift. It denotes typically an edible food that is first offered to a deity or saint, and then distributed in His or Her name to their followers or others. It is normally consumed by worshippers after worship (also spelt as *prasadam* or *prasada*)

MLA: Member of the Legislative Assembly

Kulith: Horse gram, a kind of bean

Pakhad: A type of crop

Hiriri papari: Call to bulls

Mane: A specific offering to the Rakhandar, the god of that area

Chapay: A folk dance performed by the male members of the Dhangar community

Sarpanch: An elected head of the Panchayat (*lit.* an assembly [*ayat*] of five [*panch*]), a village-level constitutional body of local self-government implemented in Goa since the early-to-mid 1960s

GCET: 'Goa Common Entrance Test' for admissions to undergraduate engineering courses in Goa, conducted by the Directorate of Technical Education, Goa

Originally written in Marathi as 'Rakhandar–Part 2, Survey No 25'.
Translated by Damodar K.K. Ghanekar.

Poor Fellow

Kiran Mahambre

W HEN Sakshi came in, mother was looking out intently through the kitchen window.

"Who is it, mum?" Sakshi asked, joining her and looking through the window herself. Outside the kitchen window, beyond the wall, the guests who had come to Ramnath Bappa's house were getting out. The people appeared new to the locality. She'd never seen them before. She couldn't understand why her mother was staring with such interest.

The people at Ramnath Bappa's seemed to be in a jovial mood. Something good must have happened, thought Sakshi.

Her mother turned around. Her glance fell on Sakshi. "When did you come?" she asked.

"Who are they, mum?"

"Some new relations, looks like..."

"Meaning?"

"Vedaa's marriage must have been settled."

"How do you know?"

"That Sushila had come day before yesterday. They probably won't announce it just yet. But then what will we do with the knowledge? Even though they are so interested in every little thing concerning others!"

Sakshi's mother surmised that Vedaa's marriage had been arranged. She wondered who and from where they were. But then, how would she find out? Sakshi was quite certain that her mother would find out from Sushila before long.

But even before she could get the news from Sushila, Vedaa's mother came with the invitation. She informed them that Vedaa's wedding had been arranged and that the date had been fixed.

"You've fixed the wedding without much delay," remarked Sakshi's mother.

"Everything happened so fast. They liked the girl. 'Let's have the wedding soon', they said." Vedaa's mother was beaming.

Everybody from the locality was invited for Vedaa's marriage. From Sakshi's house, everyone went for the wedding.

Sakshi's mother had a keen eye for detail. Her eyes roved over every little thing – the articles that had been put in the bridal trousseau, what was being served to the people. The economic status of Vedaa's house could be gauged from these things. Vedaa's body was glittering with the ornaments she was wearing. Despite the high cost of living, Vedaa's father had not stinted – he'd bestowed diamonds on her. Sakshi's mother didn't need to be told about their economic circumstances. Everyone knew that they had opened a boutique and given it to Vedaa.

Their house was overflowing up to the doorways. Nothing was wanting. Her husband was well-to-do, it seemed. Sakshi's mother was curious to see their customs and ways.

Everything was worth seeing. Absolutely nothing seemed to be lacking. The ceremonial bridal *Shalu* sari embroidered with gold thread, her needle and embroidery work were displayed there, the utensils, everything – all very classy.

Vedaa was very happy. But the bridegroom? His face seemed overcast.

Sakshi's mother tried to probe from the neighbours. 'Were they not happy with the girl? Were they perhaps attracted by the father's wealth?' Sakshi's mother was adept at extracting information.

"No, he had fever yesterday. The *muhurat* was decided exactly when he had fever. Last evening, he was in bed, burning with fever."

Hearing the neighbour's statement about the groom made Sakshi's mother a trifle disappointed. 'So his lack of brightness is because of the fever,' she thought to herself.

The marriage reception was over. The following day, Vedaa's relations were coming for the party at the bride's house. There was a lot of noise at Vedaa's. Deciding to join in, Sakshi's mother made a *mukhavayalyo aarti* for the bride.

A large convoy of big cars began to stream in. Vedaa and her husband arrived in a spanking new car. Vedaa got down from the vehicle. Everybody was waiting to catch a glimpse of the groom. Though they'd seen him at the wedding, they were anxious to see him from close by. He was handsome. Vedaa must have fallen for his looks.

Sakshi's mother commented, "In fact, Vedaa isn't very pretty. It's just that she's very tall and thin. Her face is rather plain. But her fair complexion trumps everything else." 'My Sakshi is so good-looking,' Sakshi's mother thought. 'In spite of her dark complexion she looks nice. Sakshi may not be tall but then being tall doesn't necessarily suit all women. She may be a little plump but Sakshi certainly looks better.'

She was unhappy that her Sakshi's marriage had not happened yet.

Vedaa got down from the car. Her face was wreathed in smiles. Her groom stepped out behind her. His face was still sombre.

"It seems Vedaa's husband had fever on the wedding day, right?" Sakshi's mother remarked to Vedaa's mum.

"Yes, how did you come to know?" Vedaa's mother asked in surprise. 'I wonder how people come to know these things without even being told,' she speculated

"He's okay now, I hope." There was no end to Sakshi's mother's curiosity.

"Yes, he's okay."

"It's just that I found his face a little subdued, so I asked."

Vedaa's mother was beginning to resent Sakshi's mother's questions. But she kept her peace. She couldn't understand why there should be such a hullabaloo about a simple fever. But Sakshi's mother was going on and on.

Vedaa's relations were introduced, the pleasantries were done. The dinner too was over. Sakshi's mother's gaze was now riveted on Vedaa's husband.

When Vedaa's mother found her daughter alone, she told her

about Sakshi's mother's questions, "'What sort of fever? When did it come? Have you gone to the doctor?'... she had nothing but that to ask. It looks like no one ever gets a fever."

Vedaa became a little uneasy. "He's still not well," she murmured.

"Didn't you consult a doctor?" Vedaa's mother was a little worried now.

"He went to the doctor. He's taking medications."

"It must be a simple viral fever. Don't worry. Anyone can get fever. The doctor's checked him. That's it. He'll be okay. Come home after he gets completely well."

Because of her husband's fever, Vedaa's honeymoon didn't happen – that much was true.

But Vedaa was troubled, "Why did it have to happen just now? Just at the time of the wedding!"

Vedaa waited expectantly. He'll be better, he'll be alright soon, but he didn't seem to have improved. Fever? He didn't seem hot to the touch. He seemed to have pain in the region of the stomach, but Vedaa could not surmise where exactly. When she asked, he would answer vaguely. He wouldn't eat properly, would not have his meals. There was no brightness on his face. He used to lie down most of the time. He'd even stopped going to his shop.

A month went by. Vedaa's husband was still unwell. She asked him, "What is the problem? What does the doctor say?"

"Nothing. He says that I'll improve with the medicines."

"But what do you feel? Shall we consult another doctor?" Vedaa asked worriedly.

"No. I will improve. I'm feeling better now."

But no matter how much he claimed he was better, Vedaa did not feel he was better. It was only that he did not complain.

Vedaa began to feel even more worried now. It was over a month since the wedding. Vedaa's mother phoned incessantly to inquire about his health. Father suggested that they go to a good consultant. But Vedaa's husband would just not hear of it. His home people too were not in favour of it.

Vedaa was in a quandary.

What was the problem with her husband? She couldn't understand what the trouble was, and his people too seemed quite unperturbed about it, which seemed strange to her. She was very worried just looking at him. He seemed to be growing darker by the day.

At last, she got an opportunity to go with him on his scheduled visit to the doctor. She wanted to ask the doctor why he was not improving despite taking so many medications for so long. Whether they should do some tests and get it done with. She was prepared to take him to any specialist, if need be. But she wasn't ready to just wait in the hope that he would improve.

Vedaa accompanied her husband to the doctor. The doctor inquired about his health.

"Doctor, it's now over a month. He hasn't improved. He's not well. What is wrong with him?" Vedaa expressed her worry.

"Who are you?" the doctor asked Vedaa.

"I'm his wife," Vedaa said, looking towards her husband. He sat quietly with his head bent down. Looking at him, Vedaa's mind became anguished. 'Poor fellow, god alone knows how much he is suffering,' she thought to herself.

She held his hand tight to give him support.

Vedaa looked at the doctor. The doctor kept looking at him in surprise.

"Ashish, did you get married?" he asked in astonishment.

Ashish, Vedaa's husband, with his head still bent, was silent.

The doctor asked again, "Did you really get married, Ashish?"

"Yes, doctor. We got married last month," Vedaa answered the doctor.

"Do you know him?"

Vedaa could not follow the import of the doctor's question.

"Isn't he my husband, doctor?" she came out with some response.

"No, no. What I wanted to know was whether you knew him earlier, meaning before your wedding."

"No. Our proposal took place and then we had the wedding soon. Everything happened within a month," Vedaa quivered as she replied.

When he heard this, Vedaa sensed that the doctor's mien had turned serious. The doctor did not smile. He kept looking at her grimly. She understood that something was amiss, but Vedaa did not understand what. Again, she looked at her husband. He was not prepared to raise his head.

"Ashish, you got married and that too without telling her anything!" The doctor's statement had a sharp edge to it and Vedaa could sense it.

Ashish did not say a word. He wouldn't lift up his head either.

"You people did not bother to make any inquiries before the wedding?" the doctor asked Vedaa sternly. Vedaa was in a turmoil. She stared back at the doctor angrily.

The doctor too kept looking at her. There was not a hint of a smile on the doctor's face.

"What is your name?"

"Vedaa."

Vedaa was now overcome with foreboding. Her heart skipped a beat. 'Why is the doctor asking these questions?' she wondered.

"Vedaa, I will speak plainly now. Ashish's illness is not curable. With heavy drinking, his liver has been destroyed. I had already told him this long back. Now he has only about six months."

"Meaning?"

"Meaning that he does not have long to live. I had given him and his family a very clear idea about this. Why did they have to do this?" The doctor murmured the last sentence to himself.

Vedaa felt as if struck on the head. Her head began to throb. She looked at her husband in anger. His head was still bent.

Vedaa stood up. She went home, to Ashish's house. Packing her belongings, she phoned her father, "Papa, come and take me. I'm coming home. I will tell you everything when I reach home."

The news that Vedaa, the new bride, had suddenly gone back home to her parental home, went viral. The neighbourhood began to buzz with questions.

His mother responded, "They deceived us."

"What do you mean?" Sukanti wanted to know.

"She has a brother. Just one brother, but he is retarded. They are only bothered about the brother. They had planned to bring him here. Because Ashish refused, she just got up and left the place," the mother said.

Sukanti spread the news to her buddies.

Ashish's illness was worsening. His wife did not come back. He came to know from his mother that she'd gone back to her parents' house. His mother had come to know when her father came to take her. Ashish did not have the guts to bring her back or even to face them.

Six months went by. Now Ashish would not even venture out of the house. One day the news came in. Ashish had died.

Sukanti proclaimed, "The poor fellow died of shock because his wife left him. I hope you haven't done anything wrong in your life? Modern girls are pampered. They are not prepared to put up with any little problems."

Another piped in, "They are earning independently now, aren't they?"

Glossary

Shalu: Expensive silk saree brocaded with gold and silver embroidery, earlier worn by Indian brides, but now worn by others too on formal occasions

Muhurat: Auspicious time prescribed by Hindu scriptures to perform important ceremonies such as marriage, buying property, laying the foundation stone of a house, starting stock trading or the shooting of a film, among others

Mukhavayalyo aarti: A phrase used to indicate that someone is merely trying to show off how much he/she cares for the other; the actual *aarti* is not done. The colloquial meaning of the phrase would be: 'She was trying to impress the people.' (An *aarti* is a Hindu ritual of worship using oil lamps.)

Originally written in Konkani as 'Bavddo'.
Translated by Xavier Cota.

Maria's Boutique

Brian Mendonça

ALL was still when José started walking homeward. It had been a tiring day. It was so difficult to make ends meet these days. Still, being a clerk in one of the numerous offices in the by-lane facing what used to be El Capitan theatre was the best he could manage. It used to be a movie house in Mapuça. His steps quickened when he thought of his son and daughter. They were his life and soul. The very sound of their laughter made him feel life was worth living, after all. When José was wearied by the toils of the day or the boss's heckling, he discussed the incidents with Ethan and Angeline (Etu and Anju, for short). His son was six years old and Anju, five. They would listen to him intently and then ask innocent questions like, 'Why doesn't the boss scold someone else? Why only you?'

Fed up with this idle chatter, Maria would stomp out of her kitchen, take the kids in hand and feed them their dinner. Surreptitiously, like a shadow, José would reach for the bottle of caju *feni* by the sideboard to feed the fire in his belly, but mostly to brush off the nagging from his wife for bringing in such a meagre amount at the end of the month. The winter months were the hardest when there were so many expenses. Everyone demanded a gift for Christmas these days. With so many relatives descending on the house and the sweets to be made, José wished they did not have to celebrate the festival at all! Between Easter and Christmas the family eked out their existence. They were God-fearing Catholics and inhabitants of Corjuem in Aldona.

The grand houses and the palatial *balcões* of Corjuem were a cruel riposte to José's small tenement on the outskirts of the village. He worked in the city of Mapuça, and though he tried to supplement his income by doing odd jobs like fixing broken furniture or helping in re-roofing the houses before the monsoons, the children's ever-increasing demands never seemed to end. The school fees bore a hole in his savings, which often left him wondering at the necessity of an education. He, for example, was a self-made man. In all the forty-five years of his life he never believed in taking loans to buy things. Many followed the practice so that they could enjoy using a car or a washing machine, while paying back the loan in instalments. The neighbours looked down on them with disdain and considered them old fashioned. Three generations of his family had lived there. José and Maria were already eyeing suitable matches for their children from the village.

That day José was downcast. He had been fired for no fault of his. With the new crop of younger workers, the old were not valued any more. Even the flimsiest excuse was good enough to give them marching orders. In this case, it had been the ingénue Monica who had burst upon the scene with her tight tops and flashy if somewhat vacuous laugh. But it was enough to unseat José from his job to which he had clung to valiantly for over ten years. Dropping out of school for want of finances, his father had got him the job in the company when José was a strapping youth.

"What happened, dada?" asked Anju when José entered the house. José tried to avoid answering her but Maria sensed that something was amiss. It was 7 pm – time for the Angelus – and she shepherded the family near the makeshift altar. The Lord had always seen them through, she thought. All would be well. Her devotion to Mary Help of Christians was well known. Not for nothing was she named Maria. When they could afford it, she used to take the family to Bombay for their annual visit so she could pay her obeisance to Our Lady of the Mount. If finances permitted she allowed the children a run of the Bandra fair.

Maria pushed a plate of rice towards José and ladled him some *kalchi koddi*. For the children she had prepared some weak gruel with boiled vegetables. This they ate with *rotis*.

"I am not going to work tomorrow," José said after a long moment of silence. In the darkness outside crickets were singing.

Maria had, in fact, expected this. She could discern his sullen moods by now, being married to him for over a decade. Though she was a shrew in certain matters, when it came to the upkeep of the family she would leave no stone unturned.

"What happened?" she asked, her eyes alive with concern.

"The boss asked Monica to take my place. She is a B.A., knows typing and also computers. She also makes and serves very good tea," José offered by way of explanation.

"Those *pampreles* in the office think too much of themselves these days. They have stolen my husband's job. Next they'll stoop to stealing my husband himself!" Maria thought to herself, eyes flashing.

"But they can't do this! Not after you have worked there for so long!" retorted Maria indignantly.

"They can and they just did," said José quietly.

Maria's mind was racing. "I shall stitch and embroider clothes and sell them in Mapuça market. I am good at it. My mother taught me stitching. I have preserved all her needlework books with me. Foreigners specially are fond of buying crotchet work for huge sums in the Friday bazaar."

The next week José went to collect what was due to him at his by now erstwhile office. The accountant told him with a smirk to come on Monday.

So José sat with his wife in the Mapuça market among the red chillies, the jaggery, the *solan* and the brooms and even the Moira bananas so famous in the village. The scenes and the smells assailed him. From where he sat just behind his wife he had a good view of the buxom lasses who tripped by gaily to pick up their fashion accessories. He would have never had such a windfall at office – Monica notwithstanding.

As a couple José and Maria were soon enfolded into the community of traders, merchants and local sellers – simple people who were sincere and warm-hearted. The women showed Maria how to get the best prices for her wares. José did his bit by attracting the attention of the passers-by and sometimes playing loud Konkani music, much to the consternation of those around him.

Soon José began to enjoy going to the market with Maria. He carried the bags with her clothes to the market. Sumita and Ganesh, the couple who lived next to them, brought Anju and Etu to them after the children finished their school. They also fed them with what little *jevonn* they could muster. José put the tired children to sleep as Maria stitched or knitted away. They had their tea together in the lean times before the first buyers trickled in by 4 in the evening.

As dusk fell, they would all wind their way home discussing the day's happenings. Then Maria would cook and José would peer into the school books of the children. Though he did not understand very much, he had to show he knew everything! He had stopped drinking now. They would say the rosary, and read Psalm 91 from the *Povitr Pustok* – the Konkani Bible. Trusting in Providence they would have their meal, laced with *korum* pickle, and sleep the sleep of the just.

They were spending more time as a family. Maria softened her rebuke of José now that she knew what it meant to be the breadwinner. Sitting side by side with her, José glowed with pride at seeing how his wife had turned the situation around. Soon they were able to afford a modest space to sell their work. Maria's intricate designs soon became the rage, so much so that even seamstresses getting ready for the wedding season began lining up outside her door for some advice and, of course, designs.

Soon they were earning much more than they used to be content with earlier. The charter flights come October had doubled her earnings. Foreigners did not hesitate to shell out for authentic stuff. By dint of hard work, Maria now graduated to a boutique. She was mulling over franchises in Panjim and Margão. She headed a team of nimble workers.

José became her marketing manager. Losing the job was the best thing that happened, mused José. He had lost a job but had found his family. They had not lost hope. They had persevered and prevailed. He remembered the words of Sirach 2:14 from the Bible: *Doom is sure to come for those who lose their hope.*

Glossary

Feni: A spirit produced in Goa. There are two types of *feni*, cashew *feni* and coconut *feni*, depending on the original ingredient

Balcões: Balconies (singular: *Balcão*)

Dada: Father

B.A.: Bachelor of Arts degree awarded for an undergraduate course

Kalchi koddi: lit. Yesterday's curry. Curry left over from yesterday's meal is warmed over a low flame till it condenses and thickens

Roti: An unleavened flatbread made from wholemeal flour and water that is combined into dough. It is rolled out and cooked on a griddle over a flame

Pampreles: Prostitutes, or young girls looking to climb up fast in life

Solan: Plural of *sol*, which are the dried peels (skins) of a fruit called *kokum* or *bind'nna*

Jevonn: Food

Korum: Raw mango pickle (also spelt '*korom*')

Dhirio

Mayabhushan Nagvenkar

T HE scent of blood and fresh dung hung in the air, mixed with the smell of fresh, scuffed earth.

Added to that was the chorus of shrieks from excited on-lookers demanding a 'kill' from Rocky. Rocky, the fawn-coloured eight hundred-pound[1] bull, seemed to almost understand what was being asked of him. Egged on by the shouts, he trotted jauntily in a rough semi-circle around his opponent Tyson, who stood some metres away. Tyson's neck was bloodied. His legs trembled with fear in anticipation of what was about to come.

As Rocky's pre-victory march ended, he banked with the stunning grace of a hurtling locomotive turning over curved rails and stopped. He then stamped the soft, uneven ground with his front hooves and swished his tail with an almost cat-like grace.

There was an angry crimson streak on Rocky's soiled right flank too. That's where he was gored by Tyson's sharp horns a few minutes ago. It was the only moment in the contest when the massive fighting bull had exposed himself in a moment of over-confidence.

When Tyson's right horn had dug into Rocky's flank, the latter had heard the worried gasp of his master and mentor Caitu over all the din. But in this moment, all his focus was on Tyson and the final thrust he was about to inflict on his tottering, panting opponent.

Earlier during the fight, as Rocky gored and worked his opponent's neck, battered his sides through the battle, a scared Tyson seemed to have sensed defeat and shat. The sign encouraged Rocky as well as Caitu, who was all set to collect the winner's purse,

---

[1] About three hundred and sixty-two kilograms.

as well as his winnings from multiple wagers with other bullfight aficionados. He had all his savings and his future riding on this fight.

For now, everyone, including the bulls as well as the five hundred-odd audience, went quiet, as if in deference to the *coup de grâce* which was about to be delivered by Rocky. A second before Rocky's rear legs went taut and bunched, ready to lunge, the bull heard what he was waiting for.

As the words 'Finish it!' rolled out of an eager Caitu's mouth, the bull was off the blocks. The crowd broke into a collective cheer. As he charged towards Tyson, the confident bull lowered his head, ready to ram into the scared, trembling bull.

Only, that didn't happen. A couple of feet from making contact with his rival, Rocky's front left hoof slipped into a deep pocket in the mud, a monitor lizard hole, which sucked his leg almost a foot and a half into the loose soil, softened further by the rains the previous night.

His left hoof trapped, Rocky buckled and with his head already lowered for assault, his heavy, well-muscled body cartwheeled, with the rear limbs rising almost eight feet, kicking the air wildly.

The flying hulk of the beast, still crudely leveraged by its trapped leg, sailed over a bewildered Tyson before crash landing on John Cruz, the local motorcycle pilot, and the two brothers from D'mello Vaddo, who had just returned home from a stint on a Caribbean cruise liner for a short break.

Shocked and lying sprawled on his side with screaming folks still trapped under him, Rocky's adrenalin continued to pump. He craned his neck to look at his opponent, who was standing still, perhaps in shock, despite the crowd running around him in chaos. The fight had to finish. He tried to get up, but collapsed. He tried again, using his hind legs to prop him up, but fell again. He tried to get on his feet several times, but could not. That's when he felt the familiar hand of his master on his left leg, which was by now seething in pain, before a grimy towel was placed over his eyes and Caitu's gentle words telling him 'it's all over, it's all over', until the melee around them faded away.

Caitu wasn't expected home early that evening. His wife Esmeralda and his daughter Andrea had both heard of the tragedy at the bullfight from their neighbours, who were trickling home from the venue by evening.

"Caitu was crying and was still with Rocky when we were leaving. He has called for the vet, but the left leg appears clean broken," Sylvester, a neighbour, told them, as he steered his scooter past their home.

A short distance away, at a tavern, neighbours and acquaintances gossiped over how much money Caitu would have lost in the wager.

"He is already neck-deep in debt. Caitu will have to sell Rocky to that butcher Manuel. The sooner he does, the better. Why should the poor animal suffer," tavern-keeper Agnelo gossiped to his patrons with an air of accustomed authority.

Esmeralda waited for her husband in her bare drawing room, weaving coconut fronds into thatch with her daughter. Her anxiety was obvious. Six-year-old Andrea's fingers appeared to weave faster than her own today, beating her for pace, perhaps the first time. So when she heard the pick-up truck slow down near her house, she flung aside the frond she was working on and ran outside, her face flush with anger.

"I don't want you in my house. Never step in again. You and that bull of yours. If you walk in now, I will stab that animal myself," she shouted, even as Caitu was hopping off the carriage, where Rocky lay dazed on a bed of mango leaves to cushion him from the hard metal flooring.

"Now is not the time, Esma. Nothing has gone right today. Don't start with this," Caitu pleaded.

"You lost our house, you've spent all our savings and put us in debt. I have to weave thatch for a living. We are forced to live in my mother's house and listen to her taunts because of you. You love that bull more than you love our daughter! Go away. Just go away. I never want to see you again. This marriage, whatever we had, is over," she lashed out again, before turning around and slamming the door on Caitu.

He jumped off the vehicle and ran towards the door which had just closed on him.

"Esma, please open the door. Rocky is hurt. I've brought him along. He needs care. I need the five hundred rupees which you had hidden behind the altar. I want to bring home the doctor to examine him," he implored, but to no avail.

"Esma please. I know I have never been able to give you anything a husband should, except for Andrea. But please for this once, help me out," he begged again.

This time, his wife screamed like a banshee before opening the door and emerging with a knife in her hand.

"Get out. Out. You are dead for the both of us. You and your bull. If you want to come back home, if you really want us, take this knife and put it through that beast's heart," she said, thrusting the large butcher's knife in his hand.

Caitu threw away the knife as if it had been electrified by Esma's anger, and fell at her feet.

By now, neighbours and onlookers had begun to assemble around their house, attracted by the loud noises. But Esma kept her tirade going.

"What kind of a man are you, who treats a bull better than his wife and child? When there's no milk in the house, you borrowed money to buy jaggery and gram for that animal. Now we cannot even repay the loan taken from the *posro*. And we know how many other loans you have taken just to raise that animal. Just leave. We are not your family anymore. From now on, your only family is that thing lying in that pick-up with a broken leg," she said, before finally slamming the door in rage.

Fallen and in tears, Caitu looked around at the faces staring back at him. Among them were Santan the baker, Kamat the grocer, Alex the moneylender, all of whom he owed money to. But the first to walk up to him from among the crowd was Manuel the butcher.

Manuel squatted alongside Caitu, offering him consolation, as well as a bargain.

"Look, we all know how sad you feel. You must climb out of

this hole. If you want money, I can buy Rocky. You won't get the full price I normally pay for a beast, because you owe me for all the beef you've bought on loan for six months. But it's still a lot of money, you know".

Caitu sat stone-faced, until his eyes fell on the knife he had thrown down moments ago.

"I know I owe you, Manuel, and I am sorry I have been unable to repay my debt, but if you ever talk to me about slaughtering Rocky, I will empty your guts out and make sausages out of them."

"Look, I only tried to help you. If you can't sell me Rocky, I need the money you owe me within two days. If not, I will come after you with the police and take Rocky away forcibly. Let's see how you stop me then," Manuel said, before storming off.

The other creditors also walked away for now, merging with the rest of the crowd.

As dusk swept in, the street lights switched on, as if to accentuate the tragedy. By now the only ones still left on the street were Caitu, who was sitting on his haunches by the closed door, the pick-up driver and, of course, Rocky, who lay exhausted and in pain on his side in the carrier, his eyes still trained on his master.

Caitu was roused out of his dream and his sleep by the sound of Rocky's coarse bellow. His left hoof was swollen now from the break. The veterinarian he had gone to in desperation yesterday had refused to treat Rocky because of a string of debts Caitu had piled up, ever since he had started taking the bull to him sometime back.

Caitu had hoped that yesterday's fight would help pay off past debts, but things hadn't really gone to plan.

His eyes ran from Rocky's wound to the sands of Anjuna beach, where he and Rocky had exercised for the last couple of years. Every morning, Rocky and he jogged on the beach for nearly an hour. Running was necessary for Rocky's fitness and durability, which are key qualities in a bullfight, apart from a killer instinct. By the end of the run, Rocky's flanks would gleam with sweat in the still tender sunlight. Tourists as well as children who visited the beach in the early hours posed for selfies with the mighty outline of Rocky against the Arabian Sea.

He got up, had a quick bath in the sea and picked up some coconut leaves, sticks and, with the help of some discarded nylon rope which had washed ashore, rigged together a shelter to shield Rocky from the sun, which had now turned harsh.

Rocky must be thirsty and hungry, he told himself, having gone without a meal himself last night, after being driven from his mother-in-law's home.

He went back home to find the door locked. Esma must have stepped out to the market to sell the fronds she was weaving yesterday.

He knocked on his neighbour Martin's door and borrowed a *kolsuli*, which he dipped into his well and pulled out some water. Heaving the utensil onto his head, he carried it to the beach for Rocky who drank nearly all its contents, which he had poured in a discarded bucket he found along the way. The few gulps that remained, Caitu drank himself.

Next, he checked his pockets, which still contained fifty odd rupees. He knew he needed to get food for the bull, which he arranged by buying a bag of crushed sugarcane stems from a cane-juice seller for twenty rupees.

Leaving Rocky to munch on the sugarcane, Caitu drifted off into sleep again, occasionally brushing off flies which had started to hover over the animal's wound.

In his sleep, he dreamt of the gunny sacks of gram and bags of jaggery which he had bought for Rocky just after a friend gave him the young, but majestic-looking, male calf.

"His father Paisan was the champ for five years in Morjim. No one, not a single bull could even scratch him. But Dattu, his owner, had a heart attack and his wife didn't want him to do anything with bull-fighting every again. The calf is a good investment. Look at the fire in his eyes. And the price is only rupees two lakh," his friend had said.

Bullfights, his friend had told him, were a good way to make money and clear his gambling debt. Without telling his wife, Caitu pledged his house to the local moneylender to raise the money required to buy the calf. He had seen snatches of Sylvester Stallone's film 'Rocky' in a video parlour a couple of decades ago, memories of which had stayed with him. So he decided to name the calf 'Rocky'.

However, as Rocky walked into his life, his fortune appeared to run out on him. His obsession with training and pandering to Rocky got him a sack from his job as a waiter at a beach shack. Moneylenders being moneylenders, the loan he had borrowed to buy Rocky turned out to be one with an 18 per cent interest per week, rather than 18 per cent per month, and soon the interest outgrew the loan itself. Within months, Caitu was forced to leave his own home along with his family.

His relationship with his wife was already strained because of his gambling habit and his debts. Now, with the arrival of Rocky and the new pile of loans, his marital relations soured further.

Esma and Caitu bickered every day, sometimes even hitting each other, as the husband battled for the well-being of the beast and the wife for the care of their young daughter.

One day, suspecting that Esma had mixed rat poison in Rocky's fodder, he had beaten her up with a rope harness. That was the day Esma walked out of the small hut they had rented, to her mother's house in Dando. A few days later, the couple appeared to have made up, until Caitu landed at his mother in-law's house with Rocky in tow. In an attempt to broker peace, the mother-in-law allowed Caitu to stay as long as the bull did not enter the laterite stone-lined compound wall. As a result, Rocky stayed in the open by a sheltered haystack across the road from the house.

He was suddenly roused from his sleep by a painful bellow from Rocky. The bull was staring at him now, the hurt radiating from his dilated eyes. It was late evening and Caitu knew that he didn't have much time to lose. If he couldn't find a vet for his bull soon, that would be the end of Rocky. And he had thirty rupees in his pocket.

He gently patted Rocky's face and spoke a few reassuring words in his ear, before heading for the vet's home.

Dr Gustav Fernandes did not like to be disturbed at home and, when Caitu knocked on his door, he abused the distraught visitor.

"Why do you keep a bull when you cannot afford it? I cannot treat him for free anymore. It is you who needs treatment and not the animal. Get out of my sight. Out," the doctor barked.

"You are my last hope, doctor. Please at least take a look at Rocky's leg. I will do anything you want. Just tell me how bad the wound is. He cannot stand up. He has been lying ever since he got hurt yesterday," he said.

"You will have to put him down, Caitu. But I will not do it for you. And I will not hire a gambler for any chores. I have to eat my dinner now," he said, slamming the door shut.

A despondent Caitu went back to the beach to sit alongside Rocky. Perhaps tomorrow will come with a solution to his predicament, he consoled himself as he lay down.

He squeezed his eyes shut, the balm of helplessness and pain gluing them shut. Soon, drops of rain, the size of acacia acorns, showered from the dark skies. His eyes suddenly opened to see Rocky nudging him with his moist nose. As he gathered himself and stood up, he saw that Rocky was walking gingerly towards the sea. Had the wound healed? Must be a dream, Caitu told himself.

He could see himself following Rocky, who appeared to be at ease with every stride he took. By now, Caitu was whooping with joy. He touched Rocky's flank and the beast, who was in pain just some time back, turned to look at him with a look of relief in his eyes. Caitu playfully touched his horns and his massive forehead as they walked towards the sea, which was churning like a young mountain stream in a frenzy. In a matter of seconds, the water reached his ankles and he wobbled as the force of the current caught him unawares. The dream just wouldn't end, he told himself. The water rose to his waist and after a long, long time, he felt a sense of weightlessness, as it lifted him off his feet. Rocky too

seemed to be soaking the moment in, shaking his head as the foam hit him in the chest and sprayed over his eyes and face.

A blaze of lightning lit up the seas around them and the man and his beast, still composed and calm in bearing, were swept away by the churning water. In moments, both disappeared from sight.

All that remained were their footprints along the beach. They too would not last the night.

Glossary

Dhirio: A bullfight
Posro: General store, usually tiny and village-based
Kolsuli: Pot used to carry water

This story won the third prize at the Fundação Oriente Short Story Competition, 2017.

Mother, When Is My Birthday?

Naresh Chandra Naik

W HEN he neared the juice extraction sink, the smell of cashew apple bagasse filled his nose. Swarms of insects were hovering on all sides around the hoops of discarded cashew apple waste. The branches of the cashew trees were sagging with the weight of the cashew apples. The cashews were like the fruits in the *matolli,* the arrangement adorning the idol of the Lord Ganesh during Chaturthi. He removed the heavy stone and threw away the hoop, and taking the clear *neero,* the filtered juice which had trickled down overnight from the crushed cashew apples, he poured it into the barrel. '*Hoosh... hoosh...*' He chased away any animals from around the cashew trees. This was his routine whenever he would come into the cashew orchard during his school break.

He had to come to the orchard early in the morning, before the sun came up. If he was slightly late, the monkeys would have a field day, laying waste the ripe cashew apples and even the raw ones and making a carpet of them under the tree. Or the village louts would plunder even the raw nuts. This morning he had a breakfast of chicken and *polli,* the flat bread of bran and wheat flour, left over from last night's rich dinner cooked in honour of the *zatra* of the Partagal Feast. This was the one time in the year that they had chicken. Otherwise, he would have come after having a breakfast of *pez,* the rice canji with green mango pickle to flavour it.

Today, he came to the plantation a little more enthusiastic than otherwise. Whilst returning from the fair, where she'd gone to sell flowers, grandma had brought him a toy car. On the way here, he would constantly take it out from his pocket and admire it. But none of them used to take him to the fair. *Baba* used to tell him to worship god from home. They would say that children get lost at these fairs. That was enough for his desire to go to the fair to die down. Talk about nothing but the *zatra* – this was cheap, that was expensive. Lots of blind people. The spread of the fair was big this year, it seems. His interest in the *zatra* had to be satisfied with the talk. He was also upbeat as his father would bring him new sandals after selling cashew nuts in the fair. His sandals were in such bad shape that his feet were sticking out and when he walked about in the cashew orchard, thorns and twigs would prick and poke his feet.

Picking up the bucket from the extraction sink and taking up the stick, he began to go around gathering the cashew apples. He gathered the apples that had fallen with the wind in the night and put them into the sink after removing the cashew nuts. After finishing the round of cashew trees, he would play for some time with the grandson of the orchard owner. He would come back and climb on the branch of a cashew tree. If he was bored, he would climb down and, spreading his worn towel on the ground, he would take a nap. But in between, if the monkeys were to come, there would be chaos. Holding up his tattered shorts with one hand, he had to chase them away. If he felt hungry, he would go around and eat some wild berries and jambul fruits. But the best were the raw cashew nuts carefully peeled and eaten with tender cashew-leaf shoots. The only problem was that the cashew shell liquid would cause flakes of the skin to peel off the fingers, so he had to immediately begin to crush the cashew apples to clean his hands. The whole day would pass by with this work in the orchard. At noon, mother and father would bring him his lunch. In the mornings, *aiyee* and *baba* would gather the cashews in the other orchard and, in the evenings, in this orchard. This was their routine for the duration of the cashew season and it was backbreaking for them.

He was fed up gathering the cashew apples on the slopes, so he went down towards the bhatkar's house. Shivam, the grandson of the orchard owner, was playing in the yard. Today he was dressed in fancy clothes. He had a watch on his wrist. Seeing that, he re

membered the make-believe watch of coconut leaflets he used to sometimes put on his wrist. Looking at his fine T-shirt and smart shorts, he put a hand to his ragged loose pants and tucked it into the waistband and checked to see if the pin with which he'd secured it to his shirt was in place. Imagining for a moment that all the attention would be on him, he called out to Shivam.

"*Shuth... shuth,* Shivam..."

"Hi there, Krishna. When did you come?"

"I came this morning."

"Come, let's play with the bat and ball."

"Yes, yes. Let's play." Shivam came running towards him.

"Did you just wake up? You've had your tea?"

"Yes, I had my tea some time ago. I got up early today."

"Good. And when are your results?"

"My results are on the 25th. When are yours?"

"Mine too are on the 25th. Teacher told me that I'll be going to the Fifth. I will be going to a new school now."

"I'm in the Third standard now. Do you know? Now I won't be writing on the slate anymore. I'll be writing on new books with a pen!"

"But I've been writing with a pen and pencil on a book from my KG class."

"Our teacher says that in our primary school we have to use only a slate."

"You know, today my uncles, aunts and cousins have come to our place. We're having my birthday party in the evening. Daddy has brought a lot of chocolates, balloons and a big cake. Later I will give you chocolates and some cake – see that you come, okay?" Shivam was excited about his birthday party and his eyes were shining.

Listening to all this, he was puzzled. He stared at Shivam. What is a birthday? Why is it celebrated?

"What is a birthday?"

"Don't you know? Birthday is the day you are born."

"When is your birthday? Call me, okay? I will also come for your birthday," Shivam brought him to his senses.

He was once again caught in the net of questions. 'I wonder when I was born? Why is my birthday not celebrated?' He didn't know. For a long time, he could not even talk.

"I will ask my mother today, okay?" he said slowly. He had no other option.

"You mean your birthday has never been celebrated?"

"No. I don't know," he said with his head bowed down.

"Forget it. Today you come to our place. Then you can tell your mother to celebrate yours too."

His birthday had never been celebrated even though he was quite grown up. He was trying to figure it out. Finally he decided he would ask his mother about it even before looking at what she'd brought for lunch.

"You know something, Krishna? Daddy has got a gold chain made for me. I will wear it today for my birthday party."

Hearing this, Krishna's hand went to the religious string round his neck. He felt good. As if somebody had drawn a benediction over him.

'Shivam was so lucky. His parents buy everything for him. They have everything. But we don't have anything. I wonder why mummy and daddy haven't bought things for me like Shivam's parents?' Such questions began to prick him like thorns. They began to trouble his mind. 'Am I not a child like Shivam? But I don't...'

For quite a long time, he could not speak. He did a lot of thinking but there were no answers to his questions. But I must remember, he thought, giving his ears a twist. 'Today as soon as mother comes, I will ask her all this. Otherwise, I will throw a tantrum kicking out my legs and crying loudly. But where will the sound of my crying reach? Will it go round? Will it reach anywhere or just fade away? That, only the creator will know...'

These thoughts kept going round and round in his mind. On the other hand, Shivam was comfortable. One by one, he was stringing his garland of happiness.

In that upset frame of mind, Krishna climbed up from the cashew orchard. The sun too had become hot. That terrible heat, coupled with the boiling in his mind – he found it overpowering.

He wasn't bothered about the cashews. Flinging the torn towel under a cashew tree, he drew up his torn sandals for a pillow and lay down. His stomach was cramping with hunger and he was drowning in disappointment. He turned on his stomach and didn't even know exactly when he fell asleep. Just as salt dissolves in water, he had forgotten his sadness, for the moment at least.

By this time, the monkeys had begun their *Shigmo* frolics on the cashew trees. He got up with a start due to their chattering and sat up. He saw monkeys on the tree with the king-sized nuts. He ran with a stone in his hand and flung it. The monkeys fled, shaking their tails. He just stared at the cashews laid waste by them on the ground below. They had squeezed the cashew apples and the apples now looked more like bagasse.

On the one hand, pangs of hunger were gnawing at his stomach. He greedily drank the water from the bottle. He ate a cashew apple and sat on the rim of the extraction sink. He was wondering when mother and father would come with some food to relieve his hungry belly. Just then he spotted them coming towards him with torn towels round their heads to protect them from the burning sun. He felt some relief. His eyes went towards the tiffin they were carrying for him and with the mere sight of the food he felt the strength returning to his hands and feet.

"Son, why are you sitting in the heat of the sun?"

"I've just come, *aiyee*. I was waiting for you."

"By the time I returned from gathering the cashews and finished the cooking, I was delayed. My poor son must be hungry, right? Come let's eat. We too haven't eaten as it was late. We've brought our food here too, so we can all eat together."

"Son, just a few more days of toil. These are the peak days of the cashew harvest, aren't they? A few more days, after that, the cashews will become less and the work won't be so tiresome. After selling off the cashew nuts, I will buy you some new clothes," father soothed him.

"No, mother, I am not hungry," he said swallowing his pangs, but mother deciphered his sunken eyes. She quickly served him. The aroma of the dry prawn curry made his mouth water and at that moment, at least, he forgot what he wanted to ask her about the birthday. First the stomach, then everything else.

Without any further ado, he started to attack the food, and blowing on the piping hot food, he began to eat. He was totally engrossed eating the rice with dry prawn curry on the banana leaf. Once the belly is full, everything is right. He couldn't see beyond the next bout of hunger and the next meal....

"Hey, wait a while. Let the food cool a little at least."

"Mummy, see it's already cooler."

"Sonny, we have to finish lunch and finish our work fast."

"Why, mother?" He remembered Shivam's birthday party.

"Today, we'll go to the temple at Gokhale."

"What is there in Gokhale? The *zatra*?" Hearing this, the wings of his enthusiasm began to flap.

He'd heard that there were lots of toys and things to eat at the fair. He'd only heard of it but today he would actually be going. Excited to go, he quickly finished his lunch and got up. The three of them set off with the stick and the bucket.

With renewed energy, he began to knock down the cashew apples. Mother and father too wanted to finish as soon as possible. By the time father finished shaking one tree, he would quickly climb another. Father and mother didn't have the strength to do this, but forgetting about the trouble, they continued. Calling upon the deities to help them, they quickly completed the rounds. Carrying the cashew apples to the crushing sink, they began to separate the nuts from the apples. Whilst pulling out the nuts, he remembered Shivam's birthday. He felt he should ask about his birthday too.

But mother was busy with her work, so he felt reluctant to ask. I will ask mother about my birthday in the evening at home, he decided.

When they reached home, he asked her with some trepidation.

"Mother, today is Shivam's birthday. May I go?"

"Son, will you go in those clothes? There'll be many of their relations there. We'll go for the *zatra*."

Mother was right. He didn't have good clothes. But he was looking forward to the birthday party, so he felt let down. 'Looks like I don't deserve the birthday party.' On the other hand, he tried to alleviate his disappointment with the thought of the fair he was going for.

Finishing all the work, they started towards home. The steps were taking him forward but his mind was pulling him back. Shivam kept coming before his eyes. Placing behind him the tantalising images of the cakes and chocolates at Shivam's party, he started walking on the road towards the *zatra*.

By the time they returned from the fair, it was Angelus time. Mother started the fire in the kitchen and began to cook supper. Tired with the day's work and the long distance they'd walked, mother and father were longing for some rest. Krishna began to play with his cart. He began to feel sleepy. Roaming the whole day through the cashew orchard and then to the fair, his legs were tired. He just felt like curling up and sleeping.

"Son, you're sleepy, aren't you?"

"Yes, mother."

"Wait a little while. The rice is done. I've just turned the pot over to drain the water."

Mother sat on the floor and took his head on her lap.

Seeing mother free, the embers of worry came to life.

"*Aiyee*, when is my birthday?"

"Son, our parents have struggled to survive, who ever thinks of enjoyment?"

"But, today was Shivam's birthday. When is mine? Why is my birthday not celebrated?"

Mother heard this and was silent for some time. Maybe she did not have an answer.

Rustling his hair with an affectionate touch, she said, "Son, what is our state? We earn today and spend today. Who says that these celebrations are for people like us? We can barely feed ourselves, so where is the question of celebrating birthdays?" Father was listening to all this, puffing silently on his *beedi*.

"Son, can a plain bird preen itself just because a peacock does?" father asked, leaning on the wall. Hearing all this was like spreading salt on his wound.

"But mother, Shivam's birthday is celebrated by his parents."

"Son, you're a smart boy, aren't you? We sense your enthusiasm, but we've never celebrated these occasions. We don't have the money to spend. These birthdays and such occasions are there for big shots to celebrate. Shivam's father is holding a good job. They can afford it."

"So when are you going to celebrate my birthday?" he persisted.

"Son, for this, the first thing you need to do is to study hard. You have to start working. You have to do up your house. After that, we can celebrate birthdays and other feasts."

"Son, we did not get these things. We can barely earn enough to eat. If we don't work in the fields and orchards, we'll have to go to sleep hungry," father said, looking at the rafters and exhaling the smoke from his mind.

"Son, now it all depends on you. You should show us these happy days. You should do well and enjoy the things that we could not. Our happiness lies in that. Who besides you will give us this happiness?" Mother expressed her hopes.

Seeing mother's and father's sad faces, he was speechless for some time. The next moment, his sadness dissipated. The sleep in his eyes dissolved with the bright thought of the future. He toughened his heart and with a brand new outlook, took out his school bag hanging on a peg and lit the lamp....

Glossary

Zatra: Fair linked to a village Feast

Pez: Type of rice porridge or gruel

Shigmo: A spring festival celebrated in Goa

Aiyee: Mother

Baba: Father

Bhatkar: Landlord

Beedi: Also spelt *bidi*, a thin cigarette filled with tobacco flakes and commonly wrapped in leaves tied with a string or adhesive at one end. They are inexpensive when compared with regular cigarettes

Originally written in Konkani as 'Aiyee, Birthday Ken'na?'
Translated by Xavier Cota.

The Divine Presence

Geeta Narayan Naik

To say that our Goa is a cauldron of different stories would not be an exaggeration. We've heard many such stories in our childhood. Some tales were greatly embellished – dances, demons, guardians or demon-guardians – I came to hear of them because our house was on the road to the market. In our childhood, the indigenous Kunnbi tribals from Bhutpal used to spend the night at our house. By the time they returned from the bazaar, it would be dark. They would sleep the night at our house. We heard some wonderful tales from them. We listened to their ghost stories. The stories of their experiences filled us with wonder.

"Have you heard of the *Bhesad* – it calls out Hoooo... Hooooo... If you respond to it, that will be your death knell." Their way of acting out their tales would hold us spellbound.

"Please tell us more. Tell us anything more." We would entreat them, not letting them go. We would sit on the *sopo* (the stone seats in the *balcão* – the porch that most traditional Goan houses have) and listen. We used to enjoy listening to their *ankhon dekha haal* – the virtual running commentary of their experiences.

When those people related their experiences, we would listen intently – we didn't want to miss a single word. Hearing their tales, our bodies would tingle with excitement. On one side our minds were filled with fear, while on the other we were curious.

Once in a way, Gopi *maam* (our maternal uncle) from Kollsor would come over. He was the actual maternal uncle of my cousin, but he would visit our house more than theirs. That was because he was a *caçador*, or hunter, like my father.

Sam sama sanyog – birds of a feather flock together – or some such expression would describe them. Though my father was a hunter, he would rarely go to hunt. He wasn't crazy about it, but you could safely say that hunting was Gopi *maam's* passion. Whether he had company or not, he would go to hunt – even alone. Anytime we went to their place, they always served *xacuti* – the spicy dish generally made at his house with the meat of the game that he had shot. Since both father and he shared a common interest, he would come to our place at least once a month.

Occasionally, he would come and call my father for a hunt. And sometimes he would bring us some meat of the animals he'd shot. He would gift us the entire side of a wild boar, a porcupine, hare or a small deer. Sometimes he would knock down cuckoos and other birds with birdshot cartridges. He would get at least a dozen birds with one shot. Seeing black-striped cuckoos and green *hoddio* struck down with their feet in the air would fill me with pity. That is why I had stopped eating *xacuti* for a while. Needless thoughts would bug me whilst eating: I wonder what I'm eating – the thigh or the neck? Forget it – I will not eat it! I just could not eat it.

Gopi *maam* would come to stay the night. There was always a spare set of clothing for him at our place. He would generally come around lunch time. He would go to the well, draw water and bathe with several pitchers of cool water poured over his head. He would then come and sit down. He would eat whatever was served to him. He was never fussy about anything. In our house, we always cooked for an extra person – anyone walking in around noon would be assured of a meal. Nobody needed to say 'Come, let's eat.' It was always, 'Come, have a seat, the house is yours.'

The minute Gopi *maam* came, we would feel happy. He would shower us with so many stories. We were guaranteed that like the *Akshay Patra* – Draupadi's magical utensil which never got empty – his stock of stories would never end. His stories were like a long string of tales. He would ask us, "Have any of you guys eaten crow *xacuti*? The *kavado* (wild pigeon) yields just a fistful of meat. How many can eat that fistful? But do you know that you can make a huge pan of *xacuti* with it?"

We would listen with our mouths agape. Each story was unbelievable. "You can't compare the *xacuti* of a *kavado* with anything

else. You guys will lick your fingers. The smell will not leave your fingers even three days after washing your hands."

He described it like a person who had a doctorate in cooking. We believed him totally. He had the knack of taking a four-anna bit of news and embellishing it with twelve annas of masala. He was really good at recounting.

This is one of the stories told by him when he'd come over once.

All of us children had spread ourselves in the *balcão*, while Gopi *maam* was seated in the easy chair. He began his tale. "My dear nephews and nieces, listen carefully to what I am about to tell you. This happened to me when I was a bachelor.

"One night, I set out for a hunt. There was a new moon. Mother kept telling me not to go, but I did not pay heed to her. Outside, it was pitch dark. Without a light, it was impossible to see anything. When I'm on a hunt, I'm not bothered about full moon or new moon. I had the urge to go for the hunt, so I set out alone." Gopi *maam* began his *sermão*.

"As usual, I tucked my *dhoti* firmly into the waistband. I put on my khaki jacket of many pockets. Shouldering my double-barrelled shotgun and clamping on my cartridge belt, I set out. The headlight, on the hat on my head, was on. Searching my way through, I went through the thick shrubbery of *santan-moll*. In this area there aren't any wild boars. Thinking that perhaps I may get a hare or small deer or perhaps a porcupine, I had loaded a birdshot cartridge in my gun. For a boar, I would have needed a buckshot cartridge. The tough hide of the boar does not allow birdshot to penetrate.

"I was going about from this side to that, flashing my light. Despite the headlight on my forehead, I could not pick out the eyes of any wildlife. Suddenly I sensed a small deer. Her eyes were glistening in the light of the headlight. Before she could be dazzled by the light, she darted away. I set out after her and reached quite far. I was struggling through gullies and bushes and feeling my way, as it was dark. Suddenly, my foot hit a rock and I tumbled headlong, landing on my face. My head hit a stone. I was saved but my headlight died instantly. Struggling to stand up, I finally straightened myself. Since my light had packed up, I had no other recourse but to use the small flashlight I carried in my pocket. But it soon became dim. I rubbed my eyes but I could see nothing. Not quite nothing, because on the other side of the Galjibaga river, on a *cazro* tree, there was a big bunch of fireflies glowing like a chariot. In the distance, the tuneless howling of a dog – *H-u...H-u-uu...* – could be heard. I was scared. Normally, I'm not even afraid of a tiger. I never shoot a sleeping tiger. That is the work of cowards. I throw a stone on a sleeping tiger to wake him up and only then do I take a shot at him." Uncle leaned back and gave a short laugh. He was telling us of his accomplishments and we were listening with rapt attention.

We were just waiting to hear what happened next. When he had begun, we were all spread out but now we were all slowly coming closer. We just badly wanted to know what came next. But Gopi *maam* was taking his time. Pouring water from a pitcher into a tumbler, he drank it down. He cast a cursory glance at his wristwatch. He wiped his mouth with the end of his loose shirt and, clearing his throat, sat back in the easy chair. We felt he was deliberately taking his time, which made us impatient.

"So, the *cazro* tree was decorated with the assembly of the fireflies. My ears were filled with the deafening *ki-i-i-r* of the night worm. And the plaintive howling of the dog *Hu-u-u H-u-u-u* which had scared me – and I had never been scared before that night – continued as I went forward. The atmosphere had turned strange."

Gopi *maam* began to colour his story. We were totally engrossed in the tale. We felt that we ourselves were caught up in the encounter.

"I could not understand how to find a way out of the darkness. Grasping a bush or a branch, I moved ahead. The footpath seemed unknown to me. I felt chilly. My legs were itching with the bushes that were tickling me. Suddenly, something slithered over my feet. I had no idea where I was headed! At this time, I don't know from where, I felt a cool breeze wafting over my body. My body stiffened right from my backbone. Goosebumps sprouted on my body." As he demonstrated by drawing his hands over both his arms, we shivered.

"See, even today the memory of that night gives me goose-bumps."

Truth to tell, even before his body got goosebumps, our bodies had sprouted them! We too sensed a cold wind blowing over our bodies. The light from the street lamps was throwing playful shadows on the wall. Normally it never comes to our notice. But today, the atmosphere in that *balcão* had changed. It was the effect of the story. Holding on to each other's hands, we inched closer. Soon our bodies were glued to each other. To mesmerise us even more, Gopi *maam* was liberally spicing up his tale. His yarn was now full of colour and making us tingle with excitement.

"That night I was terrified beyond belief. On a hunch, I began to walk and found a sort of footpath. I was feeling cold. In fact, I was shivering. And I was feeling dizzy. What will I do if I feel giddy and fall? Thinking this, I called out for divine help, 'Lord, Mallikar-jun, come to my aid, please.' My head was whirling. Suddenly I felt as if somebody had switched a light on. Am I hallucinating, I wondered. Swaying from side to side, I took some steps forward. The light was coming closer. I wasn't imagining it. There was a fire burning there. The embers were still aglow. Close by, at a distance of two hands I saw a *dovornnem*. The *dovornnem* is a resting pillar to aid porters carrying head-loads. I lost no time. Removing the gun from my shoulder, I rested it at the side of the pillar. Letting out a sigh of relief, I sat by the fire warming myself. The dying embers of the fire warmed me. Suddenly, something glistened. Some-body was approaching me with a firewood torch in his hands. He had a rough blanket thrown across his shoulders, a turban on his head and a loin cloth across his waist. The buckle on his belt was glowing even in the dark. As he walked, the steady thudding of his staff was audible. He came to me, 'Aren't you Shanu Porob's Gopi?'

"What! How does this guy know me? As for me I'd never ever seen this man."

"I am Janu Budhvont, the wise man, from Dando. Shanu *bab*

knows me very well. My cattle are lost. I was looking for them when I saw you. Why are you sitting here? Looks like you've lost your way. This place is not safe. Come on, get up from there. Start walking ahead, I will guide you to the edge of the village." That unknown person forcefully made me get up. There was a kind of firmness in his words. Like a puppet, I followed him. My feet had grown heavy. Dragging my feet I walked behind him. Showing me the way with his firewood torch, we reached the outskirts of the village.

"Gopi, walk on straight ahead. Take this torch. Just below this point is your house. Keep one thing in mind. Don't look back till you reach home. If anyone calls out to you from behind or hails you or if you hear the wailing voice of a woman, see that you just don't turn back to see. Start walking fast. Remember what I have told you." He lit the second torch in his hands and gave it to me.

"'Like a god, you came to my aid. Thank you very much.' I had to say this.

"Almost in a stupor, I began to walk towards home. I just wanted to reach home and flop down. My head was throbbing. I don't even know when I reached our yard. After reaching our patio, I turned and looked and looked, but there was no one there. The man wasn't there nor was the torch. Neither could I see the point from where I'd just climbed down there. All that I could see beyond, was the river Galjibaga and the lengthy row of fields along its banks.

"After this, for a few days, I had fever. It would rise and come down. Later they told me that I was mumbling in my sleep, 'Mallikarjun, save me, Mallikarjun, save me!'

"After my fever went down, I related all that had happened. My gun had to be brought. I surmised that it would be near that pillar. Father sent our *mundkar*, Pedru, to collect it."

"'Where did you find the gun?' father asked Pedru.

"'*Bhatkar*, can you imagine where I found the gun? I found it at Mastimoll near the marker pole of the *Vargatini*. It was fallen there. Do you know, *bhatkar*, it seems that on a new moon night, any young bachelor boy passing that way never returns safe! This female spirit just does not leave him. You remember Soiru's son, don't you? She finished him. She just did not leave him. Mother of Jesus! Only Our Lady knows how our Gopi *bab* was saved from the clutches of that *Vargatini* spirit. You know, *bhatkar*, this is not a plain bonfire we imagine it to be – it is the cremation place of Raya *bab*. He was cremated there on the new moon. Our Lady herself must have showered Her Blessings on our Gopi *bab*!'

"'Pedru, you have spoken the truth! I will now tell you what must have happened,' said my father.

"'After he fell into trouble, Gopi's subconscious urged him to invoke divine aid, crying *Mallikarjun help me!* Mallikarjun is the patron deity of our village. So when there is a cry of help to him, will he not come running to help? He must have sent Bhagil Paik to help him. Who do you think was the one who came with a blanket and a firewood torch? Janu Budhvont, the wise man? I don't know any Janu Budhvont. It must have been none other than Bhagil Paik. He was the one who saved him from the ghost."

"'Mallikarjun, this is indeed your divine intervention!' saying this, father joined his hands.

"He went inside the prayer room. Prostrating himself before the deity, he said, 'Thank you, Lord Mallikarjun, I will make you an offering of a cock immediately at the temple.'

"I could hear the conversation going on outside," Gopi *maam* continued with his story. "So, what I thought was the resting pillar was actually the lair of the *Vargatini*. I was very fortunate, other-wise that spirit would have destroyed me. I hadn't understood the gravity of it as I was burning with fever. I had warmed myself on the fire of the burning pyre of a dead man. Can you imagine that?!

"Many days after that, that man glistening as if with an oil mas-sage, came to me in my dreams. We immediately sacrificed a cock at the temple."

Gopi *maam's* tale had come to an end and all of us let out a col-lective sigh. I furtively joined my hands in prayer to Mallikarjun. If I get into any big problems, I only have to invoke Lord Mallikarjun, I thought, fixing it into my mind.

Just then, father ushered us all inside. "Come on, come on, go and have your supper." Inside, the aroma of *xacuti* was wafting all over. "I've just brought hot, hot loaves from the baker. Let's see how many each one can eat."

We were tackling the *xacuti* but our minds were still entangled in the shrubbery of the ghost's lair. In this distracted frame of mind, my hand, instead of eating from my own leaf-plate, had wandered into my neighbour's plate!

Gopi *maam* and my father were looking at each other and smiling quietly. That night, fearing the *Vargatini* spirit, we children hugged each other and fell asleep.

Glossary

Bhesad: Scary ghost

Ankhon dekha haal: *lit.* Seen with one's own eyes. Hindi expression for 'running commentary', used in Konkani. It can also mean 'mentioned by me'

Hoddio: Also spelt '*haddyo*'; it is a green-coloured bird

Anna: A unit of currency formerly used in India, equal to 1/16 of a rupee. The anna was demonetised as a currency unit when India decimalised its currency in 1957.

Sermão: Sermon, lecture. In this case, telling a story

Dhoti: A traditional men's garment worn in the Indian subcontinent. It is a rectangular piece of unstitched cloth which is wrapped around the waist and the legs, and knotted at the waist

Santan-moll: The plateau belonging to Santan

Bab: Term of respect for an older man

Mundkar: Tenant

Bhatkar: Landlord

Vargatini: Spirit of a woman who has died violently or unfulfilled (generally an evil spirit)

Bhagil Paik: The name of a spirit which protects certain areas

Originally written in Konkani as 'Sassay'.
Translated by Xavier Cota.

The Thief Who Left Behind His Things

Bina Nayak

MY mobile phone rang incessantly, early on a Sunday morning. I wondered who it could be as I picked it up. It was my sister, Deepti. "Somebody broke into our Goa house late last night," she said, sounding alarmed, "it was raining heavily and there was a power cut... the whole village was in darkness."

Wait, what? My heart raced. Goa is no longer as safe as it used to be – I had heard people lamenting on various Goa groups on social media, but never imagined the troubles would come home to roost. "What's stolen?" I asked her. "Not sure as yet... the neighbours and the maid checked, everything seems to be in place. The big Godrej lock on our main door was broken. Another house in our *vaddo* got burgled the same night. Theirs was a mess, all clothes lying around, cupboard doors broken, and a gas cylinder was stolen from their kitchen."

"What, a cylinder! All that trouble for a gas cylinder?"

"The maid says there is a big blue umbrella opened out and kept in our hall. It's definitely not ours. Maybe the thief left it behind."

Five years ago, whilst staying in Goa during the summer vacation, we were robbed on a stormy night. It was the end of May. The pre-monsoon showers had uprooted trees and electricity wires, plunging Almeida *vaddo* in darkness for three nights. My kids and their cousins enjoyed themselves thoroughly, playing games in candlelight, trapping fireflies in glass jars and marvelling at the stars each time the cloud cover parted. The showers had cooled night temperatures, ensuring they did not miss the ceiling fans. Three days later, when the linesmen fixed the electricity wires, they ran to switch on the TV. Eager to catch up on episodes of *Chhota Bheem* and *Shinchan*. But there was just static on the screen. Perhaps the cable wires also needed fixing. A quick call was made to the cable guy, who promised to rectify the problem immediately. However, when the TV continued displaying static till late evening, the kids' patience cracked. "Let's go back to Bombay. Nothing works in Goa!" they screamed and threw tantrums. Next morning the cable guy arrived to inspect and delivered a chilling verdict: "Your entire cable wire is missing. Somebody seems to have stolen it."

"What? Who steals cable wires...?"

"Oh, the copper component in the wires fetches a tidy sum – a few hundred bucks at least. Enough to keep petty thieves hydrated with *feni* for a few weeks," the cable operator enlightened me. I was very upset. "Why steal my cable wire for *feni* money? He could have just asked me, I would have gladly given it to him."

On the last day of our Goa stay, as I was locking rooms, drawing curtains over windows, I opened the terrace door to do a quick once over. And saw a pair of *chappals* fallen askew, skid marks on the moss-covered terrace floor where someone appeared to have slipped. Calling the kids up, I scolded them, "How many times have I asked you all not to play on the terrace? Who slipped and fell over here? Whose *chappals* are these?" The kids were perplexed. What I was pointing at were clearly adult-sized *chappals*. Besides, they had not stepped on the terrace the entire vacation. There was more fun to be had on the mango trees. "Not ours! Can't you see how big they are?" That's when I realised I was in possession of the cable wire thief's *chappals*. On a dark rainy night, he stole our cable but lost his *chappals*.

And now, some other thief had lost his umbrella in our house. I wondered if it was the modus operandi of Goan robbers to leave behind a calling card. But that would be the stuff of Sherlock

Holmes' TV serials. Chances were it was the same stupid robber. A forgetful dim wit perhaps, who didn't steal anything of value, but left his own things behind.

I fought sleep that Sunday night. Tossing and turning, I thought of ways to nab the thief. Finally giving up, making a mental note to stop watching those Sherlock Holmes serials – they made sleuthing seem too easy. At 6 am on Monday I called my sister, "Deepti, I'm going to Goa. I will lodge a complaint with the police and fix new locks on all doors. Do you want to come? We can stay for a week."

And so we sisters arrived in our little village, sans kids and husbands. All set to catch a forgetful thief.

We were *gheraoed* by the entire village immediately upon arrival. The elders offered advice and recounted sightings of the alleged thief. Everybody claimed to have seen suspicious people hanging around both houses that fateful night, but no one thought of making a note of their looks or their bike number plates... By afternoon, the village *sarpanch*, the *talati* and the *mamlatdar* had paid a visit, promising to fix extra street lights near the two houses. I was certain the promises would be forgotten the minute we returned home to Bombay. The other house's occupants were permanent residents of Australia; they visited Goa once in three or four years. At least Deepti and I, and our respective families, dropped by more often. After the onlookers and well-wishers vacated our house, peace and quiet prevailed. We sat down over a cup of tea to take stock of our situation. We walked over to the dining table, and there on top of it was the big blue umbrella.

It was an old fashioned, men's umbrella. The type that needed muscle power to open and could withstand heavy winds. A polished wooden handle and a sturdy metal tip meant it could be used as a walking stick. In Bombay, old Parsi gentlemen carried such umbrellas. This had to be one classy thief. Or a thief who had robbed an old Parsi gent? Hidden in one corner of the shoe rack were the *chappals* left behind from the previous cable wire robbery. I gathered the clues and placed them on the table. During both robberies, something had spooked the thief to make a quick getaway. This time around, he didn't manage to steal anything at all – and we had two full gas cylinders. Plus a TV, a stereo, open cupboards, a loaded drinks cabinet and some silver lamps in the *devara*.

"Deepti, you think there are ghosts in our house?"

"What rubbish, Binita! You sound like all those villagers."

"Just a thought... but something frightens robbers in our house."

"They're just petty robbers who filch small stuff, so we won't make a big deal of it to the police."

"Could it be the migrants? It doesn't seem like the handiwork of professionals... it appears as if gardening tools were used to break open the door, not drills and cutters."

"Or it could be the local drunkards who gather at Marcus bar, using sickles... oh, that reminds me, let's call the carpenter to repair the door and fix new locks."

"I still think we have a resident ghost, like a *devchaar*, who protects our house..."

"Binita, sweety, don't even mention that in public, okay? I will disown you!"

I had an idea. I quickly opened out the blue umbrella and took a picture with my mobile. I was going to make a poster. 'Found. This blue umbrella. Owner is requested to contact 9966901009 and claim it. We have no need for it as we use ladies push-button umbrellas'.

Deepti laughed at me. "Binita, it's not somebody's pet cat or dog that you've found. And do you think the thief is so stupid that he will not guess the intentions behind your poster?"

"It's worth a try, after all, he broke open a door by hacking out a locking system that cost four to five thousand rupees, and then stole a gas cylinder worth five hundred rupees... he could have run away with the fancy locks, no?"

"If you're going to play Sherlock, go find your Watson at the Mapuça Police Chowki and give him the umbrella. There could be fingerprints on it. And while you're at it, give away the *chappals* too. Don't know why we've kept them for all these years..."

"The police will laugh at us. I mean, nothing was stolen."

"Exactly, I think that's the point of these petty robberies – they are too embarrassing to report. But we must report them, after all it was a break in, and our house is compromised. But keep the umbrella, we can use it. Just as we've been using the *chappals*," Deepti said to me.

At 7 pm in the evening, the village carpenter and handyman, Shannu, arrived to fix the door. He had a day job as a peon in a bank. I went inside to make tea for all of us while Deepti gave him company, chatting about the money situation in Goan banks and ATMs. Outside, it was getting awfully windy. A huge downpour was sure to be upon us in a few minutes.

"I think I'll come back tomorrow evening and finish this, I forgot to carry my umbrella," Shannu said to Deepti.

"*Arre*, no way! How can you leave us with a door that has no locks! We are just two women living alone. What if some other robber comes and kills us tonight?"

"*Bai*, lightning does not strike twice in the same place."

"But it has! This is the second time we've been robbed. And it's the same fellow robbing us, we think."

"Don't worry, use the latch at the top of the door. Keep your *balcão* light switched on through the night. No one will come. I guarantee you."

"No, Shannu, you complete the job now. We have a spare umbrella, you can take it and keep it if you like," I persisted. After much grumbling, he agreed. As we were sipping our teas, it started to pour with a deafening roar. Leftover mangoes from trees began falling like green hailstones, hitting the freshly tarred road with a squelchy thud. Coconut branches fell off trees as they swayed dangerously close to the power lines... and, wait for it... the lights went out! Pitch darkness was heralded by the coughing sounds of a drill that had stopped.

"Now what?" Deepti asked no one in general.

"What else? We wait for fifteen minutes. If it doesn't come back, I go home," said Shannu. "Go light some candles, there are nails strewn everywhere."

"I think we have run out of candles... should have bought a new packet this morning while buying bread and milk at Anand's *gaddo*..." I said to Shannu. "Come inside and sit on the sofa. I will make more tea."

"No, I'm fine here on the *balcão*," he replied. "Do you at least have a torch?" he asked.

"Must be upstairs somewhere, I'll go look for it," said Deepti and left the hall to take the staircase. Doors and windows left open in the house were making quite a racket in the wind. I tried bolting a few, but the curtains kept whacking me in the face, and the wind was too strong. Leaving them, I went to the kitchen to make a fresh round of tea. I wondered if I should also rustle up a quick snack; it was getting close to dinner time. Thank god we had both our cylinders. My thoughts were shattered by a shrill, blood-curdling scream. A loud bang followed as the door shut and footsteps could be heard retreating on the street.

I came out running, as did Deepti, holding a torch she had managed to locate from upstairs. She pointed it towards the door and then at me. "What happened? Why did Shannu scream and run away?" Deepti asked me. I shrugged my shoulders. We both turned around to go inside and what do we see... our mother's dressmaker's dummy standing near the hall door, looking like a decapitated lady!

Mother was a much loved seamstress while she was alive. Unfortunately, neither my sister nor I inherited her skills. After she passed on, we gave away all her sewing paraphernalia – her antique Singer sewing machine, her set of needles and cutting scissors, her pattern books, box of threads... but the kids insisted on keeping her dressmaker's dummy. Every summer they would dress it up and play house-house with it. My older girl had tied roller skates to its base to wheel it around from room to room, and to jive with on the terrace...

The wind had caused the dummy to slowly roll out from the

corner room, where it was kept, into the hall. No wonder Shannu ran!

"Well, at least one part of the mystery is solved. Now we know what spooked the robber," said Deepti, as we both doubled over laughing. "*Avoi ge*, this is too funny!" We latched the door and went upstairs to sleep, grateful that mother had left us a security guard.

Next morning when we opened the main door, we found Shannu's toolkit left behind on the *balcāo*.

Glossary

Vaddo: Hamlet, part of a village

Feni: A spirit produced in Goa. There are two types of *feni*, cashew *feni* and coconut *feni*, depending on the original ingredient

Chappals: A pair of slippers

Gheraoed: *coll.* Surrounded

Sarpanch: An elected head of the Panchayat (*lit.* an assembly [*ayat*] of ve [*panch*]), a village-level constitutional body of local self-government

Talati: A Revenue officer

Mamlatdar: The head of Revenue administration; also an Executive Magistrate

Devara: Small prayer room or temple in Hindu homes

Devchaar: Benevolent spirits believed to guard boundaries between Goan villages

Bai: *coll.* Used to refer to a woman

Arre: *coll.* Oh!

Balcāo: Balcony

Gaddo: Hand-cart, usually selling road-side snacks or knick-knacks

Avoi ge: Oh, mother!

Life's Bumpy Ride

Cherie Naroo

S ANDRA quickly placed her empty cup of black tea on the table next to the sink. She would wash it later, she thought. She was running late and had to be in time to get the 10:15 am bus to Margão; it was already 9:40 am. Looking down, her chin almost touching her chest, she quickly adjusted her blouse and tried to pull together the open gaps between the buttons. She wasn't really bothered about her figure and never understood all that nonsense her neighbour Martha's teenage daughter talked about. Diet! 'What diet?' she thought. When she first heard the word, she thought they were talking about colouring their hair. Dye it! 'All rubbish,' thought Sandra. No rice, curry and fried fish?? She would die and it would be a miserable death at that! She was more than happy in her full figure. She had gained a couple of kilos, just a couple, she was convinced. It didn't bother her, after all what was life without the joys of eating well. She considered herself to be quite the *fugoti* in her village. At all of forty-two, years and waist, she could easily charm and harm at the same time. In her college days she was called 'Sexy Sandy'.

'Sexy Sandy' quickly opened the steel cupboard in the bedroom and reached for the talcum powder on the shelf. Her sister Rosalin who worked in Dubai had sent her the lavender fragranced talcum, along with bars of Lux soap, face tissues, Axe oil, Tiger balm and flat blue tins of Nivea creme. Sandra loved all things foreign. She even had a showcase full of empty perfume and alcohol bottles all in beautiful shapes, sizes and colours. She didn't have the heart to bin such beautiful pieces of glass even though they were empty. She was sure they would come in some use someday, but until then they occupied prime location in her hall, just beside her television. She elaborately dusted the contents of the talcum bottle onto the palm of her right hand and then, keeping the jar back on the shelf, she patted both hands together. Eyes closed, lips puckered in, she kept sweeping her hands across her face. She went to the mirror, looked at the reflection and liked what she saw. She didn't look her age, she thought to herself. In fact, she hadn't looked better in her life, not even on her wedding day, dressed in white and filled with excitement and anguish. She could still remember that day as if it was yesterday.

Sandra locked the door to her house. Put the keys into her handbag and slid her hand through the oversized handles. Holding it close, tucked into the nook of her armpit, she walked out of her small gate and started towards the main road humming Lorna's latest hit song from *Nachom-ia Kumpasar*, the movie made on Lorna Cordeiro, Goa's Nightingale. Sandra had watched the movie twice, once at the theatre and once on her mobile. Watching movies on the mobile was so great; you could enjoy the latest flicks seated just about anywhere, even on the toilet seat!

She enjoyed watching Lorna. It gave her a sense of empowerment in some way. She always imagined herself to be a younger version of Lorna, feisty and fun. Especially in her *festache* dress, gold high heels and flame red lipstick, she would sway her hips just like Lorna. The songs made her feel alive. That and the *feni*!

Having taken a dozen-odd steps she realised she hadn't put on her lipstick. She rarely left home without the bright red shade on her pout. "I'll put it on while I am on the bus," she thought, and increased her pace towards the bus stop. Reaching the stop she used her palm to shade her eyes as she looked towards the direction of the oncoming traffic, looking to see if the bus was anywhere in sight. It was not, so she opened her handbag and took out the foldable umbrella she always carried with her. That too was a product of the Gulf. Thank God for Rosy, as they fondly called Rosalin, her 'Gulfie' sister. With the Goan heat and scorching sun she didn't want to get a tan, it was difficult enough to stay chocolate coloured; dark chocolate is not what she wanted to be. Even those fairness creams she had 'invested' in didn't seem to work. Nothing worked except, of course, the talcum powder. Thank God for that invention!

A good ten minutes later she was sitting in the bus on her way to Margão. She was lucky to get a seat by the window. The warm breeze was sufficient to keep the sweat at a minimum. She heard Forsu the bus conductor yelling, "*Fudhe vos, fudhe vos*", making his way through the aisle, hand filled with small change notes held tightly between his fingers and smaller change coins in his palm. Unconsciously, Sandra dug into her handbag and, running the tips of her fingers over its contents, she searched for her purse. The bag was filled with so much stuff; she made a mental note to sort out and discard the unwanted contents. Her fingers found her wallet and she pulled it out, opened it and took out twenty rupees just as Forsu reached her seat. He smiled at her and said, "Sendra, *borem gho*? *Bore dista, sodhanch bashen*," and smiled with a wink. Sandra flashed him a half teasing smile and replied, "Forsu, *tu kitem hem bodbodta. Kitem bore dista*? *Haven aiz lipustick galunkus na mure.*" To which Forsu replied, "*Tum* national beauty, Sendra, no need lipstick. Always hot."

Forsu handed back Sandra's change of ten rupees with a flirtatious grin and she smiled back at him, well realising he was holding onto her palm longer than required. She let him. Nothing to lose, she thought, it gave Forsu some excitement in his otherwise "*Fudhe vos*" day.

She turned her face to look out the window, taking in the scenery that passed her eyes like the reel of a documentary movie. The colours of green monopolised the scenery and it was so refreshing to her eyes. She could see the hills in the distance. Such contrast to the road she was being driven on. Red mud made up the footpath of the road and it was strewn with litter, cow dung, stray dogs and cows. The strays moved along at their own pace not to be bothered with the everyday worries of human life. Vendors sat down to sell their wares. People stopped to buy things. From vegetables to vessels, sweetmeats to farm meats, from umbrellas to underwear, everything was available on the footpath. '*Saiba*, how can you buy underwear on the footpath with everyone around watching what size and colour you pick? Not me, *baba*,' thought Sandra. Thank God for Rosy again, because of whom San

CORTIM- MARGAO

Velankani Travels

dra wore foreign underwear, made in Bangladesh.

The bus drive from Cortim to Margão was taking longer today. Apart from the normal problem of the existing narrow roads there were also repair works being carried out. The water pipeline that ran alongside the road had been dug up, making it difficult to navigate through an already narrow road. "*Paad podom!* These governments are of no use to us common peoples, only eating up our hard earned monies," she said angrily to the woman sitting beside her. The deteriorating conditions of essential infrastructure and facilities in the villages was appalling, to say the least. The politicians who represented the villagers were hungry for money and only made promises to them when it was election time. After that, neither the politician nor their promises were in sight, until it was election time again. Sandra had always voted for the Catholic candidate from her village. This time she thought the chap would have a clearer conscience than that of his Hindu predecessor and would be partial to his community. But sadly, to the misfortune of the village, his family acquired their Portuguese passports and shifted to Europe. Now he had to make extra money to ensure they could stay there and also to pay for the frequent trips he made to visit them. So he took a bribe for any permission needed from his office. The villagers were losers in every way. They all had a long list of complains and many frustrations but none had the strength or inclination to stand up to question and fight for their rights. So they just went from one day to the next, disgusted with the corruption around but taking it in their stride, hopeful that things would get better one day soon. Sandra thought of her precious village Cortim and how it used to be when neighbours and friends needed no invitation to visit. It was so safe that the doors were never locked, day or night. If there was a problem everyone would pitch in to help. In times of celebration or death, marriage or separation, there were always people you could count on. There was never the fear of being lonely, even if you were alone.

'Times had changed,' thought Sandra sadly. Most of the younger generation had moved out of Goa looking to make better lives, leaving behind empty houses with old people. Elderly mothers and fathers, aunts and uncles whose lives revolved around the next phone call from their son or daughter, niece or nephew. But despite their lonely existence it was magical, the joy in their eyes when they spoke of their younger days when they were strong both physically and financially, days when their houses were filled with family and friends, days when their presence was valued. Sandra's eyes fogged up. She dipped into the neckline of her blouse and into the side of her bra and pulled out a crumpled tissue. The foreign tissues were so soft and absorbent as compared with the local ones which were like writing paper. As she dabbed the corners of her eyes she thought about her own life. The emptiness and sadness she felt all came rushing out as she tried to conceal a sob. Her jaw quivered and she tightly shut her eyes to stop the tears from escaping. She felt emotionally weak; she leaned her head against the bus window and held her handbag close to her chest. Slowly she opened her eyes, and her tears rolled down her cheeks onto her 'foreign' tissue. She gazed out into the scenery once again, only this time she did not notice the greenery or the gutters. Her thoughts blocked her sight and memories rushed back, eight years to the day when she walked down the aisle, when she wore that beautiful white dress, the same day she had looked in the mirror feeling like the most beautiful girl in the world, the day she entered the church and saw Caje stand at the altar.

She could still remember the thumping of her heart and the butterflies in her stomach as she took each step to reach him. There were thirty-one steps, she recalled. Everyone in church turned to look at her, smiling as she passed their pew, whispering to each other. They were married by Fr. Ignatius in a sweet ceremony, with a lengthy sermon. Priests loved to talk. Not only Catholic priests, all priests, Hindu, Muslim, Sikh and even those new self-proclaimed godmen who claimed to be in touch with the Almighty, they all loved to talk. They probably did not get many opportunities to talk, so when they did, they had so much to say. Sandra smiled slightly to herself, she could hardly remember what Fr Ignatius, bless his soul, had spoken about on that day, but she could remember the exhilaration going through her veins thinking of what was going to happen once the wedding was over and the guests had left. She was a thirty-four-year-old virgin at the time, what else could have been on her mind? Definitely not Fr Ignatius' sermon!

Her marriage to Caje was 'arranged'. She had crossed thirty with no sign of any blossoming romances in her life. Time just flew by and her job as receptionist at the doctor's clinic kept her days busy. Her mother, bless her soul, was worried that Sandra would remain a spinster the rest of her life and so she spoke to every woman in the village, who was willing to listen, that she was looking for a suitable boy for her daughter. Rosy was married to Peter and they had a daughter. They lived in Dubai for as long as Sandra could remember. Rosy was a talented seamstress and worked in a boutique while Peter worked with the airlines. They were college sweethearts and were married the day after they graduated from college. Peter's parents worked in Dubai and so they arranged to take them there. Mother had put Rosy on the job of finding that 'suitable' boy and she did. She found Caje. He worked at the airport in luggage handling.

Sandra received a brief bio-data stating his full name, date of birth, height, weight, educational qualifications and hobbies with two photographs, one of Caje standing up against the backdrop of a busy mall and the other a close up with an iPhone to his ear, at his office desk. Sandra later learnt that in fact neither the desk and nor the iPhone was his. She had sent a similar bio-data to him and a couple of photos, which thanks to Photoshop made her look slim and fair. Thus their relationship began, based on lies.

The wedding date was fixed based on when Caje would get leave. So, instead of a cool December wedding they ended up marrying in hot sweaty May. They hadn't met until a few days before the wedding when Caje arrived from Dubai and Sandra went to the airport, half the village accompanying her, to welcome the groom. With every man that exited the arrival gate Sandra's pulse raced a little faster. Then finally Caje appeared wearing a red football jersey that stretched against his noticeable paunch, tucked into his black jeans and white sneakers on his feet. He had a baseball cap on his head and a thick gold chain around his neck and an equally thick gold bracelet on his wrist. The groom had arrived!

They greeted each other cordially, hardly looking at each other, embarrassment filling the air. On the way home they were pushed into the back seat of the same car whilst Caje's brother Felix sat in the front. The rest of the village got into the minivan which followed. Neither spoke to each other in the car. Felix kept the commentary running. He spoke about the price of fish, corrupt politicians, the casinos and their neighbour Sylvi whose daughter got pregnant and had eloped with the *poder*. Caje seemed to be more interested in the local news broadcast by his brother than his to-be wife, thought Sandra. Never in her life had she imagined herself to be in such an awkward situation. She just stared out of the window, observing minute details of the scenery on a road she had passed many times before.

The wedding day was soon approaching and even though Sandra was filled with excitement there was an overwhelming sense of doubt about her soon-to-be married life. Was she making the right decision? Was Caje the person she wanted to spend the rest of her life with? What was her life going to be like once she had married Cajetan Almeida? Sadly she realised she had no answers to any of those questions. How could she? They had hardly spoken since he arrived, he had not made any attempt to contact her and her calls to him were always monosyllabic. She could not gauge if he was ignoring her or if he was just shy. So she chose to give him the benefit of doubt. It was easier to believe he was shy than to deal with the other option. Thus she married Caje.

After the wedding they were driven to a nearby resort in a neighbour's car that was decorated with flowers and had the huge initials 'C&S' which fell off somewhere along the bumpy road. Caje's friends filled the car and kept singing loudly, continuously and out of tune. They all made their way to the hotel room along with the bridal couple and didn't show any signs of leaving way past 2 am. Caje said nothing to them. In fact, when their beers were over and she thought they would finally be gone, he opened a bottle of Johnnie Walker Red Label, as if he had wanted them to stay. It was almost 3:15, Sandra was tired by the stress of the entire day, the scorching heat during the afternoon nuptials and the humidity at the reception. She just wanted to free herself from those layers of white satin and lace and the suffocating veil and the layers of caked foundation and makeup. So when she couldn't take it any longer she broke down and screamed at them. Hearing her yell seemed to make everyone in the room sober. They got up, lowered their heads and filed out in a straight line, mumbling under their alcohol-laden breaths. Caje hadn't moved from his seat; he just stared out of the balcony into the darkness, his face emotionless. The door shut behind them. Sandra locked it and walked into the washroom. She undressed and washed off the makeup. Putting on the red satin night dress she walked out of the room to find Caje still seated in the balcony. She went up to him from behind, put her arms around his shoulder and leaned forward to kiss his forehead when she heard him snore. That was the story of their wedding night.

The next day when he still wouldn't speak to her she decided she had had enough and told him she would go and tell everyone that he was a 'homo'. It was only then that Caje had told her that he was in love and in a relationship with another woman who was not only much older than him but also married in Dubai. She was not ready to leave her husband of twenty-seven years, children and young grandchildren for Caje. He had decided that he would teach her a lesson and in revenge agreed to marry Sandra. Instead of angering his lover, this seemed to make her want him more and she thought it was a great idea. This way they could both share the guilt of cheating on their spouses. It had to be the shortest marriage in the history of Cortim. The marriage was annulled before Caje resumed work; he went back to Dubai a single man, the same way he had arrived. Sandra later heard that the woman soon lost interest and left Caje for another man, married and younger. Sandra donated her wedding dress to the undertaker, to be used as he saw fit. She went back to her job at the doctor's clinic.

The bus braked, bringing it and the memories of Sandra's wedding fiasco to a stop. She dabbed her wet eyelids and turned self-consciously around. She realised Forsu was looking at her. She nervously lowered her head and walked towards the exit. Forsu caught hold of her hand and squeezed it gently. She gave him a small smile, thus leaving her sadness and adversities on the bus. She opened her foreign umbrella, Forsu got off the bus behind her and they walked to the small cold drink house where they shared a *falooda*. He made her laugh with his bus stories of how Aboli the fisherwoman had asked him to remove the bus fare she had tucked into her cleavage, and how sixty-five-year-old Santan would sit on the last seat watching porn on his mobile. It was eight years since she had been taking the bus and Forsu had become a part of her life, a part she enjoyed. Sandra and many other Goan women like her took the reality of their lonely existence in their stride, hopeful that there would be happiness and excitement, maybe even love, waiting for her around the corner.

Glossary

Fugoti: Firecracker

Festache: lit. For the Feast

Feni: A spirit produced in Goa.

Fudhe vos: Move forward, or keep moving (to the front)

Sendra, *borem gho? Bore dista, sodhanch bashen:* Sandra, how are you, girl? You look good, like always.

Forsu, *tu kitem hem bodbodta. Kitem bore dista? Haven aiz lipustick galunkus na mure:* Forsu, what are you babbling? How can I look good? I not put on even my lipstick today

Tum: You (are)

Saiba: O Lord

Paad podom: Curse them!

Poder: Baker

Falooda: A smoothie made of milk and raspberry syrup, served with a dollop of ice cream and Basil seeds

In a World of What-Ifs

Jeanette Barbosa Noronha

"OH my gosh! Tell her you'll call her back. Can we get to this already?" Alicia yelled as her 'best friend' Emmanuel spoke to his mother on the phone.

"Okay, mama, the teacher just glared at me for using my phone during class time. I have to go. Love you. Bye!" He sighed as he disconnected the call, and turned to Alicia, rolling his eyes.

"You know, no one likes it when you roll your eyes like that," she teased as she took out her lighter, "shows how ugly you really are."

Manu rolled 'em again and shouted, "I really don't like what you're turning me into. I now miss my classes and lie to my mom... not something I'm really proud of."

"Oh, but you like me," she laughed, "you're hooked onto me now, face it."

"Whatever. Now get that smoke out of my face!"

The breeze from up high the Monte never felt so freeing, yet, somehow, Manu always felt choked up whenever he was with her. He'd never been in trouble before. Being a straight 'A' student right from kindergarten till middle school, you'd never expect him to, right? But this 'new girl' who looked beyond her (supposed) years had this aura about her: bad didn't seem so bad anymore. A couple of mentally stimulating conversations later (punctuated by the lighting of cigarettes between them, of course), Emmanuel left for home, although to him it was like leaving home to go back to his place.

His mother watched as he parked his bike in the garage and, as he entered the house, pretended to be busy.

Manu belonged to a well-off, upper-caste family from Borda, Margão. His parents always made sure that he had the best of ev

erything. He attended the highly prestigious Loyola High School, which was regarded as one of the best in Goa. His parents were devout Roman Catholics who insisted on him attending the Holy Eucharistic Mass at the St. Joaquim Chapel in Borda every day. He'd meet his neighbours, who probably eyed him as a future son-in-law. Since the time Manu was old enough to walk over to the Chapel, he had been everyone's favourite. Dona Paulita and Sr. Abel, his grandparents, always bragged about him to the neighbours, much to everyone's amusement. As soon as he passed out from school, however, Manu began to change.

"Oh, you're home already? How was school, darling?" she asked, tossing leaves in the salad bowl.

"It was... uhh, it was interesting."

"I'm glad my baby is happy. Now go freshen up, I've made *porco assado* today."

"Thanks, mom. I'll be right down." He rushed up to his room, slammed the door behind him and fell flat on his bed. Alicia! Bloody Alicia Marie Colaço! He just couldn't get that girl out of his mind. She wasn't like the typical 'it' girl you'd see in movies or read about in books. Her hair didn't fall perfectly, her smile didn't brighten the room – she barely smiled at all. She was mean, condescending, disrespectful and downright hurtful to anyone that spoke to her. She socialised only to the extent that was absolutely necessary for survival, she didn't have a lot of hobbies other than sitting on hilltops and watching the world slow down before her eyes. Still, she was the epitome of perfection to him.

Later that day, Emmanuel's mother stumbled upon him daydreaming while supposedly studying. Putting her laundry basket down, she approached him.

"Son, are you alright?" she asked, indicating her worry for the boy.

"Umm... yeah! Wait, what? I'm doing my math homework" he replied hastily.

"Darling, I asked you if you were alright, not what you were up to." She began wrinkling at the forehead. "Is that girl bothering you again? What's her name? Anthea?"

"There's no girl, mama. And it's Alicia! You can't get one name right, huh?" he said, defensively.

"I'm just warning you, son. Girls like her don't usually mix around with boys like you. What is she anyway, like four years older than you?" she leaned in, eager to hear.

"Just two. Besides, it's not her fault she flunked her classes. Her dad passed away three years ago. He had..." he went on, but was interrupted by, "Let me guess. Cancer?" she scoffed.

"Ugh! Mama, could you possibly be more annoying? He had Amyotrophic Lateral Sclerosis. I didn't know what it was until she explained it to me. Bet you don't know what that is either. That's so like you: always judging people. What if that were to happen to us? Have you ever thought about that?" Closing his book on the table, he charged up to his room.

"Manu? Emmanuel William Sequeira! Listen to me when I'm talking to you, young man!" she yelled. He turned around and rolled his eyes again. "Maybe she's not all that bad, this Alicia," she added. "All I'm saying is it's a little too pretentious, don't you think? I mean, you read this kind of stuff in books all the time. Of course the parent's illness varies, but the plot stays the same. I just don't want my little boy bearing the brunt of it all."

"Whatever, mama."

The door was slammed shut.

Far off from the hustle and bustle of the city life, Alicia always preferred sitting on the edge of the Monte, in Margão, watching the world slow down before her eyes. She was 19 years of age – her dark brown eyes told stories her mouth never could. Her hair was often compared to Maggi noodles, although after the death of her father, she cut it to shoulder length. She didn't laugh at silly jokes; she was intelligent yet not so academically oriented. The girls in her school obviously didn't like her; there's something about that girl who attracts all the boys that makes her a villain in the eyes of other girls. Alicia knew when to walk away from people; she knew what it was like to be hurt. The only man in her life, at least the only one she thought she could trust, was taken away from her. When the doctors told her about her father's sickness, Alicia contacted the school's headmistress and pleaded her to ask her students to donate money towards the ALS Foundation. Instagram was full of her classmates' videos pouring ice-cold water on themselves, yet nothing seemed to help her father's case. So when her world came toppling down after his death, Alicia resorted to the one thing she thought would help her – cigarettes.

"My mom thinks you're bad company," Manu told Alicia the next day, "and she advised me to stay away from you."

"May I ask why? I told you, Manu, the women hate me!" she laughed and took her Economics text book out of her bag. A paper that was thought to be hidden secretively slipped out of her book, but Alicia quickly got rid of it – or she'd like to have believed.

"Who's Dr. Danielle? And why do you have an appointment with her this Saturday?" He was confused and the wrinkles on his forehead got even more prominent. "Is she that doctor from Curtorim your father used to visit? Do you have ALS too?"

"No, silly! Stop jumping to conclusions. She's uhh... she's just my mom's friend. She called us over for her birthday party this Saturday, so I wrote it down so I wouldn't forget. That's it," Alicia said, smiling her widest smile.

"Your smile tells me when you're lying. You're not as clever as you think you are, Alicia," Manu said, rolling his eyes. "Besides, why would you say a birthday party was an appointment? At least attempt to make your lies believable."

"Okay, fine. Dr. Danielle Miranda is this psychiatrist from Benaulim," she began.

"Oh, is your mom ill or something?" he asked, worrying.

"No. It's me. Ever since my dad died, it's like my mind has been against me. I can't think straight, and all I do is sulk for days. It's nothing for you to be worried about, Manu. She just prescribes a couple of medicines, and then I'm like a normal person all over again. She even said that if I take my medicines regularly, in some time, I won't have to take them at all." Alicia assured him as she patted him on the back. "We were learning about macroeconomics the last time, right?"

"Mama! Mama! Do you know of any Dr. Danielle Miranda from Benaulim?" Manu asked, as he came rushing home that day.

"Uhh... no. Why? Did she come to your school or something today?" Mrs Sequeira asked.

"No. Do you remember my friend, Alicia?" he asked, excitedly. "Apparently Dr. Danielle is treating her for depression. Depression, mama! How can you tell me not to be a friend to someone who clearly needs a friend?"

"Enough of your nonsense, Manu. I told you not to talk to that girl! She's a bad influence. How do you know this is not just the perfect alibi to throw you off and make you fall for her? I told you, girls these days cannot be trusted. Did you know that she smokes? Sr. Pinto told your *avó* the other day that they saw her smoking when they had gone to the Monte Chapel. If they knew about your friendship, I don't want to think about what will happen to our family," she yelled.

"But mama, will you just listen to me for once? She's not like other girls. She's..." he went on...

"Different? So you trust this unknown girl over your own mother? We've raised you to be a good boy; don't let this one girl throw all that away! Am I clear?" Furious and frustrated, she walked away.

"As clear as crystal, mama," Manu sighed.

The next couple of weeks were the most difficult, in Manu's eyes. He didn't want to betray his mama for some girl he thought was intriguing; he knew better than that. He began socialising with the other boys in his class – Edgar, Savio and Jean-Luca, the well-to-dos from his class soon came to be his new best friends. Alicia noticed this; she noticed the way he'd avoid eye contact, the way he'd systematically boycott her in the canteen, during lunchtime. She knew, now, that she could add Emmanuel's name to the list of people who had betrayed her. When Tr. Rebecca assigned them to the same group for their Psychology project, Alicia asked if she could switch groups, on grounds of being uncomfortable with one of the girls there. Manu was thrilled yet disheartened. He was happy that he didn't have to ask Tr. Rebecca to do the same or that he wouldn't have to be in the same group as Alicia; yet he was sad that the one person he could call his best friend was now out of his life forever. He knew he had a decision to make as soon as his mother said what she did, and it was now clear that he'd already made that call.

Two months later, and it was time for them to pass out of their higher secondary school. Manu did mind-numbingly well in all his entrance exams, breaking records at the national level. The most difficult thing for him to do, then, was decide which medical college he wanted to set foot in. He thought of his parents, who would feel lonely if he had to decide to leave Goa, and so he decided to opt for the ever so prestigious Goa Medical College. His parents, the elated duo, threw a grand party for him, where all his (jealous) friends were invited. They had to be invited, given that the entire cream of Borda was present, along with some of Manu's teachers from school. Speeches were made, glasses were raised, and laughs and tears knew no limit. Manu did everyone proud and went on to become Goa's first neurosurgeon, specialising in the treatment of Lou Gehrig's disease, also known as ALS. Forty-three years later, he retired, in a pool of wealth and good health, with his wife, Annabelle and three kids, Zac, Nadia and Alicia.

A sixty-one-year-old Dr Emmanuel put his pen down, took his spectacles off and rubbed his eyes. His autobiography was complete, yet it somehow lacked excitement. His eyes, portraying regret, began tearing up. Denying every tear that came his way, he looked up as he heard footsteps. His youngest daughter came running to him, told him she'd be going out to meet some friends, kissed his cheek and left.

He saw a spark in her eyes right from the time he first held her in his arms.

"We will name her Alicia," he said.

"But no one in your family or ours has that name," exclaimed his sister-in-law.

"Someone in my family was once named Alicia," he answered, smiling, "and somehow, she will always be family."

What happened to Alicia Marie Colaço, you ask? No one really knows for sure. After passing out of higher secondary school, this girl, whose name was synonymous with 'trouble', seemed to have been wiped off from everybody's memory. Before he met Annabelle, who so smoothly swept him off of his feet, Emmanuel had made several attempts to track Alicia down, but all in vain. Rumour had it that after her mother's fatal road accident, Alicia overdosed on her sleeping pills and was found lying dead on the Monte. Others say she moved to Europe and began writing songs for an artiste of that area. Still others insist she's very much in Goa, and teaches yoga and the art of self-love in a local school in Curtorim.

"Maybe one of those is true, maybe none are. I guess I'll never really know for sure. But I can still hear the lighting of cigarettes every time I go up to the Monte with my family. That distinct chuckle is all that distracts me when I need to concentrate the most. She may be gone physically, but her presence is ever so present in present time. To me, she will always be that twisted girl that taught me a thing or two about the real world. To me, she will always be perfectly imperfect, as the kids say nowadays. To me, she will always be my first glimpse of love. On the sunniest day in Goa, Alicia will always be my thunder," he thought to himself, as he slammed the book shut and walked away.

Glossary

Avó: Grandmother
Porco assado: Goan roast pork dish

Not Your Time to Go, Girl!

Dinesh Patel

T HE scarlet sun reluctantly dipped its weariness into the eager Arabian Sea, even as the evening gusts rose with gradual intensity and traversed silently over the bemused river that flowed with its ever-so-melancholic gait from deep within the hinterland into the extending sea. In the drowsy distance, the moon, paled by the brilliance of the solar dazzle, awaited the opportunity to glisten, glow and sprinkle its mesmerising charm.

The endlessly routine rendezvous of the day and night that dispersed each other during specific periods, continued without the evident animosity, though the stalemate was apparent – the sanguine day yawned a victorious smile at dawn, while the beguiled night effortlessly held its sway as dusk nestled in.

Denis looked at the amazing sunset through the trees and thickets, oblivious of the timeless battle, as he rode faster, hoping to catch the sun dip into the sea from his favourite vantage point – the Zuari bridge. He loved watching Goa's golden sunsets that were so nonchalantly common at every gazing spot in the state, day after day after day, year after year after year!

The bridge that seems to conjoin south Goa to north Goa, itself, over decades, had become the talking point for various reasons that spring from assorted perspectives. Built over the biggest river and lifeline of Goa, the Zuari bridge connects two quaint villages, Cortalim and Agassaim; the Zuari river flows through six major talukas of the state often referred to as the Rome of the East.

The soothing breeze gently blew nostalgic melancholy over Denis, as he instinctively glanced to his left, what was now a deserted spot, but where din and vehicular jostle once prevailed; the spot where he occasionally boarded the ferry, as a little boy. And even though he had enjoyed his limited trips, watching squeaking seagulls above and the muted fish below, adult gratefulness reflected as he approached the bridge.

Snaking through the traffic bottleneck, passing the extended hands of the local flower vendors and boys with freshly-snared rock crabs, he saw the sun drearily lowering itself into the horizon where the Zuari river lost itself to the Arabian Sea. So intimately interwoven was the amalgamation between the two water bodies in the radiant evening glow that they seemed unified from a distance.

Suddenly a flock of birds passed, reflecting dark silhouettes over the blushing sun, much to the delight of the nature lover perched on his two-wheeler, who instantly veered to the side to catch a better glimpse.

The youth from Cansaulim in South Goa stopped, forgetting that he was on his way to the local TV studio and was barely halfway to the capital city, Panjim, and that his guest would be waiting to be interviewed. But the creative are seldom bound by norm-clasping parameters and Denis disembarked and walked gingerly closer towards the edge, as loose gravel cascaded, frightening scampering crabs below.

He looked at the brazen bronzed sky that discarded its bright azure garb, draped in fluorescent orange, its soft vibrancy reflecting on passing strangers' faces. Soon it would cloak itself in velvety black, bejewelled with a million stars whose twinkle the moon chose to dispel tonight.

The bridge often held a mirror, reflecting wonderful memories of his life, during altering phases and diverse periods of the day and night. The image of a lonely streetlight playing silently on the ripples of the river below at 3 am while returning from the journalists' ghost shift still sparkles his mind, much like memories of vibrant sunsets which, like indelible ink, filled his mind with poetry and heart with a thousand dreams.

Denis may have seen innumerable Goan sunsets, from the rocky heights of Vagator in north Goa to the palm-fringed windows of Palolem in south Goa, but each new sunset ceaselessly infused renewed cheer within his soul, instilling vigour and distilling an unknown calm. He looked again, watching the sunset intently, as if painfully letting a dear one depart, occasionally distracted by loud tourists who made a gleeful dash for the bridge with their cameras held high and crimson radiance sparkling in their eyes.

Denis knew that feeling well. It was that very emotion that had kept him buoyed whenever he felt blue or his heart rippled with despair. He watched the group animatedly take pictures of the spectacle that unfolded before them and then rush off as their taxi driver honked noisily for their return.

Apart from the speeding vehicles on the road, the pedestrian lane, the bridge was empty except for a girl who apparently did not belong to the group that had left with glowing memories, nor displayed similar emotions.

The flavour of freshly cooked sausages still lingered in his mouth, as Denis redirected his gaze towards the smouldering ball of melting emotions, but could not take his eyes off the girl.

But there was nothing unusual, as tourists and locals often enjoyed the sunset from various points on the bridge. But the pragmatic boy did not miss the peculiarity in her stance and demeanour that stood out like a dreary dark cloud in a golden sunset evening. For, her lean structure not only ignored the wonderful sight that nature so benevolently offered, but also walked as if in a trance to achieve something her mind conjured long before her arrival. Again, though there was a curious spring in her stride, she never looked in a hurry to cross the bridge.

Now visibly distracted, the journalist within began to prop questions and once again involuntarily glanced in the direction of the girl who walked steadfastly towards the middle of the bridge. It seemed obvious that the girl, who wore faded jeans and jaded top and seemed to be from South Goa, was not interested in nature's charm or the tireless traffic that whizzed past noisily, for she did not once move her head in any direction, as if mesmerised by brimming thoughts within.

And despite her usual pace, Denis almost sensed something

unusually flawed in the new scene that began unfolding on his favourite vantage point. Something was not right! Denis could almost feel it, yet could not identify it.

The biker was now so ensnared by the situation that he began feeling a part of the event that promised dramatic consequences. Perhaps it was the way she walked with gay disdain, the way she carried herself, as if the world ceased to exist, as if a scentless flower, as if fish struggling out of water, as if lovelessness prevailed. Denis quickly snapped free of his burbling unbridled thoughts, for he knew the writer within often jostled to conjure words in such emerging situations.

"Look, they are looking askance at her too," Denis told himself as passers-by looked casually at the girl, perhaps sensing the same feeling.

Wrapped in dulled youthfulness, the local girl, perhaps in her late teens, who seemed enveloped in previously preconceived sentiments, moved as if in a trance and stopped, then slowly turned towards the fading sunset, looked longingly towards it and inhaled deeply, as if cherishing the life within.

"Wow, look, I was wrong, she does like the sunset," Denis thought to himself, and a smile finally forced itself on his face after moments of baffled confusion.

But Denis was so horribly wrong! The unknown girl with strange behaviour and a neat braid did something that none would dare imagine.

As the Cansaulim lad and some others watched, the lass reached for the walled barrier of the bridge and leaned audaciously as she looked deep below. Those watching her almost froze, for they realised she was no tourist nor an angler looking for a catch; her intentions seemed dark and dangerous for her own sake.

The young girl looked as if she had battled many marauding emotions and lost what she perhaps cherished; fear and pain seemed conquered, the way she dangerously leaned forward.

"Hey, girl, careful, you'll fall if you lean forward," somebody screamed in Konkani, as a crowd began gathering, anticipating the unexpected.

"Are you crazy, what are you doing?" another vernacular voice echoed as an elderly man passed on his scooter.

The girl half-turned at the Konkani plea but hastened to complete her predefined task. What she did next sent chilling shivers down the spines of all that had now gathered, dumbfounded, to watch her moves.

For the wiry girl nonchalantly began to move forward, then clasped the barrier and attempted to climb, but then hesitated, stepped back and reached for her pocket as if remembering a final chore.

All watched with disbelief as she placed a neatly-folded paper close to the railing, took off her slippers and went back to what she was doing. Her moves were effortless, her rhythm fluid, her intentions clear, as she looked heavenwards, arms extended.

Horror seized each face that witnessed the unfolding event as it now was quite evident what was to happen next. Some in the crowd ran towards the girl. Denis, baffled by the sudden turn of events, also ran, his heart pounding for unknown reasons.

"Wait, please wait...," they pleaded as they rushed forward in a bid to alter the inevitable.

But it seemed the utmost wrong move, for whatever minuscule doubts remained in the girl's mind evaporated with the commotion and unwanted attention. The lithesome girl with emotions erased from her face halted for a brief moment and stood as if a mountaineer on the pinnacle, but before anyone could say another word or do something and much to the horror of those watching, took a step forward into what would be her watery grave and jumped into the waiting arms of death.

A deathly gasp erupted from all that had witnessed the unbelievable episode and, like involuntary participants in a drama, rushed to see the splash of a soul that wanted to shed all unknown ignominies that life had so painfully poured on her.

Shrieks were muffled by honking cars that were oblivious of the unfolding drama on the bridge, for only a selected few were now participants of what was to be a solo tragedy, who felt the pain of an unknown stranger.

Denis felt a pang of sorrow stab him viciously and the feeling seemed to be shared in equal proportion by those that had been part of the episode. He obviously did not know the girl, her condition, her trauma, her feeling or reason for this abrupt and untimely end, yet grief, like joy, transcends all barriers and was so effortlessly transferred. It's a human trait that ensures the prosperity of our species.

The biker peered hopefully below, for he had heard tales of Zuari's benevolence from fishermen and clam collectors near St Jacinto Island. His eyes searched for signs of the distraught soul, but the girl seemed engulfed in her watery grave and had perhaps moved away to another world of perennial peace and eternal happiness.

"Oh, why waste such a precious life? Why does hate besiege us so much? Why does grief so easily entwine us into a web of consistent misery?" Questions filled the saddened onlookers.

But life seldom gives in so easily against the ruthlessness of death, even when everything is so blatantly evident. Some among the crowd that had held their nerves quickly began seeking solutions. A few members quickly darted to the other side, where the ferries once stood, and waved at a young fisherman who sat mending his net. Noticing the urgency and the situation, the man cast aside his net and jumped on his canoe that fortunately had a motor that roared furiously as he turned towards the spot.

Denis looked below again, hoping against hope for signs of life, as ripples grew wider at the spot the audacious girl had plunged from the amazing altitude.

But there was no sign of life below, except for frightened water birds, as dusk quickly began to dispel light. It appeared as if the mighty Zuari had clasped the poor girl in an eternal embrace, providing the solace which she may have searched for in her fledgling life. The very life-giver in many a region of Goa would now be falsely accused of taking a life!

Fortunately, the Zuari is anything but maleficent and soon a gasping and visibly frightened girl bobbed to the surface, screaming for help ceaselessly with her water-filled lungs.

The crowd burst into instinctive applause, life had triumphed despite the towering odds. Like others who peered below, Denis felt a gush of sudden relief and a rush of unaccounted joy but couldn't help but wonder at the complexities of human behaviour and at the relentlessness of life to struggle and survive. It was only moments ago that the girl who had thrown caution to the winds and flung herself to death, after embracing the darkness of death, wanted the return of light in her life.

"I hope she does not die when she does not want to. It's not her time to go," Denis said a silent prayer, knowing well how precarious the situation had turned again. "If the fisherman does not make it in time she would not live to tell her sad tale."

But fortunately for the girl, an angel in form of the young fisherman was darting towards her, who now championed the cause of saving a life. His alert eyes scanned for movement in water as he passed under the massive bridge, anxiously watched by several optimistic eyes above.

Denis was struck by the humanness of all the participants of this sudden plot. "Who says humans are not emotionally bound, all seemed equally connected and if one could find a measuring device, you could tell how each heart beat with equal intensity for the safety of their fellow being who struggled below," the Cansaulim boy was touched.

But soon the new-found joy turned into shudders of despair when they noticed the girl submerge, despite her rekindled desire to live. The crowd saw the wave of the hand, as if thanking all in her hour of approaching death.

But Gabriel, as Denis learnt the fisherman's name later, was not among those to give up so easily, especially when he fervently believed that River Zuari was his mother who fed and took care of him. Generations had lived on these banks and he knew the waters well. As the determined fisherman neared, he jumped into the water where he had last seen the waving palm and, lo and behold, soon emerged with the girl, as he swam towards the boat.

He gently pressed her chest and the girl sputtered to life as water spluttered from her mouth. A stranger had saved a stranger for no motive or gain!

Relieved at the appropriate end of an absorbing episode, the crowd began dispersing as quickly as it had assembled. Denis too hurried to his bike and, as it coughed to life, couldn't help but notice the note that lay motionless near her slippers, hiding within the reasons for such unwarranted extreme behaviour.

"No, I can't," he whispered, almost changing his mind.

Just then a sudden gust teased the note that fluttered to life and suddenly flew over the bridge and into the river. What reasons the lucky girl had cited remained embedded in her heart, for the mighty Zuari has held innumerable secrets in the past and was not about to reveal this one too. Ironically, the very river that was chosen to become the reason for her demise inadvertently became the cause of the girl's new life, as if giving the distraught soul another opportunity to right the wrong.

Birds nestled into the trees as the boat reached the shore. Denis could see nothing more but a small chapel that stood like a sentinel, watching fishermen's boats tugging impatiently at the ropes, aided by tiny waves that seemed to tease. Perhaps, the tiny waves could tell of unhappy tales of not so fortunate ones that jumped and could do nothing even though they had instantaneously reversed their decision.

For we seldom know, before we've bid final goodbyes, before we've reflected on our past deeds and hope to erase the ills... before we really know if it is our time to go!

Matilda's Bubbles

Anita Pinto

MATILDA smiled at the bubbles around her. Now here was Rosy in her bubble. A dirty pink that seemed about to burst. Her bubble had a sweaty odour. The bubble touched her nose. Pasqual came in bouncing. His bubble was shining. Where did she know him? "How many?" he asked, coming closer. She smelt the fresh bread on him.

"Give her one only," said Rosy. "She does not finish that also." Matilda rocked in her chair and smiled. She could smell the rain in the air. The pre-monsoon winds whipped strands of her silver hair about like a halo. The cuckoo called loudly from the mango tree, heralding the rain.

"I must tell my Tony to bring the doctor tomorrow. That Dr Bhobe, he say that you are only getting old. What he know? You must eat. You are not eating. You hear me, *mai*? Your *shanya* son, Alfred, hasn't written so many months. Where he stays? Emrica? London? Oh *mai*!" Rosy shouted. Matilda jerked in fear. Rosy's bubble came close again. "What am I going to do with you? How I can look after you also now?"

"Call her advocate," said Thomas coming in with some letters. Then he cycled away ringing the bell. A baby began to cry. "Now look," said Rosy "you woke my baby." She sat on the *soppo* opposite Matilda and popped out her ample breast, pushing the nipple into the baby's mouth. Matilda saw more bubbles as she rocked. She could hear the baby's loud sucking noises. Rosy ranted: "That old hag wants me to water the garden now. Just because she has let me stay in her small mud hut in the garden, she makes my Tony pluck coconuts; the children rub her feet and I cook for her. Now she says that I must water her garden also. Real bitch she is! Her mother adopted my husband and now I am stuck with her for life! I am not her *poske*m. Her children come visit and bring her so much of fruit and biscuits and cakes. You think she gives us? Never! She is not like you. I like to talk to you, you know. You won't repeat what I say to anyone else. I know you are somewhere else. You are kind to my family. My husband calls you his Guardian Angel. Did you have the soup I made for you? Let me see... *Saiba*, it is here only on the table! Hold my baby." She dumped the baby on Matilda's rocking lap and fed her the soup. "There! You are smiling now. My soup is good, no?" Matilda looked down at the bubble on her lap. It felt good. It was a clean, soft bubble. She touched it gently with the tip of her finger. "Don't drop him now," Rosy said, picking up the baby. "Ah here is Lourdina. Lourdina!" Rosy shouted although Lourdina was right on the doorstep. "Don't forget to give her bread and milk before she sleeps. And close the window, I am going. I will tell Tony to see Advocate Zuzarte tomorrow and call the doctor also. Good night." Matilda watched Rosy's bubble float away into the shadows. It had a little bounce to it.

Lourdina's bubble floated before her face, smiling. "You will keep me in your house, no? I am like your daughter. I will look after you. Don't listen to that Rosy, she is only a gossip. She knows nothing about you. She can't look after her own children. Three babies and no work. She did not finish seventh standard. Did the postman come?" Lourdina walked to the hat stand and leafed through the letters that the postman had brought. She pocketed one quietly. "Only bills. I will tell that Rosy's husband to pay them tomorrow. Come, I will give you a nice bath now."

Matilda liked soap bubbles. She remembered bathing her son in his blue, plastic bath tub when he was a baby. He used to burst the bubbles and laugh. She put her fingers in the tub of warm water searching for him. Then she stirred up the water furiously and began to cry and rant. "Where is he? Where is he? He's drowning!"

"Stop it! Stop it!" shouted Lourdina. Matilda quietened down. Dear god, she's really getting worse by the day. She dressed Matilda in a clean nightgown. Her nightgown had to be clean and ironed or she would try to rip it off. Lourdina had learned that when she had once put on a nightgown from off the washing line

without ironing it. How does she know, she wondered? But she knew. After the milk and bread she sat her in the comfortable armchair in front of the TV. More bubbles on the TV screen. Lots of colour and loud noises. Lourdina changed the channel to CNN News and left the room. Someone with white hair and thick lips was a new bubble. She could see him in a big bubble. His words were coming like bubbles from his lips. People around him were bobbing.

Lourdina walked into the kitchen and drew the envelope from her pocket. It was a letter from Matilda's son, Alfred, to his mother. He wanted to know why she had not written to him for weeks. Was she well? He asked her to tell Advocate Zuzarte to email him as he did not have the lawyer's email or his phone number. Lourdina tore up the letter and threw it in the back garden fire where the leaves were just smouldering. She walked into the TV room again. Matilda saw her bubble, a slight smoke odour hovering around her. It scared her.

Lourdina had a plan. She could tell that the old woman was deteriorating by the day. She would die soon, and then she would get married to her Francisco and live in this house. When Alfred came she would tell him that she would look after the house for him. And she would just stay on. I cannot stand that Rosy but I must make friends with her. I do not want her to call the lawyer or the doctor yet. I will think of something.

Matilda sat out on the balcony again late the next morning. There was a gentle drizzle and the air was crisp. Lourdina came out with her mid-morning *kanji* and said, "I'm going to Rajan's *gaddo* down the road. I shall be back in five minutes. Eat your *kanji*."

Rosy bust through the connecting garden gate like a bubble bouncing. "Where's that little tartlet gone?" she asked. "I don't trust her you know." Matilda looked at her. What was happening? Just then Lourdina swung through the main gates, hips swaying in rhythm with the overgrown grass. A bright smile lit her face when she saw Rosy.

"Look Rosy, I just went out to buy some toast for Matilda

ma'am and I bought some cake and chocolates for your children."

"But why?" Rosy questioned. "It must be your birthday or something."

"Yes," Lourdina quickly assured her, "it is my birthday and I want to go meet my boyfriend for lunch. Will you please come back and check on ma'am? I'll come home soon." She was eager to tell Francisco about her plan.

"Okay," Rosy said, happy with all the goodies. "She must not be as bad as I thought."

Matilda listened to the bubbles banter and rocked her chair in pleasure. The sun had come out and there were dragonflies whispering too. They were beautiful rainbow bubbles all over the afternoon sun.

Lourdina returned quickly in a sulk. Francisco hadn't liked her idea. "That's taking advantage of her and it is wrong of you not to call the doctor to check her up," he had told her.

The next day Rosy said she was going to send for the doctor but Lourdina insisted that Matilda was better and eating all her meals well. "What better? She's sitting there like a *lolo* not saying anything."

"I made her walk in the garden today and she admired the flowers and watched TV. She even laughed at some programme on BBC," Lourdina said.

"Yes, I know." Rosy answered. "She used to talk of England all the time before. She stayed there for eight years when she got married. She told me that she loved apple pies and something called butter crocin. How anyone can have crocin tablets with butter, I don't know!"

"Oh Rosy, that is butter croissant which is like bread. I'll bring you some from Mr Baker when I go home tomorrow. You must taste them," Lourdina told Rosy.

Rosy looked at her suspiciously. "Thank you," she said. "And she also likes to have all those soap bubbles in her bathtub."

Lourdina was avoiding the bath too often as the old lady would probably catch a chill. She wanted the house but she wasn't trying to kill Matilda. 'I'm not a bad person,' she thought. "Okay, I'll give her a warm bubble bath today."

Matilda's son Alfred had done the bathroom beautifully for his mother with a luxury step-in bathtub because his mother had always talked of enjoying a nice long soak when she lived in England.

"I'll put more soap in her bath to give her a good sleep," Lourdina told Rosy and Rosy smiled in approval before she left.

Lourdina's bed was placed across the foot of Matilda's bed. In the middle of the night her bed shook with a soft vibration. She woke up startled and lifted Matilda's mosquito net to see if she was trying to draw her attention. But she was sleeping with a gentle snore. After an hour the bed shook again. Was it an earthquake? She wondered. She sat up in her bed deciding to keep vigil. But she must have dozed off because the bed shook again more vigorously. Lourdina jumped up and looked around in fright. "Is god punishing me?" she asked herself. It was almost daylight. She sat on the chair for an hour and then went into the kitchen to get some coffee and have a shower.

At 11 am when Rosy brought some *kanji*, Lourdina pleaded, "Please can you sit for ten minutes? I'm going to the chapel to pray."

"*Saiba*! Your Lourdina is becoming a saint!" Rosy told Matilda. Matilda smiled at the pink bubble. She smelled of lux soap and detergent today. "I washed so many clothes. Here, hold my baby; I'm just going to drink some water. God knows how long that girl will pray."

When she came out again from the kitchen she heard Matilda singing softly to the baby as she rocked in her chair. "She is getting better," Rosy thought and Lourdina came just then, her head bowed low and crying softly. "What happened to you now? Somebody died or what?"

"No, come sit on the *soppo* with me," Lourdina said. "Last night, someone was shaking my bed. At first I thought it was madam Matilda but it wasn't her. Then it happened again. An earthquake?"

"No!" exclaimed Rosy, "maybe it was a ghost!"

"A ghost? Whose ghost? There has never been a ghost here!" said Lourdina.

"Sir Constantino, my madam's husband! He always came and sat here with Matilda *bai* when he was fighting with my madam. She was always fighting with him."

Matilda looked at the two bubbles bouncing against each other and heard whispers. Whispers of fear.

"You pray before going to sleep and tell him that all is well. I'll call Fr. Dominic to bless her tomorrow," Rosy said. "I'm going now, I have to cook."

"Rosy," Lourdina whispered, "please also ask Thomas to call the doctor and Advocate Zuzarte tomorrow."

"Okay, okay. I'm going now," said Rosy, running out of the gate.

That evening after dinner, Lourdina gave Matilda a nice long bath with extra bubbles and a soft, clean nightie. She spoke with her gently and kissed her forehead before she tucked her into bed. Matilda smiled at the bubble. Lourdina sat on the chair next to her and prayed till Matilda fell asleep. Only then did she go to have her own dinner.

It was nearly midnight when Lourdina finally came back into the room and went to bed. She felt more relaxed and sure that there was no ghost in the house; just Rosy's imagination and her own guilt. She immediately fell into a deep sleep dreaming of her kind and wonderful Francisco. But it was barely an hour later when she was woken up with her bed shaking. She sat bolt upright and made the sign of the cross, peeped at Matilda and saw her turn in her bed. But she was peaceful. Lourdina was trembling with fear. She looked out of the window. Rosy's little shack was at the far end of the neighbour's garden. It was too far to call her and a slight drizzle blurred her vision. No one was about. She went back to the room and sat on her bed facing the open door. She looked alert, determined to catch anyone who dared to disturb her again. "Forgive me, Lord. I did not mean to be cunning. I will tell Francisco that we will rent a flat nearby so that he can go to his office in Porvorim and I can continue to work here. They can keep a night nurse for Matilda and I can also try..." Lourdina prayed fervently with her eyes closed and fell asleep. The bed shook gently again. Lourdina found that she had fallen asleep in a foetal position. She sat up saying it was only her imagination. Anyway, it was morning.

Dr Bhobe, the family doctor, came the next morning when he was called. He was a tubby little man with a bristly moustache and kind eyes behind small rimless spectacles. "Good morning, good morning," he said walking into Matilda's room.

Matilda looked at the very round bubble, smelling of aftershave and antiseptic and smiled. Dr Bhobe's voice was gentle as he took her blood pressure, examined her chest and looked at her feet and hands for any water retention. "I think it is just senility creeping in. She is 79 years old now," he said to an anxious Lourdina. Rosy stood near the doorway with the baby and Thomas, the postman, too had come and stood nearby. Swati the cleaning woman and the newspaperman soon joined in. Matilda was well liked by all. Dr Bhobe pulled at Matilda's chin and said "Aah." She obediently opened her mouth. All good. Then he bent close and pulled down her eyelids. His moustache tickled her cheek and she put her finger into her ear and shook it vigorously. The bed shook. And Lourdina gasped in understanding. The doctor quickly shone his torch in Matilda's ear. "There's a lot of soap there," he said. "I'll clean it." Lourdina turned to look at Rosy and smiled. Rosy began to giggle and ran out of the house. So much for Constantino's ghost – soap bubbles!

Adv Zuzarte contacted Alfred and he came a week later.

"I'm sorry mum, I haven't come for a while but I was making some important changes in my life," he said bending to kiss Matilda. She put her arms around his neck and held on. This bubble she liked... she knew.

Alfred looked around the house that was his childhood home and smiled. "Thank you, Lourdina, for looking after my home and caring for my mother. I believe that you are planning to get married soon. What is your fiancé's name?" Alfred asked

"Francisco, sir," she replied.

"I've told you before, Lourdina, please call me Alfred. Will you ask Francisco to join us for a drink this evening? I would like to talk to both of you together," he replied.

"I'm in for the sack," Lourdina thought. "Why didn't he question me about not calling him or sending for the doctor earlier?"

That evening Francisco came smiling like he always did and sat out in the veranda. Lourdina came and joined him looking very nervous. It was Alfred who brought out the drinks and soda and Lourdina ran in to get some glasses.

"Let me come straight to the point," Alfred began. "I know it has not been an easy task, Lourdina, looking after my mother. But you and Rosy from next door have done an excellent job."

"I'm ssssorry Alfred, I must confess that...," Lourdina stammered.

"I know, Lourdina, you had been hiding my letters. I guessed that. But it was probably a very trying time for you when you were planning your future. I have thought about this. As you know, I am a widower with no children. I decided to come back and work from here. I will have to go back to the UK once a month for three to four days. I know you will manage and leave emergency calls to Tony."

"But we are planning to get married and live nearby," Francisco said.

"I know," said Alfred. "But I have decided to build you a small flat by extending the old rooms at the back of the kitchen. That way we can both benefit. I shall also help Tony who is my childhood friend and Rosy with some monthly income so that they are more independent."

Lourdina sat with her head bent, tears pouring from her eyes. She heard Matilda's soft call and went in and brought her outside.

Such colourful bubbles. Such joy. Alfred stood up and hugged her and kissed her. "You are the best mum in the world," he said. Suddenly for a few seconds the bubble burst and she said "Alfred, you were always a charmer."

Glossary

Mai: Mother
Shanya: Clever
Soppo: Cement seat
Poskem: Adopted child
Saiba: O Lord
Kanji: Soft rice porridge
Gaddo: Hand-cart, usually selling roadside snacks or knickknacks
Lolo: Slob
Bai: *coll.* Used here to refer to a woman

The Mango Tree

Anusha V.R.

S HE stood by the window staring intently at the fruitless spindly mango tree. It hadn't borne a single fruit ever since it had been planted fifteen years ago as though it was deriving its nutrients from something toxic. Papa had wanted to chop it down years ago but grandmother would hear none of it. The tree will stay put, end of discussion, she would say. He didn't want to disagree with the whims of a crazy but sweet old lady so he wouldn't fight her over it. It was just a tree after all. Now that grandmother was gone, she wondered if her father would finally get around to uprooting the mango tree and plant a more worthy fruit-bearing tree in its place. Her mind went back in time. Back to when the bungalow in which she stood smelt of fresh paint and the backyard she was staring at had been bereft of flora. No mango tree. Nothing. Just a barren piece of land with upturned soil, red like blood.

Uncle Mike had appeared out of the blue when he heard about the Faleiro's newly constructed home. He arrived at the sprawling whitewashed bungalow, impressed his brother had made something of himself while also hoping he could get wiggle a few thousand rupees out of him under the pretence of a lucrative business venture.

"More than a decade has gone by and not even a phone call. Hell, he didn't even attend our wedding. Why do you think he is back, Chris?" grumbled Mrs Faleiro as she sliced tomatoes in the kitchen.

Uncle Mike overheard his sister-in-law's qualms. The very next day he woke up even before the sun could invade the sky and sneaked into the kitchen. He prepared breakfast for the entire family. The smell of tea and mild spices filled the house. From that morning onwards he cooked every meal for the rest of his stay. He helped Sylvia with all the household chores. He meted out instructions to the gardeners who had dug up numerous holes to plant a plethora of saplings. Sylvia's heart thawed in no time.

"Everyone deserves a second chance. Besides, not even you help out as much as he does," she told her husband a few days later. A complete 180 of what she had previously felt.

One day, as unexpectedly as he had appeared, Uncle Mike disappeared.

"I told you he is a good for nothing. Came to live rent free and eat free food till he could find something better," said the ever-fluctuating Sylvia. Calculations fluttered in her brain as to how much Uncle Mike's two-month stay had cost her. Food, water, electricity. Not to mention that expensive watch her asinine husband had gifted his younger brother for finally coming back home. She had put up with all of it, not solely due to him helping out around the house. It had been because of that rotten business idea he had pitched to her which she now realised had been too good to be true. Michael was willing to make Chris a part of it. She had been equal parts ecstatic and grateful at what she perceived as his generosity to include her husband in such a grand project. But now he was gone and with him he had taken any hopes she had of becoming richer then she already was.

Not wanting to pick a fight with his wife, Chris replied, "Michael has always been a wanderer. He left the house when he was just seventeen, Sylvia. He doesn't like being tied down to one spot. He lives his life on his own terms. We were lucky he stayed as long as he did." Christopher Faleiro's voice was tinged with pride for his brother. He didn't care about the business. He was just happy he had gotten to see his brother after all these years.

Sylvia snorted to show her disdain for her brother-in-law and continued to nurse her glass of wine.

The couple's train of thought did not once factor in the relief that bloomed in their thirteen-year old-daughter's heart as she slept curled up in a ball in her room.

One month had gone by since Uncle Mike had arrived when she decided she would tell her mother.

"Don't lie, child! It's a sin to lie. You think this house will pay for itself? Uncle Mike's business venture will help your papa clear the loan for this house faster. Instead of dragging his name through the mud by telling lies we should be grateful he is willing to make your father a partner in his venture. And then we can finally think of getting a bigger car, instead of that metal garbage Chris drives around now..." replied her mother. Her thoughts already wandering to which car would make the neighbours writhe with envy.

Another month went by before she could gather up the courage and tell someone. But what if they responded the way in which her mother had? Maybe mummy had been right. Maybe she would ruin papa's business venture and they would lose their house like Maria, her classmate had. Maria didn't come to school anymore since her family couldn't afford it. Maybe she should just keep quiet but the pain wouldn't let her keep quiet. It had a mind of its own. It wanted to scream about its origins to anyone who would listen and not shrug their shoulders.

It was a balmy Saturday evening. Uncle Mike had driven up Panjim to meet a few of his friends and would only be back by nightfall. She slowly crept to her grandmother's room and told her everything. Her grandmother did not silence her right after she uttered the very first sentence like her mother had done a month ago. Grandmother listened to all of it. How her son crept into her granddaughter's room night after night. First it was under the pretext of giving her a new toy or a chocolate bar he had picked up for her when he had gone out that evening. Then his grimy hands would go under her frock for a few minutes before taking off his own clothes. She had tried to scream once even though his weight was crushing her ribs but he had muffled her voice with a large hand and whispered with his sour rum-stained breath as to how he would slit her throat.

"Go to sleep and pretend like nothing happened," grandma said in a flat voice and sent her away.

First a terrible sense of betrayal flooded her. Her own mother hadn't believed her. Why should Uncle Mike's? She swallowed her dinner slowly and dragged her unwilling feet to bed. Her little heart thumped in her chest waiting for the nightmare to begin when she heard her room door creak open. The usual rustle of the chocolate wrapping could be heard as Uncle Mike removed it from his pocket, followed by the sound of a zipper being unfastened. She wondered whether slitting her wrists would be as painful as listening to that sound for another night. But her thoughts were interrupted by a huge crash. The noise of something metal crashing against a hard object. A thin figure which had been previously crouching in her closet stood where the silhouette of Uncle Mike had been a few minutes ago. The moonlight filtering through her bedroom window outlined the shape of Uncle Mike on the floor. Grandmother stood over his body with a thick metal shovel the gardeners had been using all day. There was no blood but a ghastly blue bruise the size of an orange was beginning to form on Uncle Mike's bald scalp.

"Get up, and help. We don't have much time," barked grandmother.

She had no idea what they didn't have time for, but she didn't give voice to her confusion. She caught hold of Uncle Mike's feet while grandma lifted him by his hands. Christopher and Sylvia Faleiro slept soundly in their upstairs bedroom. They had had one too many glasses of wine as was their Saturday night tradition.

In the backyard, a huge pit had already been dug for a jackfruit tree which was to be brought from a nearby farm the next morning. Grandmother spent a few more minutes widening the pit and making it a bit deeper. She kept throwing glances in her son's direction making sure he wouldn't gain consciousness. And then they rolled Uncle Mike into the pit and filled it back up with soil.

"Go to bed. It's late."

"But, grandma, he was still breathing," she said, her voice shaking.

"All the better. He'll die with a lungful of dirt if that blow to the

head doesn't kill him."

The next morning she saw grandmother overseeing the gardener's work. She wouldn't let anyone go near the pit they had dug for the jackfruit tree. She said she had planted a mango seed. She wanted a mango tree. Papa wasn't a patient man. He didn't like to wait for a seed to sprout into a sapling and then grow into a tree. The entire process would take years. Wouldn't it be easy to get a miniature mango plant transported from the farm?

But grandmother stuck to her stance. She pulled out every card in the book. Right from "Won't you grant an old lady her dying wish?" to "I'm your mother and you will do as I say". Christopher finally caved in and went back inside his home, only to realise that his flighty brother had fled the nest again.

"Are you alright?" said a voice from behind, startling her. Her recollections of the past came to a screeching halt.

She nodded. Her father had come back from the funeral service which had been held at the Holy Family Chapel. She hadn't attended the service. She didn't want to believe grandmother was truly gone.

"She loved that damn tree," said her father, following his daughter's line of vision.

She nodded again, almost feeling sorry about how little her father actually knew about his own mother, his brother.

"I guess it's time for that tree to be finally pulled down. It bears no fruit, too thin and leafless to even provide any shade, it will constantly remind you of grandmother and depress you, sweetheart. Besides, your mother wants to redecorate the house, so might as well let her have a go at the garden as well, eh?"

Wings of Vertigo

Aaron S. Rodrigues

NOTHING is more peaceful or more enjoyable to me than to watch the small golden fireball in the sky end its daily reign. I love watching the sun set, the horizon tinted with a golden glow, the clouds lined with gold and the birds soaring among these jewels of the sky. It is a time of utmost tranquillity which gives meaning to even the most hectic of days. Sitting in my balcony, with just the sound of the birds crying, the light tropical Goan breeze rippling through my hair with the trees swaying lazily, the scene isn't really different from a fairy tale, but humans are by nature greedy – always wanting more and I am no different.

The heavenly view does not satisfy me. Goa is often touted as a paradise and as magnificent as it is, I have only ever seen the paradise I live in from the ground and as I watch the tiny swallows and finches fly, I envy them their freedom, their ability to leave the ground, to soar in the endless sky. Although no creature of the evening sky is more enviable than the lonely hawk. Every day I watch this magnificent creature, hunting on its own, sailing the sky without the need to beat its wings. I watch the swallows, finches and even the black ravens avoid him, giving it its space. No limit, no direction, no path. Paradise would indeed be redefined if viewed through those sharp eyes.

I like to view the world through the eyes of a normal human being. I don't believe in miracles and yet every evening I am as drawn in into the scene before my eyes as a child drawn to fairy tales. I am hardly different from your average sixteen year old. I believe in the miracles that I see with my eyes. Nothing more, nothing less. I do try to act my age and follow ideals and ideas instilled in me by people. They say the world is a busy place; you dream and you are lost in the bustle. Yet my lonely childhood gave me a lot of time to ponder and I still find serenity in the setting of the sun and the scene that unfolds with it.

I long for the freedom that wings give birds, flying around in their dozens – singing. I have longed for company, yet waiting alone for so long has made me phobic to it. I don't need it, not when I have to adapt to this busy world, but what I do desire is to be like the hawk. King of the sky, master of himself, lonely gem with no rival to steal his glory. No threat to his reign, except maybe an untimely end. Right now, there he is at his peak, emitting an aura of command the others can't match or even aspire to.

I am not, in particular, a credulous person. However, there is one habit I have carried from my delicate childhood. During the splendid spectacle of the setting sun, the enchanted time when the clouds are lined with gold, I wish for the golden fireball, as if a god, to grant me just a simple wish – to be able to view this paradise from the eyes of the hawk. It has been eleven years and my wish still remains unfulfilled, yet today seems different. Everyday seems different. I see the hawk homing in on an animal it might have spotted and as it does so, it dives sharply out of the sky... no feeling of vertigo! Does it feel no fear? At the very last moment, it pulls out of its dive and flies towards me. I guess it missed its prey. It is time for my daily ritual; I turn to the waning Goan sun on its last breath and I wish one more time to let me, if only in a dream, to see this paradise from the eyes of the hawk. Just as I make the wish, the hawk gives out a cry. A call of some sort, almost a plea.

I hear a twitter. I lift my head from my wings. I open my eyes. Everything is bleary. I have overslept and that will cost me a meal. The sun isn't up yet but some beings are and that means I am late. My surroundings are a bit foggy, I guess that's the reason I feel a little chill. I stretch my wings and ruffle my feathers. I feel uneasy but I do not have the time to ponder. My stomach does all the thinking now. I now feel the cool morning wind blow through my feathers. I still wait. I can't leave yet. I wait for a sign. I don't know why. It's just instinct. I look to my left. It's almost here now. The first glow appears from the horizon, there's my sign. I stretch my wings, straighten my legs, release the hold my claws have on the branch and I am off.

I love this feeling. It is the only time I feel at peace (except for my rumbling stomach) but even that reduces its complaints. I fly high over the plains, almost to the shore. I beat my wings a little just to get me higher up. I fly over the forest in search of a meal. The trees obstruct my vision. I must fly between them. I lower my altitude, glide among the trees. Ah... there's my breakfast – a nice plump mouse scrabbling for food.

The morning sun creates no shadows so I fly over him and prepare for a dive, time it right and I'll have my meal. But alas! My wings brush against the leaves of a tree. The mouse is alert and it scrabbles off to a hole in the ground.

Defeat! It's harder to swallow on a hungry stomach. I fly off cursing myself for being careless. I fly around a bit but nothing seems to be moving except for a couple of buffalo. It is frustrating to search when you are famished, yet that's all I can do if I wish to satisfy my hunger. I fly back to the hole where I lost my first prey, perched on the branch above it in the hope of surprising the mouse. I wait long and see no sign of movement. I start getting restless, my hunger just making it worse. I want to fly off but an inner debate calms me down – patience, I was told, is the key to an easy meal. Not long after this, I spot its nose and whiskers poking out from its hideout. I get ready, check my surroundings and space, calculate the time of my dive. Time freezes. I focus on the movement of the mouse. I home in, and the moment it leaves the hole, my claws grab it.

I clean my beak on the branch, too full to do anything. I choose a nice shady spot and rest as well as I can.

My eyes open. It's almost time for the evening flight. Sunset, the most peaceful time, turns into a battlefield. I prepare myself for another day, another battle. I scan the skies. The swallow flock is up hunting the insects, and yes, once again far away in the distance I see those cursed raven. They have come to disturb the peace again. I take off. The ravens are still far away and have settled in a tree, waiting for the perfect time to raise havoc. I fly over the shore. I see the crabs scuttling to their tiny ground caves. Near the horizon I see a flock of white swans in their disciplined ranks, their beauty enhanced by their rigid flight formation. I soar up and fly towards the sunset hill – the sun's rays blinding me. I fly high up towards the gold-edged clouds. I feel safe here. It gives me the courage I need for the battles that rage every day. Since I left my nest I often tried to reach the horizon. Long and far I flew over sea and over mountains, yet the horizon beat me with every step. I was even foolish enough as a young hawk to try to reach the sun, flying high, piercing the clouds, ever higher; until I felt so dizzy I almost fainted. I have learnt since then that wings will only get you so far. Escape from chaos will lead you to peace, for only so long. You have to return. Live in the chaos. Try to make peace a home there. Only then will it be everlasting. Tranquillity will come to you. From then on I have followed my ancestors' path, striving for inner tranquillity. Yet it is hard to do this alone, no support, no comfort, and when you've had a trying day, you sometimes lose your purpose.

Sometimes I wish for the life of the land dwelling creatures. Their life limited to the ground, the ground giving them a solid surface to move on. Our lives are as much a curse as a boon. Flying high we try to escape our fears, yet they haunt us no matter how high we fly. We view the world below us – such a peaceful and beautiful world it seems – the skies we fly in are empty except for the sun and the clouds. I swirl around and drop below the clouds, just then I spot something that makes my mind blissfully blank; I see another hawk in the distance. Judging from its flight patterns it looks like a female. Excited, I frantically beat my wings, trying to get there as quickly as possible. My failed attempts in the past offer me no second thought. I crave for the company; I don't care about the past failures. In my excitement I fail to see the black cloud rising from the trees. Curses! Those ravens have targeted me again, but this time I cannot afford to lose. I change my direction, bend my wings and rush straight as an arrow to the raven matriarch – that sadistic queen of the accursed harem. The other ravens crowd around me, seeking the right time to attack. The matriarch gives a cry and flies off but before I can give her chase I must them

ward off. I change direction and attack the ravens on my right, but they seem to have synchronised their movements. The ravens on the right swerve away while the ones on the left move in to attack. I won't get them this way. I soar up, they fall for the bait. They think I am fleeing away from them, start crying excitedly in their horrid voices and give me chase. As soon as I spot all of them in chase, I break my sky ward flight. I pull my wings closer and dive, twisting and spiralling to increase the force. Something I learnt from my elder. Like a powerfully thrusted spear, I dive towards them hitting as many as possible with my beak. They realise their mistake and break off crying in dismay at this turn of the tide in the battle. Their attack is now a rout. I chase them away, but before I can target the matriarch she has disappeared, and her accursed black army now flee in every direction possible.

I look towards the right, where I spotted the hawk. Unfortunately, she is gone too. The sun has set, leaving just a ghostly glow over the horizon. I have won this battle yet have achieved nothing. I fly back to my tree frustrated, disappointed and sickened with the taste of blood in my mouth. I screech in frustration and somehow, I feel it has been heard.

Weird! It felt so real, so detailed, not something my conscious mind could grasp. I sit up and walk to my balcony. It's a breezy, sunny Sunday morning. Yet, I just slump to the floor and rest my head against the wall. I am lost in a vertigo of thoughts and images. It was a weird dream I had last night. None like any I've had before. I felt the dives, the wind – in my wings...? The fearlessness of the height. The thrill of the hunt. My mind can't get over the experience. The very way I looked at things was different. My eyes were transfigured into lens that could home in onto things, my mouth was the lethal point of a sharpened spear, my wings... It just doesn't make sense. I can't explain it unless I convince myself that miracles exist. The whole day passed in a haze. I knew my mind would not give me any answers until the evening. I hoped that magical time would provide me with the answers I need. I remain a human. I need someone I could share this with, someone who wouldn't mock me, someone who would understand me! Or just someone who would care enough to listen to me. My mind failed to convince my heart that I could cope with this hectic hell and live through my experiences, trying to savour them alone.

I craved for company, I yearned for attention, I longed for love. Lost in this vertigo of thoughts, time passed me by. The sun mellowed down from its fiery yellow self to a delicate orange. The swallows were hunting flies, the clouds were lined with gold, the horizon exuding a heavenly glow. Everything seemed calm. In the distance, I saw a black cloud approach. Intent on disrupting the peace of the twilight. I watched them draw closer. As they did, out of the trees flew the hawk, a lonely figure against that vast army. But I was amazed to see another hawk soar after him. Like two seraphim, they charged the black clouds of ravens, breaking the evil harem. That's when I got my answer. In that vertigo of thoughts, I found it staring at me.

Miracles are not just a beautiful fantasy. Lost in the bliss of serendipity, I felt my heart getting a second wind. I will go for it just like the seraphim. Against all odds, on the wings of vertigo.

Why Rita Doesn't Eat Sausages Anymore

Clara A. Rodrigues

DONA glanced over her shoulders constantly as though half expecting a hidden lover to come out of nowhere asking her not to leave. However, the glint of love was missing from her eyes. What she was trying to hide nobody could decipher. No, not even the Customs officials at the airport terminal in Brisbane who asked her to step aside so that they could search her purse-bag. Little Angel tugging at her dress only made matters worse. Dona cringed seeing Angel scratch her hair, spoiling the neat braids she had so nicely done for her. Angel had definitely caught the lice from her cousins in Goa, thought Dona, with a little shake, knowing that her hair had by now already seen the inevitable transfer of lice during the plane journey.

The grandmother and granddaughter duo were returning from Goa after attending their village church feast of St Anne. The rains in Talaulim had been extremely heavy that year. Dona had even caught the flu after she got drenched in one of the downpours.

The lady official at the terminus offered her a sympathetic look as the bouts of coughing started. Dona hurled a few threats at her granddaughter and, when she remembered that threats never had any impact on the little one, decided to win her over with a promise of buying the child her favourite doll.

"I am from Goa," Dona said with an imploring look, knowing that she was being searched because she looked Asian. Most Asians faced this hassle of being unnecessarily searched but each time Dona always managed to wriggle herself out of the ordeal, convincing the duty officer that she was from this little part of India called Goa which was formerly ruled by the Portuguese and which was a little unlike the rest of India as it had some kind of

Western outlook which only Dona could explain so well. This usually always miraculously worked in her favour until this time when she stood facing a wide-eyed lady inspector – who, despite finding nothing dangerous in her bag – asked her to step aside to be frisked.

Dona was a cherubic looking lady. She was known for giving the inside-the-palm pinch to her children whenever they misbehaved, but with her grandchild Angel it was different. After her daughter Yvette gave birth to her first grandchild, the old disciplinarian self just melted away and she embraced grandmotherhood with a far greater genial spirit. But today, for the first time in Angel's five years, her grandmother pinched the fidgety child into quietness.

"Ouch," the poor little one cried. She didn't know how to react. A little while later the questions poured.

"Grandma, are they taking you to the outer room because you pinched me?"

The outer room was a dreaded place, where Angel remembered her cousin telling her that their teacher would threaten them that they would be sent to, if they created any mischief.

Angel shivered and so did her grandmother, the latter oblivious of any outer room, but rather at the thought of being frisked awkwardly. It had never happened to her before but she had heard stories of how outrageous some officers could get at the pat-down session.

"Grandma, where are they taking you?" asked Angel innocently again.

Dona, sensing the worry in the little one, answered, "Nowhere sweetheart. There's no need to worry. It will only be for a quick second."

Dona managed to convince the little version of her former self.

After the uneventful frisking got over, the official asked, "Is there anything to declare, madam? Weapon, sharp object, banned products that you might be carrying into the country?"

Dona shook her head in the negative. She quickly signed a declaration form and was allowed to go back to where little Angel was.

As they were being ushered out of the checking area, there was a massive commotion a little ahead. Accompanied by sniffer dogs, cops brandishing guns were making enquiries and jostling a few passengers. A wave of panic suddenly came to sweep Dona who started faltering a little.

"What's the matter, grandma?" asked Angel, but Dona did not hear the little one talk. All the time her eyes were fixed on the commotion ahead.

She froze as one cop made his way towards her, pointing at her at first and then narrowing his eyes. Dona's Goan roots no longer remained a private affair as she blurted aloud, "*Saiba pav.*"

"Ma'am, have you seen this man?" asked the officer, pointing his finger at a photograph.

Dona relaxed a little. After all, it was not her that they were after. She smiled, relieved.

"No. No... Never seen him before," she said.

The cop thanked her and moved away.

Dona was tired. The plane had taken an eternity to land and Dona hadn't slept a wink. Her visits to the loo were restricted to timings such as midnight and early dawn when people, usually asleep, don't bother about their co-passenger's business. Occasionally, her thoughts went back to Goa where she was angry with her brother for not fencing their ancestral property, as a result of which the neighbours were trespassing and tethering their cattle inside the property.

Outside the terminus and Dona breathed a sigh of relief. She walked a little distance along with Angel, looking to hail a cab. The cabs usually waited around the bend outside the airport. There was a lady with her pet dog who seemed to take to Dona rather quickly and followed her, and would have still continued had the lady not tugged at the leash firmly.

"*Mal criado,*" muttered Dona at the audacity of the dog. Henry, the cab driver, about to bite into his mayonnaise-dripping burger, stopped no sooner he heard Dona. He hastily rewrapped his burger and started his cab and slowed down near Dona. Thinking it was some driver who really needed a trip for the day, and thanking God for helping her save her time hailing one, Dona quickly pulled a tired and sleepy Angel into the cab before finally pushing herself in. She gave a soft tug at the luggage as if to check that everything was there.

She gave Henry instructions to their house in a tinge of an Australian accent, the Goan one fading in the backdrop of the rolling landscape, closed her eyes before he could even grasp it and slipped into her nap.

After they had crossed a few miles she awoke with a start when a bag slipped from her lap. She picked the bag, adjusted herself, took a quick look at Angel, who was by now fast asleep, and was about to doze off when the cab driver asked "Is it for the *sorpotel* or *vindalho*?"

Dona was stunned. She felt the same dread she experienced at the airport returning. Sweat, however, failed her because Australia was experiencing its winter.

She raised her eyebrows trying to keep a straight face and, just in time, remembered to smile. A smile really helps in rescuing one from situations and keeping composure, she had learnt.

"I didn't understand what you are saying...?"

"Those lovely Goan sausages," said Henry cheekily.

Perhaps it was her inability to keep up with the game of pretence or her plain curiosity that made Dona ask, "How on earth did you know?" she asked.

"*Aghe mai*," began Henry in heavily accented Konkani, "forgive my language skills but I am the son-in-law of your land and my mother-in-law too would sneak in *chouriço* till a few years ago when she stopped eating them. I would collect her from the airport and over the years I realised that there are always some telltale indications when someone is hiding something, especially sausages. And when you cussed out the dog like that, I guessed as much that you were from Goa."

"She turned vegetarian?" asked Dona, clearly now not interested in how Henry had deduced about the sausages but wanting to know about his mother-in-law's queer loss of appetite for sausages.

"No... She still eats other meats. Just the sausage."

Dona thought it rather strange that a fellow Goan should not like sausages.

Henry and Dona bonded during the long journey over sausages. Henry had never been to Goa and said he planned to visit the state soon along with his wife. Along the way they discussed methods of packing the sausages without getting caught by officials or smelt by sniffer dogs.

The journey took a few hours longer as they stopped over at Henry's place after he extended Dona and Angel an impromptu invite. He had insisted because it was rare to have a Goan on a visit and he knew that each time a Goan visitor came by, a peg of *feni* was inevitable. It made the Australian winters warmer.

Moreover, he said it was his mother-in-law's ninetieth birthday. Despite the jet lag, Dona obliged. She found it quite intriguing that a Goan could have stopped consuming sausages! She had to find out.

Henry introduced Dona to his wife Gisela and mother-in-law Rita, an amiable and plump woman. Dona assumed the extra weight the lady had amassed was due to her fine taste for food. Indeed, she thought, a lady of fine taste. But then, how could she have ignored or slighted the poor sausage? Each time Dona thought of it, things just appeared more complex.

Dona took to the charming lady. A small repast was served as Dona told them that she and Angel had to reach home and so wouldn't be able to partake in the main course lunch. Goan hospitality flourished in Australia as dish after dish made it to the table, except for the Goan sausage.

It was a pity that Dona couldn't eat those *chouriços* on her birthday as it always coincided with the Lent season. Being a good Christian always won over her love for these sausages but each year it was a tough battle ignoring the Goan meat dish.

After pleasantries were exchanged and it was time to leave, Dona couldn't stop herself from asking Rita, "Why don't you eat sausages anymore? Is it a sausage allergy you developed?"

Slightly embarrassed by the topic, Rita let her in on a secret.

"I just can't anymore. It's an appetite that just dissipated."

She showed Dona to the next room where she dished through the last drawer of her showcase and brought out a newspaper cutting which read 'Lady arrested for smuggling sausages'.

The five-minute plan of exchanging goodbyes lasted for an hour as Rita spoke to Dona about how she was getting these *chouriços* for the Goan diaspora reunion in Australia and how she was caught at Customs.

"I had to do community service and also pay a hefty price but, more than that, I really couldn't face the people around me," said Rita. "I just couldn't face people anymore. I was arrested! And that too for an offence of smuggling!"

She explained to a bewildered Dona how sausages were so harmless. Gone was the days of their 'banger' reputation, said Rita, referring to the days of the World Wars when sausages, because of a meat deficit, were stuffed with water, cereals and other leftovers, which caused them to make a 'bang' sound like an explosion.

"They are harmless. A good Goan sausage is never known to have harmed anyone," said Donna quietly.

Dona knew how certain foreign countries were very strict with their laws with regard to imports such as meats because of the danger – any contagion which could harm its livestock – it could bring into the country.

Dona didn't know how to react. She embraced Rita. For Rita it was therapeutic talking to Dona. This was the first time she had ever spoken about how she had felt since the incident. Until then she had always avoided the topic.

Soon, it was time to leave. At the parting, both ladies felt a lot lighter – Rita from opening up about her emotions when she had been caught and branded a smuggler, and Dona, the eternal optimist, who with the hope of reigniting the taste for sausages in Rita, had left a generous parcel of sausages behind, resulting in a bag much lighter.

Glossary

Saiba pav: God help me

Mal criado: Such a rascal; someone who doesn't have manners or is not raised well

Aghe mai: Oh mother

Sorpotel: Also called *sarapatel.* A dish of Portuguese origin commonly cooked in the coastal Konkan region of India, primarily Goa, Mangalore, by East Indians around Bombay (now Mumbai) of the former *Estado da Índia,* and in north-eastern Brazil too. Ingredients include meat and offal, and vary depending on region from pork to lamb to beef

Vindalho: A traditional spicy Goan dish, which can be made with pork or chicken

Chouriço: Goan sausage

Feni: A spirit produced in Goa. There are two types of *feni,* cashew *feni* and coconut *feni.* It is believed to have medicinal properties

Pavlov's Daughter

Noel Sequeira

D ARTING through the thicket, a chameleon scampered to the left and right and wriggled its tail at the signal of thumping feet. It froze in trepidation.

"Good morning, Hulkie! Isn't it nice to be a new person every day?" exclaimed Renuka, right after heaving a massive sigh of relief for not stamping on the chameleon who was anything but green two afternoons ago. Eleven-year-old Renuka hunched all the way down to meet the chameleon's bulging eyes.

"Would you like to crawl into today's battlefield and fight for your right to exist?" It took barely a week for Renuka to renounce the game of cricket, something she was often peer pressured by her neighbours into playing. What captivated her was the notion of a battlefield, which she had more fun extrapolating onto the game of life. In every sphere, she identified a winner and a loser. In her self-conjured battlefield, she was the referee.

The chameleon refused to budge, anchored to the fern-laced soil of Nachinola. Renuka got the hint as she tapped the air a few centimetres above his head and said, "You just be your pretty little camouflaging self while I assert your contribution to the circle of life." Today, Renuka's toys would be duelling on the battlefield of anthropocentrism.

Renuka then raced towards her tree house, a three-and-a-half minute walk from her house. She couldn't thank her stars enough for the privilege of waking up every morning to chirping bulbuls and magpies, lurking wild boar and swathes of evergreen. All the charming gifts of earth that her father lamented are ever so speedily being wiped off the face of Goa. It was the fear that Renuka would grow up associating forests with dinosaurs – miracles of the past – which drove her father Girish to vacate his quarters and buy

a house in Nachinola, nestled in the illusion of a world where concrete jungles were a trifling matter. Girish, the Chairperson of the Psychology Department in Goa University, didn't bat an eyelid at the subsequent task of driving sixty-six kilometres every day for his paycheck. Renuka's conceptualisation of Goa, his motherland, as he had known it, always came first.

One foot on the bark to catapult her to the rope ladder of her teakwood abode, Renuka craned her neck and squealed, "You matter! Everybody matters." The chameleon, however, disappeared into the blue and white cottony horizon.

Renuka eagerly sauntered into the four walls of her tree house. Scrutinising the crevices, she braced herself for a new visitor. Last week, she was pleased to unravel the conspiracy behind the binaries of fat and thin in the presence of a scorpion. What will it take for shopaholics to realise that they've been bleeding their pockets dry just because it's too humiliating to be fat? Renuka wondered as she drummed her paunch.

Renuka loved Mathematics except when it was taught in class. She emptied the contents of her geometry box onto a stool and decided to treat them as troops on the battlefield of her mindscape. The scale (or ruler, as her classmates called it) gleamed amidst the tidy sprawl of paraphernalia. A gust of animosity crept in as it suddenly hit her; she was glaring at the archetype of 'perfection'. The mighty ruler, so thin and so tall. "Setting the standards for measurement, how dare you!" she mouthed scornfully. Sliding the protractor, triangle and compass towards one edge of the stool, she roared as the shimmer of the ruler faded in its defeat.

Renuka would often eavesdrop on her parent's post-dinner altercations. Insensitive to the staccatos of discord, she found a new hobby in jotting down the indecipherable words her father would spew in verbal combat.

"Renuka will soon fall prey to the neoliberalisation of education if we don't do something about it," she heard him rant. "Do you realise some of these words don't do more than clear out the wax in here?" her mother Esmeralda retorted, as she gestured towards her earlobe. 'Parents in love' would soon be the first example of an oxymoron to exit Renuka's lips when her tenth grade English teacher would quiz her on literary tools. The memory of her parents' last embrace was beginning to blur and hence, Renuka would fritter away considerable time decoding the conundrum that was their marriage.

Her maternal grandmother Vovo dropped a few clues when six-year-old Renuka pressed her right ear against the closed doors of the *sala* in her ancestral house in Loutolim, the hub of the elite.

"*O teu marido vai roubar o meu,*" she bickered to Esmeralda.

"*Mãe, por que pensas assim? Ambos têm interesses comuns,*" Esmeralda shot back. "*Tu vais arrepender-te. Havia tantos bons rapazes de boas famílias.*" Vovo rested her case and dawdled to the kitchen.

Vovo refused to speak anything other than Portuguese, leaving Girish with no option but to sign up for a course. Besides, he was thrilled to raise a trilingual daughter. Unfortunately, his fervour to build a rapport with his mother-in-law proved futile as Vovo would never settle for a Hindu.

Vovo's acrimonious words confirmed Renuka's suspicions. Swayed by the eloquence of Esmeralda's father who was an ardent historian, Girish asked Esmeralda to be his wife. Even though he wasn't from a *boa família* (which Renuka eventually gathered was a euphemism for upper-caste Catholic), he braved the Vovo tides.

In spite of a few Google searches, Renuka never figured out what Girish meant by neoliberalisation. What did tickle her fancy was his flippant use of 'genderless'. Only after a third glance of her school dress code did she confront the word 'gender'. The loss of ventilation by converting a skirt into a pair of shorts was never a fair justification for submission to thought control. If one morning she felt like trousers, she'd like to dive straight into them.

Renuka's intellectual wars began when she lit a candle in her tree house and accidentally confronted the shadow of her head which kept expanding as she retreated. A frozen spectator, she watched a spider swing from one end of a cobweb to the other and two beetles fornicating until the lady beetle resisted the grasp of the not-so-gentle-man-beetle, sending him all the way down and out of the angular contours of Renuka's head-shadow.

Unable to turn away from the spectacle in spite of the million voices in her head, she noticed a synchronous pattern in the two. "All wars begin and end in one's head," she gasped, her brain cells shrieking 'Eureka' in unison. Every night-long quarrel between her parents was an echo of two simultaneous wars occurring deep down in the contaminated canals of their minds. "That's not a war, it is chaos," she discerned, staring at the battleground venue for approval. The shadow of her mind deserved an identity, not that of a human entity but of a venue, a battlefield. She impulsively christened it *Brainshed*.

Renuka got to work. She carefully cut out the faces of her family members from a portrait and hung them through a hook attached to the ceiling, finally putting the yarn of wool her mother thrust into her utility kit. She fondled the yarn, suppressing the butterflies in her belly, fluttering in anticipation to watch the war unfold. As she pulled out some thread, she recalled the sparkle in her mother's eye as she emotionally blackmailed her into knitting a pair of socks.

"You know orange is my favourite colour and my birthday is just around the corner. Prove to Mrs Ezilda that you can catch a skill faster than she'd catch a cold in the winter." It didn't take more than seven minutes of Mrs Ezilda's despotic sewing instructions to seek greener pastures. Her stifled mind drifted to a "course in carpentry for kids", giving her impetus to insist on a vocational switch.

"But she's a girl!"

"Renuka is Renuka. Besides, I can hear the sobs of the slaughtered Asoka tree. It says: "*Why did the municipality usurp my place? I'm sorry for rescuing you guys from the blistering heat. Sir, before a truck transports me to further obscurity, would you accept my offer to hold your cup of Darjeeling tea? I reckon your wife scolded you for dripping some on the carpet,"* impersonated Girish.

"Renuka, I'll call up the Carpentry Facilitator and fix a spot for you. And then we'll haul the branches into our courtyard. But first, promise me a rustic little table, will you?" he winked.

Snapping out of the flashback, a slight chill crept up Renuka's spine at the sight of her aunts and uncles lurking in the plateaus of this battlefield, ready in combat. The women gravitated away from the men, building an army and sizing up their ammunition.

Renuka would light a matchstick and fling it with her imaginary bowstring every time an aunt annihilated an uncle's Achilles heel. Armed with a mini toy fan, Renuka would leave the possibility of the flames charring the images of her defeated uncles to the winds of circumstance.

"Do you even realise that with my qualifications, we could've been eating lobster every fortnight? But no, it was more important that YOU weren't the one changing diapers!" Renuka mimicked Aunty Amita's shrill voice and quickly lit a matchstick which struck the edge of Uncle Ravi's moustache.

"Maybe if you had the foresight to drape your saris in another room, Viren would've been unzipping trousers instead of..." Uncle Ravi trailed off, but the blades of Renuka's toy fan condemned his patriarchal entrails and allowed the ashes of his existence to disperse far away from the landscape of the battlefield. Renuka later regretted her eagerness to drown out Uncle Ravi's harangue as she missed an opportunity to flaunt a word she recently acquired. Rumour had it that Viren relinquished the right to use his tool as preferred welcoming foreign objects into a particular 'orifice'.

No victor was determined as, soon enough, it seemed that the opponents were mongering over a lost cause. But as the rays emanating from the candle wick criss-crossed back into the labyrinth of Renuka's mind, a cloud of remorse engulfed her. She suddenly felt a wave of empathy towards her cousin Viren. The only cousin who didn't thrive on the sadistic pleasure of bullying her. From the hushed conversations amongst the oldies, she gathered that Viren had dropped some sort of an earth-shattering revelation.

"You're a world-class psychologist. Please fix our poisoned

son," beseeched Viren's parents one night.

"I don't think he's the one who needs fixing," Girish smirked, offering free sessions where he'd help them 'deconstruct heteronormativity'.

Renuka as well as the distraught parents had no inkling of what that meant. Three sessions down and she grasped much more from hiding inside a cupboard during her father's counselling sessions than the *gratis* clients did. "Love knows no boundaries" resonated well with her but "gender is just a construct" proved to be a cumbersome code to crack.

Squinting at the last few strands of her Aunt Flavia's tresses melting into grey feathers, the memory of Renuka's two-day suspension from school flashed before her eyes. It was the day she had walked into class with no hair on her scalp. "Do you think you are a boy?" barked her Geography teacher. Renuka wondered if teaching Geography impaired one's logical abilities. Her flashbacks oscillated to a more recent episode. That of her dad's jaw dropping in disgust at the sight of a concrete monstrosity built over what was once a quaint playground, not just for her but her squirrel McKenzie. "Ugly constructions, ugly constructions everywhere!" her father muttered to himself in exasperation. Ever since that day, 'construction' always had a negative connotation in Renuka's troubled mind. Perhaps a synonym for something superficial, something dispensable. *Is gender something the world can do without?* She pondered and pondered.

"*Poi, hanv tuka lagun kitem hadla!*" Sanga's singsong voice delicately punctured Renuka's reverie. She turned to see Sanga hanging from a branch with one hand and clutching a gorgeous orange-and-black striped butterfly between her left-hand thumb and index finger.

Renuka was about to reprimand her for what she would translate as animal cruelty but succumbed to the impulse of flicking Sanga's left hand, inviting the butterfly to navigate the non-erected battlefield. Renuka quickly slammed the open half of the oval-shaped window and said, "Thank you, Sanga. *Aiz borem friend mevlem battlefieldan mhajekade war jhogodpak.*"

Renuka nostalgically recalled the time Sanga volunteered to be the rival puppeteer during the 'Battle of Pigments'. It was the period when Girish was actively keeping tabs on the #BlackLives-Matter movement in the U.S.A.

"These blacks are just attention-seekers," interjected Esmeralda while Girish was intently scanning the news.

"How I wish you would read more than speak," he replied, shifting his concentration back to the news.

Girish had a penchant for reproaching her History syllabus. "Why would anybody waste their time on eight pages of Gandhi? Now, I'm not denying his indelible mark in the freedom movement but nobody talks about his latent racism. Why doesn't anybody here talk about Martin Luther King?"

Daddy's bedtime stories soon turned out to be crash courses in structural racism and white supremacy. Renuka did observe how the people of Nachinola would ostracise and alienate Sanga. Sanga identified as Siddi. Her ancestors were African slaves shipped in by the Portuguese rulers. She spoke flawless Konkani, miles better than Renuka ever could. Nothing angered Renuka more than people whispering racial slurs every time she and Sanga would cycle past the narrow banks of Pomburpa Lake.

The symphony of Sanga's dangling earrings and mellifluous shrieks every time her cycle would glide downhill sent a surge of affection through Renuka. The sporadic breeze would bring her jet black ringlets to life, often tickling her perfectly symmetric nostrils. And then she'd giggle, involuntarily revealing the world's most enchanting smile. Renuka never quite understood why the riffraff swoon over pale Bollywood divas.

One overcast evening, Sanga scooped up a cardboard box brimming with Barbie dolls, most of them missing a head or a limb. Together, they painted some Barbie doll torsos multiple colours of the spectrum. Hanging by threads, the uncoloured torsos entered the battlefield to vanquish the coloured torsos. It didn't take her much time to realise that in the end, all the torsos would collapse and find semblance in one another.

On this particular day, Renuka stared at her emerging shadow on the wooden surface of her tree house ceiling, waiting for the last few traces of sunset to ebb away. She remembered the carvings on the antiquated furniture and tapestry in Vovo's ancestral house. Some depicted battles between the conquistadores and the indigenous people. If not in reality, then in her imagination. After all, it was the colonised who toiled for days to produce these exquisite artefacts.

She watched the butterfly flutter around and the chameleon gingerly inch its way to its vantage point. She retrieved a few Barbie doll heads, now mauled by her puppy Zombie. Added a few of her soft toys to the troop that was to vanquish the human race. This had been on her mind for a while.

Renuka's hands trembled as she manoeuvred the strings gripping the toys representing the wild and the Barbie doll heads representing the humans. The butterfly occasionally swooped down the battlefield, a mystical voyeur. The chameleon lingered at the bottom end, almost with the flair of a clairvoyant.

She stared at the Barbie doll heads. The menace in their eyes piercing the scent of the room. She contrasted that with the trusting eyes of her stuffed cow toy. There was only one way this war would end with a smile on her face.

Twelve years on, not only did Renuka become the mastermind behind Goa's largest beauteous menagerie but she also earned the reputation of a wedding crasher. She'd lovingly wrap her homemade contraceptives with goofy collages of her animals and deliver them to variable newlyweds. Of course, she'd punctuate her perfunctory remarks of gratitude with: "*Hai Saiba, kitlo kalor zata!* Global warming, I tell you."

"We deserve it for spouting babies faster than pretty papaya and coconut trees." And then she'd slide the breadth of her handkerchief down her armpit for dramatic measure.

Renuka made her father very proud. When she wasn't tending to her animals or vegetable garden, she'd be agitating against the mining tycoons. When her beloved pigling Tyronne failed to rouse Renuka out of her slumber, she'd bounce back to reality with her alternate alarm clock melody – the absurd yet ingenious lyrics of her favourite Regina Spektor song:

> *Pavlov's daughter woke up in the morning*
> *Heard the bell ring*
> *And something deep inside of her made her want to*
> *salivate*
> *So she lay there drooling on her pillow*

It reminded her how easy it was to become a brainwashed puppet. She encountered them by the dozen. She knew the future of Goa wasn't entirely in her hands but she also did know that the battlefield of resistance was ripe with promise.

Glossary

Sala: A living room, typically conforming to Portuguese architecture

O teu marido vai roubar o meu: Your husband is going to steal mine

Mãe, por que pensas assim? Ambos têm interesses comuns: Mother, why do you think that way? They both have common interests

Tu vais arrepender-te. Havia tantos bons rapazes de boas famílias: You're going to regret this. There were so many good boys from good families

Polle, hanvem tuje khatir kitem haddlam: See what I've gotten for you

Aiz borem friend mevlem battlefieldan mhajekade war jhogodpak: I've found a good friend to fight the war with on the battlefield

Hai Saiba, kitlo kalor zata: O Lord, how hot it is

Pavlov's daughter ... drooling on her pillow: Taken from the track 'Pavlov's Daughter', by singer/songwriter Regina Spektor, from her album *11:11*

Mary Had Not Come

Shantan Sukhtankar

P ETER was sitting at the airport waiting for his flight. He was experiencing strange emotions, as he was going back to Goa after many years. Peter was tall, dark and slim. He had time to kill, and seeing a magazine on the nearby table, he picked it up. Today he had a thick gold bracelet on his hands whereas ten years back, it was the bread bangle from the baker!

Peter was going home after several years. No matter how many years one spends abroad, the pull of Goa never leaves you. Their house, which was on the verge of collapse, was repaired and maintained by his friend Remy with the money that Peter had sent, but he couldn't maintain it any longer. He didn't have the strength in his limbs any more. Peter had planned to come home several times. But if the first year went to earn enough money to repair the house, the next year his savings were exhausted as he remitted it to look after the failing health of his father. The third year, the bakery oven had to be repaired. The years just went by.

Some things don't have an answer. Life takes its turns and we do not know why. In this search, in an instant everything changes. Peter remembered that he was nearing forty now. There was no answer to Peter's problem. The only question Peter had was, why had Mary not come? The rays of the evening spread across the runway of the airport, making the soft glow of the setting sun very beautiful. It draped its colour all over the sky. In his mind's eye, Peter could see the sun of twenty years ago. He'd seen many sunsets, but today he recalled clearly the sunset he saw from the doorway of the chapel, ten years ago.

Peter was the son of Seby, the baker. Seby was well known as an excellent baker in Curtorim. The bakery of the D'Costa family had been running for several generations. Seby and his wife carried on the business. But one day, when all of a sudden his wife passed away, Seby was left all alone. Peter was then in the Tenth standard. Seby was finding it difficult to run both the household and the bakery and also manage Peter's education. Somehow, he pulled on for another two years to enable Peter to finish his higher secondary. Seeing his father struggling with the bakery, Peter decided to help him. The death of his wife had left Seby heartbroken and lonely and this had aged him much more than his actual years.

Just like any other day, Peter was on his trip around the village with his *pao*. Near the gates of the landlord's house he saw some girls passing by. Since they were right in the middle of the road, Peter pumped his horn. Startled by the loud blaring, three of them reacted by jumping and uttering 'Oh my God!' But one of them just laughed. Dusky complexioned and slim, the girl had on a white dress and was smiling. "Did you girls just get scared of the baker's horn?" she asked, laughing out aloud. Peter liked her from that moment on. From then on, he began to deliver an extra two loaves at the landlord's house. The same day, on the way home, he met his close friend Remy who told him that the girl was Mary, the *bhatkar's* sister's daughter. When his sister died, the landlord had brought her to his place and was looking after her, as his own daughter. He paid for her education and boarding in a good college in the city. Now she had completed her studies and had come to stay at their place.

Every day, as they saw each other in the evenings, Mary too, had begun to like Peter. They were now meeting quite often. On the slope of a hill was a chapel. Mary would leave the house saying she was going for a walk. There was a world of difference between them in their status. But not in their outlook or in the future that they envisaged together. Days went by and soon a year had gone by.

A day came when Mary was scared. She told Peter that the *bhatkar* wanted her to get married. The landlord would never agree to allow her to marry a baker. Besides, he wasn't well off either. He thought that if he had some money, the *bhatkar* may relent. Peter decided to go to Dubai to struggle and make a fortune.

He confided his plans to his close friend Remy. He began to make the arrangements to go. He planned to come back within a year and meet the landlord to ask for Mary's hand. Remy helped him to contact an agent, find a job and organise his accommodation.

He pawned a couple of his mother's gold bangles. On his return, he planned to redeem them and put them on Mary's hands as a wedding gift. Being a motorcycle taxi pilot, Remy had a lot of contacts. At a time like this, his wide range of acquaintances came in very handy. Noting that Seby was handling things very bravely, Remy comforted and encouraged the old man.

All the preparations for the Dubai trip were done within a month or so. The day for his departure had arrived. The soft glow of the setting sun had bathed the chapel on the hill with its rays, making everything so beautiful. Peter had come and was waiting for Mary as usual. Remy would be dropping him to the airport that night. Thousands of questions were crowding Peter's mind. The job abroad, leaving his father to fend for himself, missing and remembering Mary and Goa. Steeling himself, he waited. He made one last effort to meet Mary before he went. But Mary did not come!

A long time went by as he waited for Mary. Remy was waiting for him at home, to drop him to the airport. But what could he do? Peter was waiting for Mary in anguish. Peter had prepared himself to give up everything to go and make a name, and money, for himself. He had no option but to go. It was late in the evening. Searching anxiously for him, Remy landed at the chapel. Peter's face had drooped. "Mary has not come," he told Remy.

"Let's go, Peter, we'll be late!" Remy tried to calm him down. "Something must have happened. We'll phone from the airport."

Peter repeated, "Mary hasn't come."

"Have you seen the time, Peter? It's past 7. You might miss your flight!"

Mary had not come! 'Something must have delayed her. We should have waited for a little more time.' The wind was rushing past them as Remy rode his motorbike fast in order to reach in time for the flight. Preoccupied with thoughts of Mary, Peter was silent. Mary used to be late sometimes but something must have happened, otherwise she would never have done this on his last day. Poor thing, she must have come late. Had they planned to meet in the morning, this would never have happened. Peter was feeling awful. He was overcome with regret.

Mary has not come! 'Mary must have cried a lot. Because I was going abroad, she must have clutched our photo to herself and cried the whole night.' Peter remembered how one day, they had stealthily gone to a studio out of the village and had a photo taken. She must have cried her heart out. Her mother, meaning her aunt, must have seen her crying. 'Who is this, Mary? Seby's son? The baker? What is this? Are you flirting with a baker?' She must have scolded her a lot. *Bhatkar* was known for his temper, and his son, young blooded that he was, was even worse. 'I will teach that baker a lesson. I will grab a crowbar and make both Seby and Peter disappear. They must have said this,' Peter thought. Mary may have begged them. 'Please don't harm him. I will have nothing to do with him.' She may have hardened herself.

Mary did not come. Peter was scared to travel in a plane for the first time, but his heart was crying. Remy embraced him and tried to instil confidence in him: Don't worry, be brave, go and come back in one piece. The words reminded him that he was actually going away. He submitted his passport and ticket and soon it was time to board the flight.

Mary did not come! The plane had now taken off. Looking down from the window of the plane, he saw the ground below looking so small. Peter realised for the first time what a tiny person he was. Did Mary not want him? 'The bottom line is that I am poor. A baker's son. What can a baker do? Could a baker be famous and shake up the world? Mary must have pondered over this. My love must have lost against money.' Mary's brother may have brought a proposal of a rich boy. Probably a handsome, rich, educated guy. They must have arranged a proposal with the son of Costa the landlord. Mary, dressed in pretty clothes and brought up in a landlord's house. Peter felt anger and ill-will at the same time! 'Mary acted out a romance with me. How mad I was!' Peter was seething because he had even pawned his mother's gold for the sake of Mary. Peter, who loved Mary so much, was very enraged with her now. 'I'll earn a lot and teach her a lesson one day. She will realise whom she has abandoned. I'll have a big house, buy cars. She will come to know one day,' thought Peter.

Today, Peter was coming back to Goa after ten years. He felt a strange exhilaration whilst entering the plane. Going back to Goa meant going back to his soil. He felt happy that he would meet his father. Twenty-five years old when he left, Peter was now thirty-five. He'd been on a contract with his boss in Dubai. What would he do when he gets back to Goa? It's better to be far away, he was thinking. Remy used to phone him occasionally. He would give him news of his father. He felt grateful to Remy. Remy had advised him – work hard, make a lot of money and come home. Every time, Peter's first question would be, "Why had Mary not come?" But Remy had never answered his question.

Today, Peter was returning home after many years. After sitting in the plane, Peter was bothered by another question. He remembered Mary. He could see before his eyes all that had happened more than ten years ago. Would he ever know why Mary did not come? 'Will I get an answer or not?' he thought.

Glossary

Pao: Bread
Bhatkar: Landlord

Originally written in Konkani as 'Mary Ailem Nam'.
Translated by Xavier Cota.

The Devil Inside Me Smiled

Preethy Sunil

O N the appointed day, when mama walked away from me towards the waiting taxi, after loosening my tight grip on her hand, I could feel the growing distance between us, both physically and emotionally, and something inside told me that after the baby's arrival, things would not be the same for me again. I remembered how all these days I had longed to have a kid brother to play with and share my life but now I was not sure that things were going to be good for me.

Immediately after his birth, Michael started having breathing problems, caused by swallowing meconium. Medically known as Meconium Aspiration, it occurs when a baby breathes in amniotic fluid containing meconium, the baby's first stools. When the thick meconium mixes into the amniotic fluid, it is swallowed and breathed into the airway of the foetus. As the baby takes the first breaths at delivery, meconium particles enter the airway and it is inhaled deep into the lungs.

He started turning blue with difficulty in breathing. There was hurried activity in the operation theatre of the Cottage Hospital in Chicalim. Soon a serious-looking nurse called dada and informed him that Michael needed to be shifted immediately to the Government Medical College (GMC), which was about thirty kilometres away from there. Dad requested one of his friends, who had accompanied him to the hospital, to arrange for an ambulance. Luckily the hospital had an ambulance and my dad, with Michael bundled in his arms, sat nervously throughout the journey.

My mother could not move from the bed as the Caesarean operation she had to undergo to deliver the baby, the second one in succession, my birth five years back being the first, wouldn't make her fit for walking for at least another week. In a way I was glad, as with Michael away in another hospital, I got all my mother's attention and love, thought I hated it when she enquired with the doctors attending to her about when she could see her newborn child. She held me in her arms and cried for him.

Meanwhile dad kept shuttling between the two hospitals for various requirements, one of which was to take the milk squeezed out from mama's breast and collect it in a sterilised bottle, to feed Michael who was admitted in the Neonatal Intensive Care Unit (NICU), in the GMC.

Then the day came when the doctors told mama that she could visit her newborn baby provided she did not walk around too much or move the portion around her operated area. Mama was all set to go to see her loved one lying in a hospital far away from hers. Her face glowed and she kept singing her favourite lullabies all day. She showered me with kisses and hugs whenever she found time for it. On the doctor's advice, dada called a taxi to take her to the GMC which was about an hour's drive from the local hospital.

It was only later that I realised that I was not included in the plan; I was to stay behind with mama's sister who had come to take care of me. I begged mama to take me along as, more than anything, I wanted the ride in the taxi; sitting in a car was a privilege that came rarely in the family. But all my pleading went in vain and in the end mama lost her patience and yelled at me.

"You are only a small child, and you cannot be taken along in certain places," said mama. The hospital authorities had earlier informed her that children would not be allowed inside the neonatal ICU. Later I was told that mama and dada had to wear sterilised hospital gowns over their clothes and change their footwear before entering the neonatal ICU and they could wait there only for a few minutes.

Mama came back from the GMC, and from her expression one could make out that she had been crying a lot. Her face was puffed up, eyes reddish and she kept on wiping her nose all the time. She had found Michael lying on his side, sleeping, his body shrivelled with tubes running through his nose and one attached to his penis to drain his urine. She started wailing in front of him. It was only after a lot of persuasion from dada, the nurses and the duty doctor that she was ready to leave the neonatal ICU, after being assured that Michael would be discharged within a week, the same time when she also would be allowed to go home. However, much to everyone's surprise, the hospital called and said that due to the good progress that Michael showed, he would be discharged on the third day itself.

Michael's homecoming, or rather, coming to the hospital where his mother was admitted, was a big affair as all the relatives descended to see him and came with their hands holding presents for him. This was the first time I realised that I would no longer get all the attention I used to get and a new chapter in life was unfolding for me. The night after being discharged from the hospital, at home, I was told to sleep with dada on the extra mattress laid down by the side of the bed, and mama slept on top of the bed hugging Michael to her bosom, a position that had been reserved for me till he came along.

Things started changing rapidly for me. I was getting used to being what I coined for myself, '*the second most wanted child*', in my family. I ached for my mother's warm embrace, holding me close to her, kissing and pampering me. Now it was always Michael who got all the attention.

"You are a big boy now," mama told me once when I tried snuggling up to her in Michael's absence. I was also getting used to my relegation to the mattress on the floor, while mom slept with her arms around Michael on the bed. I was also getting used to doing small chores for Michael like getting his nappies, collecting the toys thrown around by him, singing songs for him, dancing to keep him amused and so on. I did this with pleasure not because I liked Michael, but because after every chore I did for him I was hugged and kissed by mama. Later on when Michael turned two and the incident at birth was a faded memory, Michael's dependence on mama reduced, especially after mama stopped breastfeeding him a few weeks after he turned two. However, my position of being the '*the second most wanted child*' remained.

Before he could start talking, Michael, like most children his age, got most of his needs fulfilled by howling and crying. If he was hungry he cried, if he was full he cried, if he wanted anything he laid his eyes on, he cried till he got it. If he had a fall he cried, for anything and everything he bawled and got his work done. So much so that the neighbours were wondering why the child was screaming throughout the day. This improved after another year and around the age of three the tantrums reduced.

After Michael started school it was my duty to take him to school and bring him back home every day. We both studied in the same school; he was in the primary section and I was in the secondary. The distance from our house to the school was hardly a kilometre but there were two roads to be crossed to reach the school. These roads were very busy and there was a continuous flow of traffic, especially during the afternoon when all the nearby schools ended their classes at around the same time. It was also the time that the next door shipbuilding yard, 'The Goa Shipyard,' ended its lunch break and the staff resumed their duty post lunch.

Michael never held still for a moment and was always prancing around. I had a hard time holding on to his hand and crossing the roads safely. Many times I threatened him, saying that I would let go of his hand if he continued his antics.

On that day I had had a bad day at school. First I was pulled up by the class teacher for not completing my project work, which again was due to Michael. All such activities could be done at home only when Michael was fast asleep, for otherwise he would demand that my parents buy him all the things that they had brought for me to do the project. He would also end up spilling gum and other articles of the project work all over the place. The previous night, Michael had slept late and it had not been possible for me to complete my project. I also got bullied by the senior students in my school during the recess. One of them blindfolded me with his hands over my eyes and five other friends of his took turns at using their knuckles on the back of my head.

It was in this mood that I was holding onto Michael's hand while I was escorting him home after school. While attempting the first road crossing near the school, I saw the school bus of the neighbouring school heading in our direction. At first, I thought that we could cross the road easily before the bus reached us. However, Michael's fidgeting delayed the process and it was too late when I realised that we had to pull back.

I tried to pull Michael back to the sidewalk but he was blindly going ahead. In the last desperate move I yanked my hands from his grip and rushed back to safety. The bus driver applied the brakes in time to save Michael's life, but one of the rear wheels ran over his right leg. His leg was a mangled mess below the ankle.

What followed in Michael's life next was a series of painful corrective surgeries to his wounded leg, followed by strenuous physiotherapy. Naturally the affection and sympathy ratings for Michael rose rapidly and mine hit rock bottom. Though no one spoke about it directly, I was held partially responsible for the mishap. Though mama never brought up the topic, the look in dada's eyes, for many days in a row after the accident, told a different story.

Michael was once again reduced to the crying and bawling mess that he was earlier in his infancy. In the hospital as soon as the doctor, nurse or any other medical staff entered his room he would start howling and crying. Most of these medical visits to his room were either for an injection or a change of dressing, the pain of which Michael dreaded. After the accident, being subjected to intermittent pain also became a part of Michael's life.

A few weeks after the accident, on the day of the removal of the plaster cast on his leg, Michael created such a racket that he brought the whole hospital down. He refused to allow the doctors to touch his injured limb. They then decided to do it later on after he calmed down. They informed my parents that they should try and convince the child that whatever is being done was for his own good. However, no amount of reassuring or cajoling by the family members could bring an end to Michael's sobs. Then finally mama decided to take things in hand. She told the hospital staff

to come back after half an hour and that she would keep Michael ready for the procedure by then. Only dada and I remained in the room watching close by. Mama then suddenly slapped Michael hard across his face. This unexpected shock brought an end to Michael's weeping. Everybody in the room was silent for a while.

Then mama sat on Michael's bed and held him in her arms. In a very firm voice she asked, "Michael, why are you crying all the time?"

"It's paining," said Michael.

"If it is paining, then it is healing," said mama.

"If it is paining, then it is healing, my child," she repeated, rocking him in her arms.

No one saw or heard Michael cry from that day onwards. He swallowed pain, he fought pain, he spat the pain and he did everything to beat the pain. This attitude further increased his ratings. He was the talk of the family, the talk of the school and finally the talk of the town. In the meantime my ratings took a beating and were pushed further down. He braved it all and slowly his wounds healed. However, due to the cutting away a part of smashed bone and other related damaged muscles, Michael could not walk on his own without external support. After trying a lot of contraptions, dada was lucky to find a master craftsman in a remote hospital who made modified shoes for children with polio. After wearing his shoes Michael could manage to walk and do things on his own.

The shrill sound of the alarm woke me up. My dream was so real that I instantly lifted the bed sheet covering Michael, who was sound asleep on the cot next to me, and felt his legs from the knees to the ankles. I was relieved to find they were intact. I got up from the bed and stood for a moment in front of Michael and watched him sleep peacefully. The devil in me smiled. Finally I had found a way out of my pitiable situation.

I had made up my mind. The plan was to be executed that day itself. Michael and I went to school as usual. After the final bell, I waited for Michael in front of his classroom. As soon as he got out from the class I took his hand in my own and gripped it firmly. We proceeded out from the school compound into the street. I waited on the pavement beside the road till I could see the school bus of the neighbouring school coming down the road towards us. I slowly loosened my grip over Michael's hand and placed both my hands on his shoulders.

I waited for the right moment and, when the bus neared us, I turned Michael around, gave him a violent push towards the pavement, and then jumped onto the road, in front of the oncoming school bus.

Glossary

Dada: Father
Mama: Mother

AARON S. RODRIGUES is a writer, avid reader and restaurateur who has recently completed his Master's Degree in English Literature. Both prose and verse writing are deeply influenced by the natural beauty and the clash of the elements surrounding his hometown of Dona Paula. The imagery and themes are often tinged with fantasy and are also inspired by observations made during his travels and his deep immersion in various genres. The short story 'Wings of Vertigo' was conceptualised during his stay in Scotland, out of his diasporic yearning for Goa.

ANITA PINTO writes for children. The eight books she has written are much read and treasured. She aims to bring knowledge and understanding to youth and children and feels the drive to tell them how to discover the world, to look into the depth of the sea, to wonder at the flight of a bird or to love the heart and mind of people. She is also a lecturer of Communication, Creative Writing and Emotional Intelligence at the BBA level. She is a part of the Goa Writers, and the Garden City Creative Writers, Australia.

ANUSHA V.R. is a twenty-three-year-old chartered accountant (CA) and CS with a penchant for travelling. She derives inspiration from her aunt, C.Y. Bharathi. Anusha's story 'Scattered Pages' was shortlisted at the Fundação Oriente Competition, 2015, and included in the anthology *Monsoon Winds* (2016).

BINA NAYAK is a graphic designer who has been working in the advertising and media industry for twenty-seven years. She spends time between Mumbai, Pune and Goa. But you are most likely to catch her in a Neeta Volvo bus!

BRIAN MENDONÇA, PhD, self-published two volumes of poems while serving in Delhi where he was an ELT editor of school books for children. *Last Bus to Vasco: Poems from Goa* (2006) was followed by *A Peace of India: Poems in Transit* (2011). He has been anthologised in *Goa: A Garland of Poems* (2017) – a collection of thirty poets from Goa which has also been translated into Irish. Currently he teaches English language, and lectures in English at Carmel College, Nuvem, Goa.

CHERIE NAROO considers writing more than just an expressive hobby. It allows her to stare into space – or at her laptop – while seeming busy and very profound. She recently got spectacles to add to the effect. As an ex corporate communications professional in Dubai, she gained valuable knowledge in the fine art of creating corporate communications that were focused, articulate and clear. With her move back to Goa in search of a calm country life of motherhood, her writing skills were put to use in cleverly crafted shopping lists and notes to husband and children. She felt she had more to offer. Naroo now actively pursues social activism across social media platforms, and has stories, articles and observations on life. Her writing recipe usually calls for generous dollops of humour, served on a base of reality and garnished with wit and sarcasm.

CLARA A. RODRIGUES wrote her first short story while in high school, knowing her world would come to revolve around words. After college she worked as a journalist in local media houses in Goa before becoming a senior correspondent with a national daily. Her interest is writing about culture and environment and animal welfare. Besides, she has also scripted short films and documentaries. She finds baking and gardening therapeutic and loves to go on long drives when not occupied with work assignments.

DINESH PATEL is a poet and author of several books; he is also an assistant professor, assistant editor, motivational speaker, travel buff, fitness enthusiast, PR consultant, advertising professional, photographer, rock climber, yoga instructor, chef, trekker, multilinguist, half-marathon runner and master of ceremonies. His educational qualifications include a Masters in English Literature, PG Diplomas in European Studies, Journalism and Mass Communication, Creative Writing, Yoga, Teaching English, and Guidance, among others.

FRANCESCA COTTA completed her BA at Symbiosis School for Liberal Arts, with a major in Anthropology and a double minor in English Literature and International Relations. She currently works as a travel writer, exploring the theme of slow and sustainable travel in her writing. She is crazy about books (both hoarding and reading them) and enthusiastic about language, libraries, bicycles, the wild outdoors, ice cream and feminism.

GEETA NAIK is an author based in Margão, Goa, and an avid traveller. She writes frequently for many local newspapers and has published books of essays, an autobiography and travelogues. Her story 'The Whiplash' won the Konkani Special Prize (in Memory of the Late Hirabai Durga Gaitonde) at the Fundação Oriente Short Story Competition, 2015, and was included in the anthology *Monsoon Winds* (2016).

GOUTHAMI has been writing since she can remember. She currently lives in Pomburpa, North Goa. The natural beauty and interesting people she meets there inspires much of her recent writing, which includes short stories, poetry and blogging.

JEANETTE BARBOSA NORONHA is a 21-year-old from Borda, Margão. Currently pursuing her Master's Degree in Portuguese and Lusophone Studies, she enjoys singing in English and Portuguese. She gravitated towards writing less than two years ago, when her work of poetry won her accolades. This is her first attempt at writing short stories and she wishes to go further in the field.

KIRAN MAHAMBRE is a Konkani writer and a translator by profession. A Konkani Bhasha Mandal awardee, Mahambre has several titles to her name, namely *Anapekshit* (short stories), *Balkatha* (stories for children), *Saimanganat* (poetry for children), *Anant Antarang* (fantasy for teenagers), *Dana Hakim* (translated from Urdu), *Venchik Kanayo* (translated from Hindi for the Sahitya Akademi) and *Nepali Kanayao* (translated from Hindi for the Sahitya Akademi). Her story 'The Blessed Man' was shortlisted at the Fundação Oriente Short Story Competition, 2011, and included in the anthology *Shell Windows* (2012).

MARIA DO CÉU BARRETO is a former faculty member of the Department of Portuguese of the Goa University, in the CLP-Camões, Goa, and Dhempe College, Panaji, Goa. She holds a double Master's Degree in French and Portuguese from the University of Bombay and the Goa University, and a Bachelor's Degree in Education (Univ. of Bombay). She is the co-author of five books currently used in the Secondary Schools of Goa, a member of the Board of Studies of the Department of Portuguese of the Goa University, and a founder member and the first president of Goa Association of Teachers of Portuguese.

MAYABHUSHAN NAGVENKAR, a Goa-based journalist, writes for the Indo-Asian News Service. He lives in Anjuna and is currently preparing a new book of short stories entitled *Anjuna Tales.*

NARAYAN MAHALE is a Goan Marathi writer with several published books, among which are *Savli* (a novel), *Rang Matiche* (a novel), *Ashtiva, Homekant, Amori, Ragavani* and *Horavani* (short stories' books). He has won the Goa Kala Academy Prize and Poet B.B. Borkar Award given by the Goa Hindu Association, Mumbai.

NARESH NAIK is a Konkani assistant professor and a published author. He has received the late Madhavi Sardesai Yuva Shikshak Puraskar, 2017. He is also a National award winner of the Sahitya Akademi Yuva Puraskar, New Delhi, 2014.

NOEL SEQUEIRA is a jack of many trades, a master of a few. He has dabbled with journalism, linguistics and storytelling, only to find himself most comfortable with babysitting dogs. His latest mission is to practice everything he preaches.

PREETHY SUNIL is a homemaker. Reading is her favourite pastime. Encouraged by her story 'Acrobat' being shortlisted for the Fundação Oriente Short Story competition, 2015, and included in the anthology *Monsoon Winds* (2016), she took part in the competition for the second time. Very excited at seeing her name in print again, she feels that Fundação Oriente is doing yeoman's service in encouraging new writers by organising this competition and publishing the anthology.

RAJYASHREE DUTT lives in a quiet village in Goa. For many years she wrote and edited for the development sector. Then, a while ago, she compiled and edited *Chicken Soup for the Indian Couples'*

Soul and contributed stories to other volumes in the series. Passionate about wildlife, she now has a regular travel blog. When she is not hammering out short stories and plays, she teaches drama or watches birds.

SHANTAN SUKHTANKAR is an architect by training but is very inclined towards literature, especially Konkani. He has written other stories such as 'The Humann of Shetka' (shortlisted at the Fundação Oriente Short Story Competition, 2013, and included in the anthology *Coconut Fronds* [2014]) and 'Vojem' (shortlisted for the Fundação Oriente Short Story Competition, 2015, and included in the anthology *Monsoon Winds* [2016]).

SUNIL DAMODARAN is a safety officer and an electrical engineer by profession. An avid reader of books, writing is something he has dabbled in recently. He took it up seriously after the first short story written by him was shortlisted in an international competition. He intends to devote more time to writing as he is encouraged and elated on being selected for being published in this anthology.

SUVARNA BANDEKAR is domiciled in the heart of Goa, that is, Panjim. Her occasional writing has been published in the local Marathi daily *Gomantak*; her story 'Marline Fisherwoman' won the second prize (Semana da Cultura Indo-Portuguesa) at the Fundação Oriente Short Story Competition, 2015, and was included in the anthology *Monsoon Winds* (2016).

VITHAL GAWAS, born in 1956, is based in Desterro, Vasco da Gama, Goa. He has three books to his credit – *Catharin*, *Lavan* and *Ozhe*. Gawas has won many awards and his writing has been included in the Goa University postgraduate (MA, Marathi) syllabus. He has been deputy chairman of the Gomantak Marathi Academy. His story 'The Deal' was shortlisted at the Fundação Oriente Short Story Competition, 2013, and included in the anthology *Coconut Fronds – Short Stories from Goa* (2014). His story 'São João' won the Marathi Special Prize (sponsored by Augusto Pinto) at the Fundação Oriente Short Story Competition, 2015, and was included in the anthology *Monsoon Winds* (2016).